MW00929959

Two Doors

C. S. Nagdev

Text copyright © 1996 C. S. Nagdev
All rights reserved.

ISBN: 1533097585
ISBN 13: 9781533097583

Dedicated to humans for their ageless curiosity and quest for answers.

Table of Contents

Preface

SO, YOU KNOW who you are and why you are here. Well, if you don't or are unsure or open to a new perspective, *Two Doors* is for you. It uses the lives of five disparate individuals to walk you to a stunningly logical and unambiguous conclusion. As you enjoy the easy read, you'd find yourself being provoked into revisiting your own beliefs.

The genesis of *Two Doors* took place decades ago when I watched a late-night TV commercial of emaciated and starving toddlers with large, sad eyes and distended bellies. Those images have never left me.

Two Doors is a fiction.

Two Doors has elements of fantasy.

While all persons and events are fictional and any resemblance to reality is purely coincidental, a few iconic names, locations, and institutions have been used to provide general context to the story.

Despite the professional edits and the rewrites, this novel would not have been possible without my wife Susan's countless reviews and critiques, painstaking proof-reading and unwavering support.

1
Somewhere

THE SCREAM PIERCED through the fog of sleep enveloping Steve Zeller. Startled, he opened his eyes wide. He noticed his hands weren't gripping the steering wheel and he wasn't in the car: He was part of a crowd in a wide-open space that had a deep-blue sky devoid of sun, moon and stars. Despite the darkness, he could discern the people around him were a mishmash of the old, the young, the children—even infants. And it was eerily quiet.

What the hell? His body tensed. He looked around. "Don. Where are you?" he shouted, fracturing the prevailing tranquility.

There was no response. A few people turned their heads toward him; but only for a moment and then looked away. It was as if they were going to address him—admonish him for his noisy behavior, perhaps—but decided not to.

Where am I? Who're these people? Why are we all wearing white gowns and sandals? Goddamn it, what's going on? While questions sped through his confounded mind, he realized everyone was in motion and moving in the same direction toward the only visible object in the distance: a mammoth white dome. He tried to stop, but couldn't. *We aren't walking;*

we're floating . . . levitating. This can't be happening. Damn it, it just can't?

His heart started pounding; he took deep breaths to calm down. "I'm having a nightmare; I must wake up." He shook his head to clear it. Then, he touched his arms, chest, and face. "I'm here . . . I'm physically here."

He observed most people around him were shaken as he was; however, some did seem relaxed and at peace, with a sprinkling even looking happy.

A voice interrupted his mounting anxiety: "Steve, welcome. You've returned from the earth. You're on your way to the Life Critique Center to participate in a closing assessment, and then you'll proceed to your final destination." The voice was calm and caring.

He looked around to pinpoint the voice's source, but couldn't. *Am I actually hearing some weirdo or am I going nuts?* From the reactions of people around him, he surmised they too were hearing the voice. He noticed another peculiar behavior: Individuals were turning around to stare at something—or someone—and then exhibiting a gamut of emotions; but, infants and children were spared that experience.

He fought to maintain his poise. "Who are you and what's this bull about returning from the earth?"

The voice said, "You're not on the earth now—you're dead: You crashed your car into a tree and were killed instantly."

"Look, whoever you are, I'm not in a mood for your crummy jokes. Okay? So, cut the bullshit and tell me what's going on? How the hell did I get here . . . wherever 'here' is?" Steve spoke with bravado—his trademark, whenever he felt trapped or faced a situation in which he wasn't in control.

"This is not a joke. You're dead. Please turn around and see for yourself," the voice said in an even tone.

He hesitated.

"Go ahead. Turn around and look." The voice was more forceful.

He sensed the voice wasn't making a request. For the first time, he felt a surge of fear; so he turned around. What he saw made him freeze and his eyes bulge. He exclaimed, "Jesus Christ!"

His powerful black Porsche was smoldering; its driver-side front end was crushed back by an ancient, immovable tree sitting by the side of the road he recognized; the passenger-side headlight was still on; and a sheriff's cruiser with flashing lights was parked at a distance.

Inside the car, he saw the steering column was pushed deep into his chest; a large blood stain on his pants was spreading; his contorted face was visible over the inflated air bag; and his lifeless eyes were looking back at him.

His attention shifted to Don McCoy in the passenger seat: His head was resting on the dashboard; his eyes were closed; and blood was trickling out of his mouth and nose. A deputy sheriff held a flashlight fixed on him and was speaking into a mike on his shoulder: "Injured passenger's a male; appears to be in his thirties. He's wearing a seat belt, but passenger-side airbag is not deployed. Subject's experiencing significant blood loss. I'll attempt to move him away from the car: There's a strong smell of gas and the potential for an explosion is definitely high."

The gruesome scene of blood, twisted metal and flashing lights sickened Steve; he shuddered. "Don screamed to warn me."

The voice said, "Yes, he did. But you didn't have time to wake up and react."

"The airbag . . . it should've saved me."

"It could have, but your foot was bearing down hard on the accelerator at the time of impact."

"I dozed off . . . had one too many drinks . . . Don's airbag didn't open. Will he die also?" he spoke in a pained whisper.

The voice replied, "No. He'll survive the accident despite the airbag's malfunction."

The guilt-ridden Steve was ecstatic. "Oh, God! That's great, just great." Then, his mind turned quickly to the well-being of his own two sons; he was relieved that Don would be there to take care of them.

His eyes remained riveted to the gory scene, and he began to shake: Seeing himself dead was having a profound emotional impact on him.

"Steve, are you all right?" the voice asked in a gentle tone.

He took a deep breath: Resignation was setting in. He said in a hoarse voice, "Okay, okay, I really screwed up. And, now I'm dead. I guess that's why all these strange things are happening—like hearing you without seeing you, and moving without walking or . . . riding something."

The voice said, "That's right."

With deliberate effort, he turned around and once again stared ahead at the approaching white structure. "So, who are you? *What* are you?"

The voice's reply was calm. "All your questions will be answered shortly after you enter the life critique center just ahead. Please be patient."

Though his fear had started to wane, his confusion and anxiety remained unabated. Also, becoming aware of his new abilities added to his unsettled state. For one thing, he could feel his power of observation growing: Anything he looked at—far or near—adjusted into sharp focus. Initially, he found his enhanced visual acuity disconcerting even though it enabled him to see in the darkness that surrounded him. Also, he was hearing sporadic, disconnected words and half sentences, akin to a poorly tuned radio station. That aggravated him. He looked at people around him; but no one was speaking.

At that moment, a scrawny woman bent with age, turned her wrinkled face toward him and gave him a kind, toothless smile. "Relax, Steve dear. Soon we'll meet our Maker and things'll be all right. So, quit your worrying and rejoice." Her dark eyes seemed to be alive with anticipation.

His mind was racing to keep up with what was happening. *Good God! I heard her, but she didn't open her mouth; her lips didn't move. She knows what I'm thinking; she knew my name without my telling her. Damn . . . we have telepathic powers. Wow!*

He concentrated on others in the crowd; they looked back at him. Suddenly his mind started to interact with their minds: The fragmented sentences he'd been hearing now became complete sentences. But the simultaneous thoughts rushing in from numerous people, though coherent, proved to be unbearable—painful, actually—for his brain. He shut his eyes tight, hoping that would stop others' thoughts from bombarding his brain. The noises in his head stopped in an instant; and, the old woman and others looked away. He was relieved by that discovery. "That's better. I can block others out. I can choose to be alone . . . alone with my own thoughts." He tried to sort things out in his already cluttered mind; but his efforts failed. Frustrated, he muttered, "To hell with it. I'll just wait and see what happens." Then, he directed his attention to the approaching life critique center.

The dome-shaped structure was six stories high, and its width appeared to stretch over a mile. It was made of white crystalline blocks; it had no windows, and its oversized, arched entrance was open, allowing a hazy warm light from inside to reach out and welcome people. Most people continued to float into the center; others, like Steve, stopped gliding and walked in.

Once he was inside, he had an unobstructed view of the vast space in front of him. He paused and took his time to scan the interior from end to end. He could feel the atmosphere created by soft lights and cream colors having a soothing effect on him. He was able to study in minute detail any part of the dome or any activity taking place by simply focusing on it.

He saw the dome area was divided into thousands of small sections. Each section had six brown tub chairs placed in a circle. The staff in light-blue body suits greeted people entering the dome and directed them to sit in five chairs, with the sixth reserved for one of their own. A multitude of group sessions were in progress under the direction of these staffers, whose demeanor was pleasant and non-confrontational. No one was rushing; everything was happening at an unhurried pace.

His attention was drawn to the opposite side of the dome where two massive doors stood twenty feet apart. One door was red, the other white; and above each door a sign in black letters read "Exit." He saw people standing in a line to leave through those doors.

While the people awaiting their turn were of every age—from the very old and infirm to the newborn—things such as wheelchairs, crutches or strollers were nowhere in sight. The soft and flowing white gowns did little to hide the contrast in individuals: A well-groomed, handsome, middle-aged man stood behind a man in his seventies, who had stubs of beard on a heavily-creased face and a prominent hump on his back; and, in front of the old man waited a young sun-tanned brunette. Generally, people appeared to be calm or resigned—some even looked happy. However, there were more than a few whose faces betrayed a state of turmoil. For some of those, the stress brought on by fear and anxiety was debilitating enough to require a helping hand from others.

At the head of the line was a doorperson wearing the same light-blue body suit as the rest of the staff. She'd whisper to the person ready to depart; and then she'd escort that person to one of the two doors a few yards away. She'd open the door and a stream of brilliant light would rush in. Nothing beyond the door could be seen, and only the form of the individual walking into the light would be visible for a brief period before that, too, would disappear. Then the door would close, taking the shaft of light with it.

Worrisome thoughts hounded Steve: *Why two exit doors? Does one lead to heaven, the other to hell? I bet that's it . . . certainly explains all the apprehension in the room. Damn, what's the right door to heaven? Huh, wonder what door I'll leave by?*

One of the staff interrupted his thoughts. "Welcome to the Life Critique Center. Please follow me." He led Steve to an unoccupied group area and said, "Four other people and a staff member will join you shortly. Please take a seat and make yourself comfortable."

Steve shouted, "Want me to be comfortable? Then, for Christ's sake, answer my questions—now." An oppressive pressure had been building in his chest. Nothing in his thirty-five years on the earth had prepared him for what he now faced as one of the dead: the astonishing new powers; the frustrating stonewalling by those in control; the intimidating and macabre surroundings; and, of course, the most critical of all, the impending judgment that would either reward him with heaven or condemn him to hell. He felt powerless.

His outburst attracted the attention of other returnees around him. More than a few nodded in sympathy with him.

The staffer was calm but firm. "Everything will become clear to you soon. There's absolutely nothing to be concerned about." He motioned the onlookers to move on.

Steve's residual fear had evaporated by then. He locked his eyes with that of the staffer's. "Yeah, sure. What's there to be concerned about? It's just the Judgment Day for us dead people. That's all. Am I right?"

The staffer didn't reply.

Steve continued, "I'll take that as a loud and clear 'yes.' So let me tell you how I see it: After one of you finishes playing my judge, I might end up in heaven and have a ball; but, then again, I might not, and get shoved into the fiery hell forever. You're right: There's absolutely nothing to be concerned about—not one goddamn thing." With that sarcasm, he turned around and dropped into one of the chairs.

"I'm sorry, but there's nothing more I can say." The staffer bowed his head to him and walked away.

He sat there motionless. After his agitation subsided, he started to reflect on the recent events. His thoughts were interrupted by a growing commotion in the group behind him. He turned around and saw an agitated middle-aged man addressing his group.

The man's gestures were vehement. "What the hell do you know, huh? I killed him because he killed my son. Do you hear? He killed my son. The punk pushed my son into the river; he couldn't swim . . . he . . . he drowned, and that bastard just stood there and watched and . . . and did nothing. Yes, I strangled the miserable life out of that son-of-a-bitch."

A taunting, high-pitched voice said, "Your son instigated the fight and threw the first punch."

"No, he did not. He was defending himself against that bully."

"But you killed a kid; he was only fourteen years old."

The man's growing irritation was apparent; he shouted, "My son was only eleven, you moron."

"How come you didn't say that before?"

"I did... I don't know ... I'm confused—too much going on. Leave me alone." It was obvious the persecuted man was losing the battle to collect his thoughts.

Someone else joined the needling. "You're a murderer. You were fried on the electric chair because you were guilty. Now you'll go to hell for sure, and—"

An authoritative voice interrupted, "Please, lower your voices and calm down. Stop the personal attacks."

The shouting stopped.

Steve settled back and his immediate reaction was the goons on that poor slob's team were trying to crucify him by exploiting his confusion; they were betting that, by making him look bad, they'll appear better by comparison and improve their odds of heading to heaven. He felt pity for that man.

With time to kill, he started surveying the endless arrival and departure of the dead and tuning into the discussions of groups displaying a wide spectrum of emotions—especially the outbursts of anger, fear, remorse and defiance, which he found to be quite unsettling. But, soon he got tired of these activities.

He refocused his attention on his own predicament and getting a sense for the event in which he was about to participate. He was anxious to get started, but none of the dead or the staff was heading in his direction to join him. The stress of waiting around for a trial and not knowing what fate awaited him began to cause a serious malaise in him. He realized that the only way he'd stop drowning in despair was to involve his mind in a rigorous exercise.

While he mulled over his options, his competitive nature and survival instinct kicked in. He thought, *I can't just sit here and do nothing. Hell no. For Christ's sake, this is the end of the line: I've only one shot at winning heaven and staying out of hell. I don't know what's going to happen. But somehow I must come out on top—I always have.*

His mental transformation invigorated him: He now had a mission to accomplish, a challenge to overcome, a problem to solve. The clutter in his brain was gone.

He decided to prepare himself for the upcoming trial. But what was he going to prepare, and how? Then he remembered the group attacking one of its members: *The emotional schmuck in the group behind me was jerked around with things taken out of context to confuse him and trip him up. That crap must not happen to me: I must be ready to squash any shithead in my group tempted to take pot shots at me.*

After considerable pondering, he concluded he'd use an objective, third-party approach to take a quick look at his life with the help of his recently-acquired powers. That approach, he argued, would help him organize his thoughts and give him a dispassionate perspective of himself: How did he become who he was? What did he accomplish? How are his shortcomings and sins mitigated by his surroundings and the rotten behavior of others? The more he thought, the more sanguine he became about his strategy; the only question was whether he'd have sufficient time to execute it before one of the blue suits would show up and start the inquisition.

He rested his head on the back of his chair and closed his eyes. He took a deep breath and felt himself relax. His mind switched on like a television and a rerun of events from his thirty-five-year life commenced.

2
Childhood

TERRYTON WAS A small town in southern Illinois. A long way from the restless large cities, it was surrounded by lush rolling hills peppered with farms, and enjoyed close proximity to one of nature's finest gems: the scenic Shawnee National Forest.

A lightly-traveled county road ran north and south through it. A traveler, approaching from the north, would be greeted by a hillside cemetery and a sign "Terryton, population seventeen thousand five hundred eighty-three, established eighteen hundred fifty-seven." The meticulous cemetery, studded with pots and wreaths of flowers at the graves, projected the town's pride and character developed over generations by families of the settlers who built it.

The county road was the town's main street. It was lined with buildings that had a log-cabin look. Prominent signs advertised a gas station, a real estate agency, a drug store, a barber shop, a souvenir shop masquerading as an Indian trading post, a candle boutique, a pub and grill, and a general store.

The general store had a half dozen antiquated rocking chairs on its oversized, covered porch. Two senior towns-folk were lounging there, enjoying a cool breeze on a sunny afternoon; they were also taking advantage of the bottom-less cups of coffee the store offered its customers. Worn and stained hats covered most of their white hair. Jeb Schultz sported a crescent-shaped beard and overalls; Sam Black wore suspenders to hold his pants up around his lanky skeleton.

Jeb and Sam, regulars at the store, were following their routine: Their conversations involved lazy small talk sprinkled with long periods of silence, and punctuated with occasional sips of coffee.

"Traffic's calmed down," Jeb observed as his eyes followed a passing blue sedan braking repeatedly to slow down to the posted speed limit of thirty-five.

Sam nodded. "Yeah. Fall's comin'." He took a sip of coffee, then leaned down and put the cup on the floor. "Makes it nicer to hang out here."

"Yeah, it does," Jeb agreed.

The screen door opened and Martha Cullen, the portly storeowner, emerged with a coffee mug and sat down in a rocker near Jeb and Sam. She wiped her forehead with her white apron. "Time for a short break."

Sam said with a knowing smile, "Cleanin' the storage room's hard work."

Martha sighed and nodded.

Jeb asked, "Anything new going on, Martha?"

Martha took a sip of coffee. "Not really. No, wait. I heard some scuttlebutt."

"What?"

"Heard the Zeller clan's at it again."

"Yeah?"

"It's hush-hush. This time ol' Stan's involved; you know he ain't partial to talk about him and his family."

Jeb nodded. "Boy, I'd just as soon leave town than make that tight-lipped mason mad."

"Well, you know what? That'd be sound advice for his nephew," Martha said, inspecting the nail of her right thumb and rubbing it with her index finger.

"Is that so?"

Martha looked at Jeb with raised eyebrows. "Yes. Stan's warned that twerp to shape up or else."

"No kidding?"

"Andrew's bent on selling the family house to get his share, and the money he says he's loaned his mother. Does he care that it'll put his poor mother and two little sisters out on the street? No, he doesn't. All he cares about is money."

Jeb pushed with his feet against the floor to coax the rocker into a gentle, squeaky motion. Then he said, "That lawyering slime's already cleaned out the family coffers. Did that right after his father's death."

Martha took a sip of her coffee. "Yes, he did, and now he's eyeing the family house," and continued as she raised her hand to her neck, "and of course Stan's had it up to here with him."

Jeb shook his head and said, "Andrew thinks he's smart; but he's really stupid. He should've known Stan will get riled up. So what happened?"

"Marge . . . well, we all know how our sweet little Marge—"

Jeb interrupted, "She's a classy French lady—a bit timid maybe."

"She ain't timid. She uses her charming manners and humor, you know, to put up with Stan's gruff personality. Stan scares others, not her; she's the one who makes sure they're raising a God-fearing family. Anyway, I was about to say that she aimed to talk Andrew out of selling the house. So, here's what she did: She invited him to dinner with the family; but she didn't figure on her Stan doing what he did. When Andrew showed up, everybody was there—his mother, sisters—everybody."

Jeb and Sam grinned in anticipation.

Martha smiled and continued, "Stan met Andrew just as he entered the front door; he grabbed him by the arm, and marched him right outside, to the back of the house."

Jeb said, "Wow."

"They came into the house a few minutes later, and Stan calmly told Marge to serve dinner."

"And Andrew?"

"I heard he was shaking like he'd seen a ghost—his father's ghost, I'd reckon." Martha laughed. "His hands shook so bad he couldn't keep food on his fork long enough to get it in his mouth; and he kept sipping water, trying to calm himself."

Jeb sighed. "That damned weasel's sure messed up his family."

"I reckon now Andrew knows that selling the house ain't right for his health. All this is hush-hush; so don't go telling other people." Martha got up and headed back into the store.

Jeb raised his eyebrows and called out after her, "You know I don't do that."

Sam, who'd been sitting back and listening, smiled and said, "Of course you do that, Jeb; you love it." Then, making a sweeping gesture, he continued, "The whole town loves to gossip: All of us patriotic, superstitious, church-going, well-off and not-so-well-off people have our noses planted deep into one another's business."

Jeb shook his head. "Aw, Sam. Stop exaggerating."

Sam's eyes sparkled with mock indignation. "I'm not exaggeratin'. Secrets are our town's lifeblood. Don't you see? We all have secrets—nice ones, sometimes juicy ones. But the thing is: Everyone knows them. We figure it's our moral duty—"

"Jeeez, Sam, you're plain mistaken. Folks are just being warm and sympathetic—"

"Yeah, yeah, that's all well and good; but they're also the ones with big ears and runny mouths that whisper a lot." Sam seemed to relish Jeb's defensive reaction.

Jeb shook his head without saying anything.

"C'mon, Jeb. You liked hearing about the Zellers, right? They make a great soap opera—better than TV. Clans like that make this rustic place pretty interestin', and because of them life here moves at just about the right pace—not so slow as to put you to sleep, but not so fast as to give you high blood pressure."

The squeaky rocker telegraphed Jeb's uneasiness. "Enough of that talk. Guess what I heard about Alma. You know she's been fainting lately. . . ."

• • •

Terryton School and the Zeller house were at the opposite ends of the town. The seven-year-old Steve and his eleven-year-old twin sisters rode bikes to school. His six-year-old twin brothers and other kindergartners and first graders were transported to the school in a bus.

The twin sisters took sack lunches and ate with their friends. The twin brothers were home from school by lunchtime. Since Steve shared classes with his cousin Tony, who lived across the street from the school and went home to eat lunch, his uncle Jim had insisted that he come with Tony to eat lunch at the house. That sounded like a good idea to Steve and his parents, and Stan was appreciative of his younger brother's thoughtful gesture.

Jim hadn't consulted with his wife Amy before committing her to feed Steve: He suspected she wouldn't agree. He was right. When she did find out, the fury she aimed at him almost gave him a permanent facial twitch. While she was unable

to undo his offer to feed Steve, she vented her seething displeasure in other ways. Steve's lunch—sometimes soup and
sandwich, but mostly cold leftovers and a glass of water—was
always ready and waiting for him at one end of the kitchen
table. Aunt Amy would admonish him to eat right away; the
reason—she'd established it the very first day he'd turned up
for lunch—was that she wanted to make sure he wouldn't be
late going back to school.

Amy prepared Tony's lunch fresh, just as the two boys
would enter the house. She'd pour juice or milk for him after
Steve had hurried through his food and drank the water; and
often, as the two boys would be getting ready to return to
school, she'd make an excuse to prevent Tony from leaving
with Steve. Once Steve was out of the house, she'd treat her
beloved son to a candy or some other dessert.

She always asked Steve, "Did you have enough to eat,
dear? Would you want a larger portion tomorrow?"

Steve wasn't fooled for a minute; he told Marge all about the
treatment he was getting from his aunt. "Ma, I like milk; but she
gives me only water. Tony gets milk or juice, sometimes both."

Marge said in a pacifying tone, "I'll give you more milk with
breakfast; you can also have it when you come home after
school. How's that?"

Steve ignored the bribe. "I want sack lunches."

"That would indeed be very rude to Uncle Jim; and your
father would be so hurt. No, dear, we mustn't appear ungrate-
ful by complaining or giving you sack lunches," Marge said.

"She gives Tony candy and cookies and pies, and I get
nothing."

"You poor darling, I'm sorry. But don't worry. I'll make
sure you have plenty of sweet treats after school. Okay? Now
be a good boy and come here." She hugged him and kissed his
forehead. "There, now run along, dear."

Even before Steve complained to his mother about Amy's antics, he knew she'd remain true to her character: She'd avoid confrontation at all costs; and she wouldn't risk creating ill-feelings among relatives, even though it meant he'd have to bear the humiliation of being fed lunch every school day by Aunt Amy, who resented every morsel he ate.

• • •

"Ma, Ma! Steve hit me in the tummy. It hurts bad," screamed one of the twin boys as he ran down the stairs.

Marge called out in a stern voice from the family room, "Steve, come down here this minute. I told you to keep away from the boys, didn't I?"

"But, Ma. They broke my GI Joe," said Steve, then a tall, lanky eight-year-old, as he pushed his red hair away from his face, and followed his twelve-year-old twin sisters down the stairs.

The sisters were looking back, and making faces at him. One of them said, "No, Ma, Steve broke it; I saw him do it."

"Why do you kids have to fight all the time?" Marge's question was rhetorical; her tone exasperated.

Steve, still descending the stairs, repeated his protest, "They broke my GI Joe first."

Steve pushed past his snickering sisters and stomped toward his mother, who was sitting on the couch in the family room, consoling the teary-eyed twin. But before he reached Marge, his father, Stan, who'd been reading the newspaper, jumped out of his lounger and delivered an open-handed wallop to Steve's buttocks. The stinging blow stunned him. He froze; his eyes bulged and his lips quivered.

"Lots more where that came from. Don't hit your brother. Get it, boy?" Stan said with a disgusted look.

At that painful instant, Steve knew he'd lost his case and the only prudent thing left for him to do was to start bawling, and hope for minimal further punishment.

Stan's voice was soft, yet menacing. "Stay in your room till your mother calls you for dinner. Now, disappear."

Steve ran upstairs, relieved to have escaped further assault on his behind; he almost knocked down his second twin brother, who was standing on the stairs, smiling and taking in the drama unfolding below. Steve closed the bedroom door, picked up the GI Joe and its severed leg, and fell back on his bed. He held the leg piece where it belonged against the body piece, and watched his prized toy with tears trickling down from the corners of his eyes.

Stan had returned to his lounger and become engrossed in the newspaper. Marge continued to hug and comfort the twin; and the two sisters, sitting next to them on the sofa, exchanged impish smiles.

Similar scenarios played out all too frequently at Steve's expense for another eighteen months. Although he felt his parents desired to provide the same love, care, discipline and security to all their children, he blamed them for not seeing through the ruses of their other four angels. But he didn't vocalize his feelings because experience warned him that the swift and sure response from his father's hands would be detrimental to his health.

Steve realized very early in his childhood that growing up sandwiched between a female sibling clique and a male sibling clique wasn't going to be easy. His older twin sisters always sided with his younger twin brothers. He didn't know why that was, except that it was a fact. First, he sought acceptance as an equal from his brothers and sisters; that relationship was a non-starter. Next, he tried to earn their good graces through appeasement and offerings of his meager belongings; that attempt, too, failed and they ended up with most of his possessions. Finally, he resigned himself to absorbing their unmitigated abuse, not to mention their conniving and sneakiness designed to keep him in trouble.

The strain of almost incessant obnoxious treatment at the hands of his siblings and shenanigans of other relatives was too much for the young Steve to cope with. It spawned in him an unfortunate defense mechanism: He encased himself in a barrier of apathy that left him unaffected by emotional ties and relationships. He became selfish and learned to be wary of his enemies and kin alike. He'd participate faithfully in all family gatherings and functions; but, with the exception of his parents Marge and Stan, he stopped being close to anyone in the Zeller clan.

• • •

By the time Steve turned ten, he'd made progress in mastering the art of countering his siblings' abuse and deceit; and life at home was becoming somewhat tolerable.

While he remained a good student, he was no longer self-effacing, sensitive and accommodating; instead, he'd become out-going, quick-witted and persuasive. His self-confidence had received a much-needed boost from the physical attributes he'd acquired: He was taller, stronger; his wavy red hair, penetrating blue eyes and emerging sharp features were collaborating to give his oval face a handsome look. He discovered he was a natural athlete with talent for playing baseball, a game he loved.

He'd also turned into a bully—a role he began to cherish, much to the dismay of the twins and other kids. The resulting notoriety put him in a different league and squarely in competition with the other mean characters in the school.

One day, his unprovoked, smart-alecky comments led to a confrontation with Jody, an oversized tough kid in his class. When the school ended, the two clashed once again on the school's basketball court; Steve wound up with numerous bloody bruises, a fat lip, and torn shirt.

Steve was afraid to face his father. By the time he could muster enough courage to go home, it was already dinnertime. He sped home on his bike; he jumped off it before it stopped, allowing it to roll into the porch. He bounded up the steps, entered the house and closed the front door behind him. He was breathing hard. He saw his family was at the dinner table, staring at him.

With a look of shock, Marge got up from her chair and rushed toward him. *"Mon Dieu!* What happened? Look at your face."

Steve started to cry, and his body began to shake. "Jody did it. I . . . I didn't do anything . . . that fat pig started it."

Marge held him close to her and said in a comforting voice, "Now, now, dear. It'll be all right. Let's clean your face and take care of those nasty bruises."

Steve continued to sob for the benefit of his father.

His brothers and sisters were laughing and chanting: "Steve got beat. Steve can't fight. . . ."

Stan, who sat staring at Steve, said in a calm but stern voice, "Shut up. Shut the hell up, everyone."

The house went silent.

Without taking his eyes off Steve, Stan continued, "Son, stop that damn whining, huh? Can you do that, son? When there's a fight, people really don't give a damn or remember who's right or who's wrong; they don't even care who started it. The only thing that matters is the result—the winning— you hear? The winning. You let that fat punk beat the hell out of you; that's all there's to it. You lost the fight and that, my boy, is a fact. Now, clean up and let's eat."

That night, sleep didn't come easy to Steve; his mind wouldn't stop replaying his father's words. The broader message of "win, no matter what" finally started to sink in, and he could see how it applied to his situation with the twins: Whenever his brothers or sisters instigated confrontations with him, he was the one punished by his parents; his siblings always ended up gleeful observers—and winners. The undeniable truth, he realized, was that he allowed himself to be set up by them. *To win, I must plan and be sneaky—and patient.* With that lesson seared into his mind, he fell asleep.

• • •

Mister Bixley, a respected aging history teacher, dressed in a brown tweed suit and a black bow tie, walked into the classroom. He placed his worn, black briefcase on his desk and opened it. Students were settling in their seats; the class was about to begin.

"Hey? What happened to my history book?" Jamie asked in his high-pitched voice as he rummaged through the mess in his desk. He was loud enough to be heard over the normal din that prevailed at the start of every class. "All right. Who's the wise guy? The book was here this morning. Damn it, this isn't the first time someone's taken things from my desk."

Mister Bixley, who was busy cleaning the blackboard, turned around. He looked with raised eyebrows in Jamie's direction, and then went back to his activity.

Venting to no one in particular, Jamie continued, "Last week it was chewing gum and a pen; week before, it was a notebook. My parents are going to kill me—history book's expensive." He had tears in his eyes.

Other kids, who'd been ignoring Jamie—as was normal for them because of his nerdy appearance and mannerisms—started to pay attention to his tirade, and some of them started to chime in with their own complaints:

"My notebook disappeared three weeks ago."

"I lost a dollar last week."

"Someone swiped my eraser yesterday."

And the litany continued.

Jody, who was watching the show, smiled and said to Steve sitting in front of him, "Hey, Steve, what happened to Jamie's book? C'mon, pansy, tell us." Then he laughed.

Steve clenched his teeth and remained quiet.

Mister Bixley completed cleaning the blackboard. He faced the class, wiped his hands with a handkerchief, and said, "Jamie's history book is missing. Has anyone found it, or taken it by mistake? If you have, please return it; or, if you know where it is, speak up now."

The class became quiet.

Mister Bixley continued, "I urge you to speak now, before I take the next step. Judging from the comments I've just heard, it appears that pilfering has been going on for some time."

No one moved or said anything.

With a determined look, Mister Bixley said in a measured tone, "All right, time's up. Everyone get up and come to the front of the class."

The class complied in silence.

Pointing to two students at random, Mister Bixley said, "You and you, walk with me and help me search every desk."

The students watched with anticipation as their desks were opened and inspected.

"Jody, come here. What's this in your desk?" Mister Bixley asked as he looked in Jody's open desk.

Jody walked over and saw two history books in his desk. His shock was obvious. He lifted the hard covers of both books; one had Jamie's name written in it. His face turned red; long seconds passed before he could muster his senses to protest. "I don't know how Jamie's book got in here. I didn't take it. I . . . I didn't take it."

Jamie pointed a finger at Jody. "He took my book; he's a thief."

Commotion broke out. Most students, obviously relishing Jody's plight, shouted their own accusations and insults at him. He simply stood there—stunned and speechless.

Mister Bixley raised his hands. "Stop that." Then, he motioned to Jody. "Follow me to the office, please."

• • •

After a summary dismissal of Jody's vehement denials, the school gave him the most severe punishment it could short of outright expulsion: He was put on a six-month probation, barred from all classes for a month, and excluded from all sports and other extracurricular activities for a year. The grapevine chatter was that his father, incensed and embarrassed, rounded out his punishment with a severe beating at home.

Demolished and shunned, Jody lost his spirit; soon, he became a mere shadow of his past, confident self.

• • •

When Steve had watched Jody being led away to the principal's office, he'd felt overwhelmed with excitement, but hadn't shown it; the only outward sign had been the glitter in his eyes as he stared at the crumbling Jody and thought, *Gotcha, you bastard. Go ahead and explain Jamie's history book I put in your desk. Try to mess with me, will you?*

Critical to his plan was recruiting Jamie, a gangly wimp who was a regular target of Jodie's harassment. He'd cornered him a week before at lunch break. "Hey, let's have some fun with the pea-brained dork Jody. What d'you say?"

Jamie shook his head. "Nah. He's a mean son-of-a-bitch. Do I look like I'm stupid or something?"

He said in a coaxing tone, "C'mon. Let's get him. He picks on you all the time."

Jamie said in a shrill voice, "He'll kill me."

Steve put a protective arm around him. "He won't know a thing. You won't get hurt. Guaranteed."

Jamie's laugh was derisive. "Guaranteed by you? Yeah, right. He whipped your sorry ass—"

"That's bullshit." He fought to hide his anger. *I need this weak-willed jerk; I must not lose him.* He blurted out, "Tell you what: I'll give you two bucks."

Jamie's eyes widened. "Two bucks? I'm in—but only if he won't find out I helped you."

The bribe was steep; but it worked. He breathed easy. "He won't find out. Here's the plan. . . ."

He didn't care that Jody wasn't going to know who was responsible for his downfall. The only thing that mattered to him was he'd won and was in control; and finally, learned how to get and use power. Also, one other realization hit him: *I'm going to keep running into jerks like Jamie and Jody; I'll always be able to persuade one to help me crush the other.* He was pleased with himself.

He derived other benefits from the Jody incident: Jamie became his loyal and grateful subject who promoted him at every opportunity; and, he also spread the word, especially to other tough kids, that Steve had ways to take care of his enemies like Jody, and that Steve was his best friend. The message got through: The bullies started avoiding confrontations with Steve, and stopped picking on Jamie.

Months later, while he was still buoyed by his triumph over Jody, he expanded the role of bribery because it had worked on Jamie.

He used ice cream as a tool to control others. By giving free ice cream to key boys, he was able to: extract favors that caused some kids' faces to be smashed if they crossed him; instilled fear in others that made them eager to please him; make yet others his "friends." He was amazed at the payback on the investment in ice creams. He learned that most kids were willing to be exploited; all he had to do was come up with the right incentive. From his perspective that was a win-win situation.

One day Steve and his friends couldn't get ice cream because no one had cash. Steve saw an opportunity to bolster his image because he knew where to find cash. That day he and his friends ended up enjoying quite a few chocolate and strawberry cones.

• • •

"Hi, Ma. Hi, Pa." Steve closed the front door and, as usual, started to bounce up the stairs to disappear into his bedroom.

"Steve, come here." He heard his father call out from the family room.

"Coming," Steve said. By then he was at the top of the stairs. He dropped his schoolbag and headed down. He saw the twins' ascending the stairs hastily and heard their room doors bang shut.

In the living room, Marge sat in her usual, comfortably padded, high-back cane chair, knitting a shawl. She looked up and, without saying a word, acknowledged Steve with a faint smile; then went back to her knitting.

Steve faced his father sitting in his favorite lounger. "Yes, Pa?"

Stan was watching him over the newspaper he was holding. He hadn't taken his eyes off Steve from the time he'd entered the room. He asked, "What's new in school?"

Steve shrugged and replied, "Nothing much."

Stan's eyes narrowed. "I hear you've been buying a lot of ice cream."

Steve was caught off guard. He said without thinking, "I didn't eat any today."

Stan's voice remained calm. "You had a lot yesterday."

Steve felt his neck getting warm. A thin film of perspiration appeared on his forehead. *How does he know? Who told him?* He managed to say, "Had . . . had a few."

Stan's eyes bored into his son; his voice quivered. "No, son, not a few—a lot. You had a lot, didn't you?"

Steve's armpits were wet. *How did he find out? God, what do I do now?* He replied in a faint voice, "Yes. I . . . I had a lot."

Stan got up from the lounger. "How did you pay for them?"

Fear made Steve queasy and confused; he couldn't come up with an answer. He froze. He didn't see his father's open left hand connect with the right side of his face. The force of the stinging slap turned him around and sent him staggering onto the hardwood floor. He started shrieking from shock, pain and pure terror. But before he could get up, sharp lashes from his father's heavy leather belt started raining on his back and buttocks.

As Stan kept swinging his punishing belt, he shouted with rage, "Why, you stupid . . . Steal from your mother, will you? I can't believe you did that ... My son stealing to buy ice cream ... to show off at school. Think you're a big shot, don't you? We'll see about that. No kid of mine'll become a thief. You hear? So help me, Steve, if you steal again . . . I'll kill you . . . You hear? You'll be dead."

By the time Marge could intervene, Stan had delivered lashes too numerous to count. Once she managed to force herself between her enraged husband and her wailing son cowering on the floor, Stan backed away without a word. He settled into the lounger, held his hand out over its side, and let the belt he was holding drop to the floor. Then he went back to his newspaper.

Marge's voice was full of love and compassion as she hugged and consoled Steve. "Now, now, dear. Everything will be fine. You know stealing is a sin. It's the God's commandment: Thou shalt not steal, right? So, don't ever steal, my son. Next time you need money, come to me and I'll give it to you. All right? Good . . . that's a good boy. Now let's go and wash up." Marge put her arm around her sobbing, puffy-eyed son and led him up the stairs.

That evening, Steve couldn't wait to get away from his family. So, right after a tense dinner, he sought the privacy of his bedroom. There, he stood a long time in front of a mirror—naked—surveying the red and burning welts on his entire back and buttocks. Stan had lived up to his reputation once again: The havoc his wrath could cause was in plain view.

He was disgusted with his own stupidity and overconfidence. While focusing at length on the physical aspects of the painful encounter with his no-nonsense father, he kept repeating in his head: *I got to make sure Pa can't find a reason to beat the shit out of me—ever again.* Then his mind moved on to reinforce the recently learned survival lessons. *No more spontaneous stealing: I must plan, plan, plan before I pinch something. I must not get caught taking other's things—ever again.* He also concluded that his mother was incapable of playing the role of a protector or rescuer: When faced with delicate situations involving her husband and their children, she tended to remain a neutral, though concerned and loving, observer.

Stan's willingness to dispense fatherly beatings convinced Steve to put a heavy emphasis on self-preservation, and sharpen the God-given skill to lie and make it a part of his arsenal.

Steve learned his lessons well. By age eleven he was using lying and scheming to augment his quick wit in all conflicts. He was manhandled a few times by irate losers; but that didn't deter him because he'd always end up winning, which meant everything to him. He also realized that altering truth packed a much greater punch if it was practiced with discretion—only to deliver a final blow.

At home there was a complete role reversal: His four brothers and sisters—his perennial tormentors—were the ones on the defensive, and targets of his surreptitious assaults. His parents were unaware of the profound changes occurring in the sibling relationships under their very noses; all they saw was a relaxed and confident Steve getting along with the twins. They were delighted—and relieved—to see their conflict-prone son was finally a happy, athletic, well-adjusted child with admirable academic performance.

At school, the change was no less dramatic. His popularity soared; his enemies feared and avoided him; and the baseball team and coaches loved his natural, all-round talent for the game. And then, another remarkable thing happened: The upper class in-crowd welcomed him into their clique.

With all the wonderful things going on in his life Steve didn't notice adolescence creeping into his body. Then, all of a sudden, one day, at age fourteen, the intensifying hormones unleashed within him a new sensation—the awakening primal urge. He didn't understand it, but enjoyed the titillating effect it had on him. Also, his attitude toward the girls underwent a profound change: They went from objects to ignore or punch to objects of desire to explore and share sensations with— freckles, pimples, and all. Unfortunately he didn't feel close enough to anyone to confide in about his confusing emotions and transformation. So, he didn't.

One spring evening, after a crushing loss to the school baseball team of a nearby town, Steve was too dejected and tired to go home right away. He stretched out on a bench, closed his eyes and listened to the ballpark empty out.

The darkness was settling in.

"Are you all right?"

He opened his eyes and saw Jane standing close to him. He barely knew her: She was two grades ahead of him and focused exclusively on seniors. And he was just a lowly freshman.

"I'm okay." He sighed and sat up.

Jane sat down next to him and dropped her tennis gear on the ground. She was a sixteen-year-old with a seductive body and streaky silver hair. She was tall as Steve. Thanks to her affluent parents, she was well-traveled, liberated, and had permission to drive the family car.

"No you're not okay. I can see the score board from the tennis courts. You guys got your butts kicked." She smiled.

"Yeah, it was a bummer. We just couldn't get our offense going . . . only three lousy hits, and nobody made second base. We really stunk." He leaned back, clasped his hands behind his head and closed his eyes.

"Want a ride home?" she asked.

"I could use one today."

Minutes went by without conversation.

Jane was hunched forward, with arms straight and hands planted on her knees. She looked at him and broke the long silence. "Steve, I'm wondering."

He opened his eyes and brought his arms down. "Wondering? About what?"

Without taking her eyes off him, she said, "About you."

His eyes narrowed. "What . . . why?"

She said in a matter-of-fact tone, "I see you hang out at school with some of the seniors I know. But I've never seen you with them when they go on dates around town. You do date, don't you?"

"Date? Uh . . . no," he said in a soft voice.

Jane appeared surprised. "You mean, not ever?"

"Well . . . I . . . I mean—"

She smiled and interjected, "I see you eyeing girls in school. I've caught you checking me out; I don't mind, really, because I check you out. You're cute . . . nice buns. You know . . . sexy."

He was speechless. Jane's directness in revealing her desire and coming on to him caught him off guard; his mind turned to mush, unable to process the situation at hand and offer an adequate response.

He sat there embarrassed with a grin and stared at Jane.

She broke the awkward silence. "Let's go out sometime."

He couldn't believe what he was hearing. *She wants to date me.* "Wh . . . what?"

"You know, go out and have some fun."

His pulse was racing and his mind was refusing to cooperate.

Without waiting for his response, Jane lifted his arm and put it around her neck as she slid closer and turned toward him. "Let me show you what I mean by fun. Kiss me."

Steve got home two hours later; he laid awake all night remembering and savoring the explosive experience.

• • •

From that day on Jane gave Steve rides home on a routine basis. Their torrid adventure went on for over two years, until she graduated from school and left for a college on the West Coast.

Besides imparting her blasé attitude toward sex, she introduced him to one other thing: The Big Apple. She described in detail her luxurious, fun-filled visits to New York City and told him about the towering Empire State Building; the unshackled, free-spirited scene of Greenwich Village; the exotic Chinatown; the sophisticated Fifth Avenue; the decadent nightlife; and, above all, the concentration of power and wealth on Wall Street and Park Avenue. Her vivid description of the city was compelling. Steve was sold; somehow, he was going to experience New York.

• • •

"Steve, you have a letter; it's from New York University," Marge called out to Steve who was upstairs in his bedroom. Her quivering voice betrayed the emotions she was trying hard to control.

Stan pulled himself upright in his lounger, and watched in anticipation.

Steve had excellent grades and SAT scores. Those credentials and his baseball-playing ability would've made him eligible to go to a good state college in Illinois. His parents could've covered his tuition and most of his room and board.

But his heart was set on going to New York, where the college tuition and the cost of living were horrendous. He'd applied for admission to New York University, a private institution with liberal arts campus located in Greenwich Village, the heart of a vibrant and free lifestyle Jane had talked to him about.

He hurried down the stairs. He reached for the envelope and said, "Thanks." His palms were sweaty; he was shaking as he made clumsy attempts to rip it open. After what felt like an eon to him, he held the open letter in his hands.

The first line read: "It is my pleasure to inform you. . . ."

He shouted, "I'm in! I'm in!" He gave Marge a joyous hug.

Marge held her son's head in her hands. "I'm so happy for you . . . and very proud." She pulled his head down and kissed his forehead.

His heart was pounding as he ran toward his father. Stan had a smile on his face; he appeared to be savoring the moment. Their handshake was vigorous.

Steve was animated, and his voice loud. "Pa. I made it. I'm going to New York!" He bent down and hugged Stan.

Stan squeezed him back and said, "Yes, son. Congratulations. I'm proud of you."

Steve rushed out of the house to announce to his world that his cherished dream was coming true.

• • •

Stan's eyes became moist as he watched the front door close behind his son. That was the only outward sign of his emotions brought on by the fact Steve would be the very first member of his family to go away to college.

Deep down, he'd carried a gnawing concern about Steve ever since he'd stolen money from Marge. And Stan knew that, among his five children, he'd been particularly hard on

Steve, even as he'd excelled in studies and sports. He had to admit Steve had grown into a fine young man.

Now his fervent hope was Steve would not only cope with the college life in New York City, but thrive.

He used his shirt sleeve to wipe away a tear drop from each eye, pushed the lounger back and closed his eyes. He had a smile on his face.

3
Growth

STEVE EMERGED FROM the Port Authority Bus Terminal in midtown Manhattan on an early September morning carrying a bulky suitcase packed by his mother. His clothes were rumpled; his eyes red. The uncomfortable eighteen-hour Greyhound bus ride, with stops in several cities, wasn't conducive to a decent sleep and left him exhausted. The traffic was light at that hour of the morning. He stopped on the sidewalk and pulled out a paper with directions to the YMCA. As he was deciding on how to proceed, a passing street sweeper truck spraying water doused his trousers—not the welcome he expected. But that didn't dampen his enthusiasm: He was in New York.

As planned, he checked into the Y on Forty-Second Street. After wolfing down a stack of syrupy pancakes in the Y's cafeteria, he wandered around the Times Square area. What he saw at that time of the day did not impress him: A mob of New Yorkers in a hurry and cars making forward progress through a combination of frequent lurches to stop and aggressive acceleration. The glamor he expected was absent. He retreated to the Y and spent the rest of the day lounging with the street map and other information provided to him by NYU to work out the logistics of getting around the city and the Washington Square campus. At night, when he lay in bed in his small, windowless room, he was engulfed with a sinking—almost nauseating— feeling of doubt about his decision to come to the megacity. He couldn't shake that funk until sleep intervened. That self-doubt, however, never returned.

His pent-up desire to explore was initially tempered by the city's size and oddities: the ever-rushing pedestrians; the towering skyscrapers; the maze of graffiti-adorned subways with riders expert at avoiding eye contact; the disparate races and colors; the glitter and nightlife on Broadway and Forty-Second Street; the ever-present street people; and, of course, the impatient cars that clogged the arteries of the city. But within a month he became jaded and nothing fazed him: He'd become a New Yorker who loved the city.

Steve was aware of his parents' inability to provide adequate financial support. His father Stan had told him he'd get full tuition and a fixed amount toward living expenses for the first year, and just a partial tuition subsidy thereafter. But he was confident that he'd find a well-paying job within a year and, after that, wouldn't need any money from his parents. To conserve cash, he decided to live near Greenwich Village so he could walk to the classes and avoid transportation costs.

The New York University's business and liberal arts campus and student housing were a cluster of large and small buildings around the famous Washington Square Park, a magnet for locals, visitors, and the artists who claimed the park as their art gallery. With the least-expensive rental options such as student housing and sharing large apartments already gone, Steve was fortunate to find a small studio apartment, carved out of an attic, with its own outside entrance, on Third Street. The rent for that tiny box brought home to him exactly how costly living in The Big Apple would be; he concluded he must find a job without delay if he was even going to survive—let alone have any chance of enjoying life—in the city.

His job hunt immediately revealed that positions available to students were scarce. He learned another unpleasant fact: businesses don't consider a college freshman very employable. Even a job as waiter, busboy or laborer seemed to be beyond his reach. *I must find a job. I must.* His desperation was growing, but he couldn't let that get in the way of his studies: Flunking courses was not an option for him. So he hung around daily in Loeb Student Center to study; to check on job-postings on the bulletin board; to keep out of coffeehouses and bars because he couldn't afford to socialize; and to escape his claustrophobic apartment.

He'd decide not to share with his parents the anxiety he felt over his fast-shrinking bank account; his crimped lifestyle had stretched into the third month, with no prospect for improvement.

One early evening after classes, he took his daily trip to the student center bulletin board to check for new job leads, he saw another guy about his age, with black wavy hair and a closely cropped beard, staring at the postings. He'd made a point of making small talk with the fellow scanners. So, he asked, "Anything new?"

The stranger continued to study the bulletin board. "Oh, I don't know. I'm just looking at the posting format."

"Huh?"

The man turned his head and looked at him. "I want to post a job."

Steve was startled, but regained his composure instantly. "Well, I'm looking for a job. You might save yourself the trouble of posting it if I'm your man. My name's Steve Zeller, Business major." He smiled and extended his hand toward the man with a job to offer.

The man smiled back and shook his hand. "Hi. I'm Don McCoy, Philosophy major. Don't get too excited about the job: It's part-time and temporary."

Steve wanted to shout: "Who cares, man? It's money!" But he said, "That's fine. Let's chat in the lounge."

Don eyes narrowed. His face and voice clearly displayed uncertainty. "Okay, I guess."

The student lounge was a spacious, wall-to-wall carpeted room. It had an extensive network of floor-to-ceiling tinted glass to bring in the outdoors, and the remaining wall space was covered with abstract art of exploding bold colors. Modern furniture with earth-tone fabrics was strewn around the lounge for small gatherings, individual quiet time or studying. Steve and Don sat in a couple of oversized bucket chairs, away from other students.

"So what's the job?" Steve asked with a smile.

"So who're you?" Don retorted, staring at him with a grin that lifted his dark beard.

"Fair enough," Steve said, still smiling. At that moment, he realized that the sturdy-looking, average-height, bearded man sitting across from him was a confident, no-nonsense individual. He asked, "Have you heard of Shawnee National Forest? No? Okay, how about Illinois? Yes? Good. Let's start there."

With that he proceeded to give Don an overview of himself, which took quite a while because Don felt free to throw out questions. By the time he finished, Don even knew about Jane and her role in his sexual awakening. He was amazed at Don's quick mind and ability to extract information. He sensed most people who met Don must find him unnerving and coarse. But he wasn't intimidated or put off by him; in fact, he found himself totally relaxed with him.

Steve decided they'd digressed enough. He leaned forward and asked, "Okay, now the job. What is it?"

Don responded, "It involves basic clerical stuff in an old financial firm located on Wall Street."

Steve wanted details. "What clerical stuff?"

Don didn't answer his question, but said, "Wolfe Financial Services is a thriving private company founded by Helmut Wolfe. It has a specialized niche: It matches its stable of investors with entrepreneurs; and, when an enterprise is ready to go public, it handles the IPO."

"What's IPO?" Steve asked and studied Don's face for signs of disdain, but there weren't any.

Don replied, "IPO stands for 'Initial Public Offering.' That's when shares of a privately-held company are offered to the general public and, magically, the private stock holdings of investors, entrepreneurs and people like Mister Wolfe become worth millions of dollars. Nice, huh?"

"What do you do?" Steve's pulse was racing; he could feel the excitement of working there, close to all that wealth.

Don gestured to him to indicate he wasn't going to be rushed. "Helmut, with two sons and a younger brother, runs the entire business. There are two secretaries and two other permanent employees—the financial specialists—they're not family."

"And what do the financial specialists do?" Steve asked with remarkable patience.

"Their job's to research, compile, massage, and organize the financial data on startup firms picked by Helmut for review. Once a company passes the financial scrutiny and receives Helmut's blessing, the specialists prepare proposals for investors, *et cetera*. You're looking at the only other outsider there; I do the exciting work for the specialists: I compile and organize reams of data for their review, run copies, arrange sections of proposals, make bound copies of the proposals for distribution, and handle any other crap they throw at me. Of course, I work part-time." Don stopped speaking.

Steve took advantage of the pause to ask, "How does the new position fit in?"

"My job's too damn big for one person to handle; I've decided it needs two people. You're in if you want the job."

"You've decided? Come now. What about the big guy, er . . . Helmut, right? You think he might want to have some say in what you drag in?" Steve was beginning to doubt his newly-found potential benefactor.

Don replied in a matter-of-fact manner, "I told Helmut I was going to find someone to share the shitload of work I have; he didn't argue. My father's one of his big investors. You know what I mean? So, don't sweat it. The firm can afford the piddling amount you'll get paid."

Steve had to restrain himself from jumping up and hugging Don; he could feel the crushing weight of his financial glacier melting away. He asked in an even tone, "Will I be able to afford a beach house on my pay?"

Don laughed. "Nope, but you may have enough for Helmut's twelve-room penthouse on Park Avenue. It's a super place; he uses it for business and private purposes. Negotiate with him; he's always looking to make a buck. But seriously, you'll start at the minimum hourly wage."

Steve liked the way Don stretched the first syllable of "super." "When do I start?"

"How about tomorrow? I'm swamped."

"Tomorrow's good." He was intrigued by Don and wanted to know more about him. "Tell me, why is a rich kid like you working your butt off? Chintzy father?"

Don sighed. "Just the opposite, man. My father would like nothing better than to finance me completely—you know, control me. Who needs that? I want to be independent, as much as I can be. I mean, it's a matter of self-actualization and, of course, personal pride. You understand?"

Steve scratched his cheek. "Look. Just tell me about your-self and save me the wrong guesses."

Don shifted in his chair to get into a more comfortable position and said in an appeasing tone, "Not much to tell. I'm a sophomore; I like the philosophy major, and share student housing with an introvert."

Steve shook his head in mock exasperation. "Don, stop. I'm suffering from information overload. Really, man, that's too much detail."

Don relented. "Okay, okay. I was born and raised in Westport, one of Connecticut's premier bedroom communi-ties for New York. My old man's a plastic surgeon; he has a sinfully lucrative practice on Fifth Avenue, and repairs high-society, wealthy clients only. He's also, as Mother puts it, 'blessed with a bit of Irish blarney—'"

Steve interjected, "You mean he's a bullshit artist."

Don nodded. "Yup. The combination's made him a *nouveau riche,* and quite popular with the old-money crowd."

"Sounds like a winner," Steve said and added, "But, you have a problem with that, don't you?"

Don's voice turned serious. "He was an absentee father to my younger brother and me—always working or socializing or traveling, rarely ever home. I don't know how my mother's put up with him—security, I guess. He and I don't get along; we never have. He's absolutely sure I'm wasting my time and opportunity—not to mention his money—by taking philoso-phy at NYU. He's pissed I'm not in medical school and won't step into his exclusive snip-'n-stretch practice. The situation's a bummer, man."

"So you're getting even with him for ignoring you during your childhood?"

"Beats me. Hey, that's super. You're playing the shrink." Don laughed. "But really, it's more than that: I want money of my own so I don't have to rely on him. Okay? I don't give a damn about his money or what he thinks. I really don't. I want to be in control of my life—not him; and that's why I got this crummy job."

"And you got it by using your father's power and influence, of course," Steve said with a smirk on his face.

"Did I say I was stupid?" Don asked with a smile.

Steve grinned. "Anyone who doesn't give a damn about wealth should get tested for a brain disorder."

Stroking his beard, Don said, "One other thing: My father hates my beard."

"Another sign of rebellion?" Steve asked. "You know, it does nothing for you; looks kind of grungy, I think. Listen to your father, and get rid of it."

Don laughed and changed the subject.

Their chat continued into late evening. Both seemed to be comfortable with each other; they ended up sharing a pizza and a couple of beers before saying goodbye.

That night, as tired and sleepy Steve lay in bed, he marveled at the critical event that had taken place: *Got a job, finally! I don't care what I have to do or put up with, I'll make it work. Now, I have a chance to at least not starve. Don's a hell of a character. And that Helmut guy? I'd love to know how he made it big. . . .*

• • •

Otto Wolfe was thirty-two years old when he immigrated to America from Germany with his wife, Hilda, and their two-year-old son, Helmut. They were from a small town near Berlin; he'd been an accountant in a privately-owned tool manufacturing company around which the town had grown. The factory and the town were dying a slow economic death when he was laid off. He decided his family's future lay in the United States of America and used his meager savings to sail to New York.

Upon landing in New York, Hilda announced that her morning sickness on the ship wasn't motion sickness—she was pregnant. Otto found a cheap, but decent, apartment in the Bowery, an impoverished area in lower Manhattan. Also, because of his accounting background, within days he snared a clerical job with a stockbroker on Wall Street.

Life was good for Otto and his family. Hilda had given birth to another son, Victor. As his sons graduated from high school, Otto was able to get them well-paying clerical jobs in brokerage houses on Wall Street. Both brothers married school sweethearts at early ages, and moved into their own apartments to raise families. Of the two, Helmut, the older brother, was by far the more thoughtful, motivated and aggressive.

A day before leukemia ended the retired Otto's contented seventy-six-year life, his long-time employer and friend visited him. He brought with him a locked metal box that looked like a good-sized briefcase.

That night, when the bedridden Otto was alone with his seventy-two-year-old wife, he pointed to the metal box on the floor next to his bed and said in a weak voice, "This is for you." Then, he waved a key in his hand and added, "Open it."

Hilda lifted the box onto the bed and sat down next to it. She shook the box and asked, "What's in it?"

"Securities. Stocks. Here, take the key and open it."

Her eyes narrowed as she took the key and proceeded to unlock the box. "Stocks? Otto, now where did you get money to buy stocks?"

He said with a faint smile, "I told my boss to do me a favor; he agreed. Every time I got paid—for what . . . thirty-five years?—I gave him a little money, about twenty percent of my pay, to buy stocks of big, solid companies and keep them for me; and, when I got dividends, I asked him to buy more stock."

Her face and voice betrayed her shock at what she was seeing in the box she'd opened. "God! Otto, I . . . I can't believe this. So many stocks . . . why didn't you say anything before?"

He was enjoying his beloved's reaction. "I decided I must tell no one because . . . because I wanted to save the money only for you. If I didn't keep it a secret, you would've spent the money on the children and me—poof, it would've been all gone. You must have security when I'm not here to take care of you."

"Oh, my dear, dear Otto," she leaned over the box and hugged him.

Then, through welling tears, they looked into each other's eyes for a long time, and savored their life-tested, enduring love in silence. Both knew their time together was about to end.

● ● ●

Hilda walked up to her son and said in a low voice, "I must speak to you . . . in private, in the bedroom."

Helmut noticed her dignified beauty that persisted despite her age and grief. He said in a gentle voice, "Sure, Mother. I'll be there in a second."

He looked around the living room of his parents' small apartment. Most people attending the gathering after Otto's funeral had left; but, his family, Victor and his wife, and three close family friends were still there talking and eating. He put his plate and glass down on the coffee table, and walked into his parents' bedroom.

Hilda was sitting on the bed and staring at her clasped hands in her lap when Helmut entered the room. In a soft and trembling voice, she said without lifting her head, "Son, I miss him; he was such a wonderful, caring husband and father. We loved each other so much."

Helmut saw two teardrops trickle down his mother's cheeks and fall on her hands. His heart was breaking for her. He was aware of his father's utter devotion to her. He didn't say a word; he sat next to her and hugged her.

She started to sob, and so did he.

Finally, looking into his eyes, she said, "Do you know what your father was doing secretly for all the thirty-five years he worked? He put aside some money from each and every paycheck to take care of me after he was in heaven. Here, let me show you." She walked over to the bedroom closet, brought out the metal box, placed it on the bed near her son, and opened it.

He couldn't believe his eyes. He pulled out a handful of certificates from the box and thumbed through them. His heart started to pound. "Father did this? They're shares of blue chip companies. Oh my God, Mother, there's a fortune here!" he said in an excited whisper.

She put her hand on his shoulder and said, "Helmut, dear, I don't know what to do with all this stock your father has left. You must help me. I need only a few dollars to live on—that's all; and when I'm gone all this will belong to you and your brother, anyway. Son, please look after your father's savings, and take care of everyone: You must take care of Victor and his family, your family, and me. Promise me Helmut. I want you to promise you'll do that."

Still in shock, he was trying to digested what his father had accomplished; it took him a while to answer. "I'll take care of everything . . . everyone, I promise. Mother, I don't want you to worry about a thing—ever."

He reached over the box and hugged her, and once again both broke into tears.

• • •

Helmut turned out to be an astute businessman. He worked his father's investments and Wall Street contacts to ease into a lucrative niche of finding investors for start-up companies. He established Wolfe Financial Services and, understanding the importance of a proper address, located it on Wall Street. Also, he moved his mother, brother and himself out of the New York ghettos to elegant estates in Westport, Connecticut.

As time went by, under his strong, hands-on leadership, Wolfe Financial Services saw exploding growth in business and reputation. It was quite clear to him that he needed people around him who were capable of sharing his decision-making pressures, responsibilities of managing the sheer volume of clients and maintaining the firm's stellar reputation.

His only brother, Victor, who didn't have children, was content to remain a good, solid soldier and execute tasks.

The disconcerted Helmut also observed lack of leadership, ambitious energy and business acumen in his two sons, Alan and Jack. He'd brought them into the firm as they earned their bachelor's degrees in liberal arts. Alan was egotistical and was comfortable with the fact that the family was wealthy, and his father was the boss; and Jack, who was two years younger, followed Alan's lead in everything. His youngest child, Erika, who was attending Yale with an undeclared major, showed little interest in the business.

He had a dilemma: He didn't have a family member who could be groomed to take over after him and lead the successful firm he'd created, and he didn't want to entrust outsiders with its control. While he anguished over the problem, the money kept rolling in.

• • •

Steve, Don and their dates were at one of the city's hot night spots and enjoying folk music when abruptly the music and singing stopped and the entertainer started speaking to the audience.

"So, fellow cosmos-travelers, why is there so much physical pain and suffering in our lives? Does anyone here know? Have you even thought about it—ever? Be honest now. At least we all do agree there's much pain and suffering, don't we? Yes? I see a lot of heads nodding. Okay. Now I'll share exactly why each and every one of you endures a painful existence. I'll tell you because I'm here to bring you peace and love, man. The answer is simple: Most diseases and muscular pain are the direct result of our unnatural posture. Yes, brothers and sisters, our unnatural posture. Hard to believe, isn't it? But it's the truth. Man wasn't meant to walk on two limbs. No, he wasn't." The tall, lean young man in a yellow, flowing robe was addressing his audience from a corner stage large enough to hold him, a chair and an oversized speaker system. His eyes were open so wide that they seemed to bulge out of their sockets. He reiterated in a subdued, but emphatic, tone, "No, he wasn't."

The entertainer's narrow, tanned face was draped with shoulder-length blond hair. He had dark and bushy eyebrows and sunken cheeks; and he sported a scraggly, blond moustache. He put his guitar down on the chair next to him, stepped off the stage, and dropped on his knees and hands. Then, he raised his knees and buttocks and said to the audience, "Children of God follow me . . . to nature, to love, to peace. Get down on all fours and walk toward me. Listen, what do you have to lose? It won't hurt you. Just get off your chairs and try; you'll feel good. Trust me, people."

Steve and Don looked at each other and broke out laughing. Their dates had already left the table and, with a majority of the audience, were heading toward the stage on their fours; the mini-skirts revealed their creamy buttocks and some evidence of panties.

"This is super," Don said.

"Super? Hell no, more like kinky."

The two friends took in the sight with obvious relish. They'd come to that bar—one of the many tourist traps— because of its reputation for the unusual and always-weird entertainment; they weren't disappointed. They watched their giggling dates crawl back to the table and stand up, struggling at the same time to straighten their bosoms and clothing.

The entertainer approached their table and addressed them. "All this may appear to be amusing; but it's really not."

Don's face hardened. "Sure it is. Man, it's hilarious."

"There's a whole scientific and philosophical basis for what I'm offering here."

Don's eyes twinkled. "Hey, wait a minute. I remember now the research you're referring to. It isolated a defective gene that causes dimwits to crave walking on four limbs. Right?"

With his shocked eyes fixed on Don, the entertainer moved away to the sanctuary of another table.

Steve wasn't surprised at what happened; to him, that was Don—gruff and direct. He decided it was time to leave. "We all have suffered enough in life—walking on all fours deserves a shot. So, let's go to my place and try it," he said with exaggerated solemnness.

The part-time job had brought him enough financial security to afford the social scene. With Don's willing participation, he started experiencing all that Greenwich Village and New York City had to offer: the pulsating night spots, plenty of free love, the haunting blues and progressive jazz, and much, much more.

The chance meeting four months before had sparked their friendship. At Wolfe Financial Services, they shared an office and together worked and butted heads with the financial specialists. They also socialized with the same group of friends.

Their bond, however, was made stronger and deeper by the classes they attended together in psychology, philosophy and logic. Because they had divergent value systems, the subject matter of these courses forced them into many lively discussions: The college experience was making both attuned to each other's needs and motivation.

Steve couldn't care less whether it was fate or luck that had introduced Don to him. All he knew was, he'd found a solid friend, even though Don was different from him in many ways. He considered Don's philosophical views and observations of life amusing and, sometimes, intriguing; he admired his painful straightforwardness and impatience with mediocrity; and he also liked his supreme confidence. He felt that trying to impress Don with credentials, position or bank account would be like someone sitting under a tree teeming with birds: Droppings would fall on that person . . . sooner than later. But, above all else, he credited Don with handing him an opportunity of a lifetime: He'd brought him into Wolfe Financial Services, where wealth and power were concentrated in one person—Helmut Wolfe—and the path to the top was short, though steep and blocked.

● ● ●

Don McCoy was at ease talking about anybody or anything except himself or his family. It was only after he and Steve became close he allowed Steve to get more than a glimpse of his world.

He and his younger brother Les grew up on their luxurious family estate in Westport, Connecticut. A loving and dedicated English nanny raised them; she made sure they went properly dressed to their exclusive Catholic school, did their homework, and didn't miss church or Sunday school. Sometimes, their parents, Fred and Jessica McCoy, accompanied them to church. But usually they had no time for activities with their children: Fred was busy with his social life, and performing lucrative facelifts and tummy tucks; and Jessica kept her schedule overloaded with beauty parlor appointments, shopping sprees, golf and, of course, socials for charities. Their lack of involvement and support hurt him deeply. But he hid his feeling of emptiness with a mask of an unconcerned youth, who didn't need proud parents cheering on his efforts and accomplishments.

He was an average-sized, sturdy kid; but he wasn't athletic. Though sports didn't interest him in the least, he let his friends talk him into joining the school wrestling team in the junior year. While he tolerated the physical contact in matches, he realized the time-consuming, strenuous training wasn't for him and dropped out after two short months.

On the evening of the day he quit the team, he was in his room sprawled on the bed, reading; the music was on loud. His father entered the room and turned off the music. "Wrestling's a great sport, son; you've got to hang in. McCoys don't quit. You don't want to be a quitter now, do you?"

He lost it; he couldn't contain his resentment toward his father and exploded. "So I quit. Big deal. What do you care? You haven't come to a practice or . . . or a match—not one. You're never around, and neither's Mom. So, stop lecturing."

There was silence; the conversation was over. Fred's face turned red. He studied his son for a moment, then turned around and walked out of the room. Don turned on the music—even louder than before.

Fred never mentioned the subject again.

Though Don lacked a gregarious personality, he led a surprisingly active social life with a small circle of good friends. He enjoyed writing essays and performing scientific experiments; and he grew into an intense, introspective and confident young man. His intelligence, logic and in-your-face honesty imparted an unsettling message that warned people to be careful what rolled off their tongues when he was around, because he couldn't help pouncing on anything irrational.

When he first met Steve, who was financially strapped and struggling to survive in the city, he wasn't impressed—it was a common condition faced by most students. But what made him take notice was the honesty with which Steve answered his questions; and the fact that he had a job to offer didn't earn him Steve's reverence—fake or otherwise.

He understood Steve's preoccupation with money. But he was amazed at the gusto with which Steve threw himself into his job at Wolfe Financial Services. He knew right then that Steve craved money and power, and would do anything to get them. In that respect, he thought, Steve was a lot like his father Fred; he found it to be ironical that, though he scorned the same addiction to wealth in his father, he

readily accepted it in Steve. But he couldn't explain his conflicting feelings.

. . .

The finals were only a month away; cramming for exams was
in full swing, and so was a last batch of quizzes with which the
professors loved to torture students. Steve met Don in the
student cafeteria after one such quiz. They sat in a booth with
bags of potato chips and sodas.

Don's shoulders drooped; he looked physically drained.
"Phew. The logic quiz was a killer. I worked my brains out all
night, but I don't feel good about the grade in this one. Damn,
I tell you, I should've worked out a deal with the Man upstairs."
He sighed as he rubbed his bloodshot eyes.

"So, now I'm to believe God makes deals with you," Steve
said, humoring him.

Don took a long sip of his drink. "Sure he does. As kids, we
always made deals with Him. Didn't you?"

Steve was munching on chips. "You're kidding, right?"

"Nope. You've got to understand one thing: I grew up with
religion all around me; Nanny made sure of that. My friends
were religious, too. We carried on extended religious discourse, usually—no, especially before final exams on tough
subjects like math or science. You see, we felt that remembering the Almighty would help us get passing grades."

Steve rolled his eyes. "Did you shit-heads consider something a bit more practical, like getting a sneak preview of the
exams—you know, stealing, whatever?"

"Too risky."

"You mean too scared." He snickered.

By then Don appeared to be relaxed and the memory of
his unsatisfactory performance on the quiz seemed to have

faded. "Okay. Now try to follow the kids' thinking. The belief hammered into us was that God loves and rewards those who remember Him and pray. So, temporarily, we'd get very religious. There's nothing wrong with that. And, while we were being pious, we'd naturally become generous. You know, religion—"

"Yeah, yeah, I know, religion and charity go together." He made a fruitless effort to contain his laughter.

"So you do get it. Super," Don said with a straight face and continued, "Look, there's no downside to this. Strong affirmation of the Lord and His generosity, a few trips to the church to get the priest on our side, and throw in some testimonials from the beneficiaries of our charity; that's got to mellow down any god enough to bump up a few grades."

"And, did God bump up your grades?"

"Yes . . . sometimes."

Steve was shaking from laughter and trying to get at the last potato chip in the bag. "You morons could have gotten the same results just by studying a bit harder."

"Of course we did that; but, we were looking for extra insurance—just in case. It wasn't as if we were requesting something for free. After all, we did what God likes: He likes us to remember Him and pray to Him. That's more than what most people do. Don't forget, we'd spread a lot of bucks around too, you know, to the needy and the church."

Steve said, "Sounds like you don't need any lessons in hypocrisy."

Don grimaced. "That *was* my introduction to hypocrisy; I haven't had much use for it since."

Steve, well aware of Don's values, acted as if he was surprised. "That sorry experience taught you one good thing and you don't use it. You're crazy. I think hypocrisy's a great tool—underrated, but very valuable."

"How so?" Don was scowling.

Good. I'll play with him a bit, he thought, and pointed a finger at Don. "You just gave an excellent example of how hypocrisy props up churches and charities that quite frequently wind up helping the poor. That's got to be okay in your book. Right? Now, what about the rich? What makes it possible for them to be completely comfortable with enjoying the luxuries of life, while telling the masses to be satisfied with merely existing as cogs, turning endlessly from paycheck to paycheck? Hypocrisy, man, hypocrisy—what else? And, of course, you know it's also a safe haven for politicians. Where would they be without it? They'd be lost completely." He paused to get Don's reaction.

Don smiled. "You may have a point or two."

"What do you mean *may* have? Take me, for example: I use it a lot; I'm totally comfortable using it."

"You're the type."

Steve shrugged. "So what? People feel comfortable when I use it. Actually, they welcome it, and want to be fooled and expect it. Hypocrisy doesn't hurt anyone. Trust me, it's—"

"You're nuts."

"It's great, really."

Don shook his head. "You belong in a nuthouse; shrinks would just love to get hold of you."

He was having too much fun to stop. "Aw, come on. It isn't deranged to practice hypocrisy: It takes smarts, and lots of it. Guess what?"

"What?"

"I think lying—a very, very close relative of hypocrisy—is also wonderful."

Don raised his eyebrows and threw his hands up. "So now you're going to defend lying. Man, do you know how stressful lying can be? On top of that, it corrodes the psyche and . . . and sucks out self-esteem."

"Hey, cut the crap—I mean, how would you know? Do you lie?"

Don's reply was emphatic. "No."

He said with a hint of defiance, "Well I do; and as far as I can tell it doesn't suck out anything."

Don rubbed his forehead and sighed.

He continued, "I'm sick of people who are always trying to maintain a sanctimonious posture; they're being either ridiculous or dishonest. Is the pressure of never lying really worth it? Not to me, it isn't. But like everything else, I don't overdo lying. I use it sparingly; it's much more effective that way."

Don raised his eyebrows. "Have you heard of something called morality?"

He chose to finish his thought. "The way I see it, most lying's not only minor in nature, it's necessary and humane. What good is it for a spouse to admit having an extramarital affair to a jealous mate or even an understanding one? Not good at all."

Don leaned forward and stared at him. Then, he raised his hands and brought them down on the table as he mouthed every word with clear diction: "What about the conscience?"

Steve was ready: He'd confronted his own conscience a number of times in the past. "Ah, yes, the conscience. Okay. So it's a big deal to some people. Actually, they're terrified of it; and, instead of controlling it, they're enslaved by it. These people get ulcers just thinking about lying—even when lying may save their butts or, perhaps, their lives. What a bunch of morons." He put the straw to his lips and took a sip of his drink.

"That's simply the conscience doing its job. But, of course, you have to have one to appreciate that," Don said and bit down on a noisy potato chip.

He ignored the sarcasm. He said, "Screw it. By the way, instead of using labels such as 'lying' and 'truth,' we should just use a plain term like 'reaction' or, better yet, 'response.' If a response to a situation was helpful, then it was good; and, if it caused problems, then it was bad. Simple, isn't it?"

Don's tone remained sarcastic. "Yeah . . . sure."

He felt he needed to bolster his argument. "You make small talk, don't you?"

"Sure."

"Well, most people do. But how much small talk would there be without lying? Without lies and exaggeration, a lot of sports-talk—and not just about fishing or golf—would simply vanish. And then what would happen? The social interactions will become a lot more boring indeed. You do see that?"

Don smiled. "Gosh, thanks for opening my eyes to the virtues of hypocrisy and lying. This is super. How could I've been so ignorant, for so long? We definitely need to talk more about this." Then he held up a textbook and continued, "But now, let's tackle something a bit more pressing and quite incontrovertible: tomorrow's history quiz."

● ● ●

"Steve, come in. Please take a chair." Helmut Wolfe pointed to one of the three black leather tub chairs surrounding an oriental coffee table. The sitting area was near an arched window that provided a splendid view of lower Manhattan.

"Thank you." Steve looked around the office as he sat down. It was the first time he'd been invited into Helmut's office in the year he'd worked at Wolfe Financial Services; he'd peeked in twice, when no one was around. The only word he could think of to describe what he saw in the spacious room was "majestic." He hadn't been told why the Big Boss wanted to see him; he was excited—and nervous.

Helmut got up from his high-back, black leather chair behind the massive cherry desk and walked over to join him in the meeting area. He carried a three-inch-thick document with blue bindings. He placed it on the coffee table. Steve recognized the document; he'd put it together for one of the financial specialists. His heart beat faster. He studied Helmut, who was not a towering figure, but had a thin face with sharp creases and rosy cheeks that betrayed a determined and tough character.

Helmut smiled at him and said, "Victor tells me you discovered a twenty-one-million-dollar error in the NPV of the candidate company in this proposal."

All right! So that's what this is about, thought Steve. He was relieved, and said with modesty, "The Net Present Value became overstated because for some reason the multipliers remained unchanged in the computer when the discount rate, along with the economic life and revenue projections, underwent final revisions."

"Oh, well. Someday, we'll build computers that'll eliminate human errors in number crunching. I understand what happened. What I'm interested in is how you found the mistake." Helmut looked into his eyes.

"Sir, I don't understand." He maintained an uneasy eye contact with Helmut.

Helmut said, "Let's see if I have this right: Your job is to help collect data for the specialists; they do the analyses and prepare the report; you, then, assemble the report for distribution. Right?"

He was unsure about the thrust of the conversation. His instant assessment was that the situation could easily become detrimental for him if he said the wrong thing and he absolutely couldn't afford to get caught in a lie. So, he decided the prudent thing would be to state everything he did with the documents. "Yes, sir; but I also read the report to pick up obvious typos and collating problems; and, while doing that, I try to understand business analyses and strategies, investor psychology and such. I do it for my curiosity and education, I guess."

Helmut nodded. "Huh. What do you think of the financial world?"

His response was quick. "It's fantastic. I love it."

"It's nice to see someone doing what he likes. I understand you've decided to work here part-time on a permanent basis."

"Yes, sir." He was relieved; the knot in his stomach was gone.

"I'm sorry your friend Don has passed on the summer job with us."

He felt obligated to say something in support of Don. "The time required to do well in the philosophy major is just unbelievable." He was aware of the unpalatable consequences to Don for quitting his job: He'd have to ask his father for more financial help.

Helmut rested his elbows on the arms of his chair and brought his fingertips together in a light touch. "He's a nice young man. I was with his father last evening. Get this: Fred still thinks Don should be in medical school. I wish Don all the best. Anyway, my daughter Erika is going to be his replacement; she'll work with you. She's a Yale freshman, has a good head on her shoulders, and she needs the money," Helmut said with tongue-in-cheek.

He managed a faint smile. "I look forward to meeting your daughter, sir."

"Good. Young man, you've saved us from a very embarrassing situation, and I think, potentially, it could've seriously damaged our reputation. Victor and I won't forget it. There'll be a small token of our appreciation in your next paycheck. Thank you for stopping by." Helmut stood up, signaling that the meeting was over.

"Thank you, sir, and good-day to you." He walked out of the office with proper composure and closed the door behind him. *Wow! He's impressed, the Big Boss's very impressed,* thought Steve. The level of excitement he felt made his head float and hands tremble. He wanted to be somewhere alone in the worst way; he wanted to raise a fist and shout "Yes!"

• • •

"Hi. I'm Erika Wolfe, the summer intern."

Steve looked up from a report he was poring over; his eyes froze. Smiling down at him was an oval face with high cheekbones, deep hazel eyes, full lips, and flowing blonde hair. A mole the size of a black pepper seed adorned her left cheek. He came out of the momentary trance, stood up and extended his hand to the tall German beauty in a navy blue dress. "Steve Zeller. Nice to meet you."

Erika shook his hand. "Uncle Victor isn't in. I'm supposed to check in with him. But I'm early. Would you please direct me to a Coke machine?"

"I'll take you to it," he said, walking around the desk.

"Thank you."

As they started walking, he smiled and said, "Coke, bright and early in the morning. Quite refreshing."

Erika's eyes narrowed. "You mean, quite odd."

He laughed. "Coke, tea, coffee—what's the difference? A caffeine fix is a caffeine fix," he said and added, "I get mine from coffee."

"You're a very solid and very traditional sort of a guy, aren't you?"

He grinned at Erika's lighthearted dig.

They reached the break room located in the back of the office complex. Since it was early, the two had the room to themselves.

He dropped two quarters in the Coke machine. "The Coke's on me." Then he walked over to the coffee machine and, feigning superiority, said, "And a cup of fresh-brewed, strong coffee for a very solid and very traditional sort of a guy."

Both broke out laughing. They carried their drinks to a small round table with four chairs and sat across from each other.

He was eager to make the most of the opportunity and get close to the boss's daughter. "I don't dare steal Victor's thunder by talking about the office and work. But, heck, we can discuss other things, like our hang-ups—you know, get to know each other a little."

"I definitely agree. After all, we're going to be working together."

They enjoyed their drinks while chatting and recounting experiences at Yale and NYU until Victor showed up. Erika greeted him with a warm hug and, after the three chatted briefly, she left with him.

Steve sat there savoring coffee and reflecting on what had just transpired. The good news was he was off to a great start with the Big Boss' daughter, who'd be sharing the office with him. Putting aside that critical fact for a moment, he found her quite refined, yet unpretentious and fun, which made her all the more appealing to him. But, all those positives of the situation couldn't stop him from worrying about self-preservation. He was aware he'd have to exercise extreme caution:

One false move with Erika and Helmut would turn any chance of his succeeding in the financial world into a mirage. Under the circumstances, he decided the prudent thing for him would be to establish a friendly, but professional, relationship with her.

• • •

Erika won over everyone with her warm and easy-going personality. She enjoyed working with the hardworking Steve. She had a sharp mind that quickly absorbed the concepts and routines of the job. She didn't complain about the drudgery that typified their work. Also, she liked earning money and what she could do with it; but, she didn't crave it, and wasn't the least bit interested in coming into her family's fortune-making business.

Most of her and Steve's work had to be done on the day it was presented to them by the financial specialists. To meet deadlines, sometimes, they had to work after everyone else had left for the day—even Helmut. That presented Erika with a problem: She preferred being driven to and from work with her father because she detested driving among the New York commuters. The antics of speeding and impatient maniacs on the highways left her tense and unnerved. Therefore, when she had to work later than Helmut, she'd choose to spend the night at the Park Avenue penthouse. She'd eat takeout food, watch some TV; then curl up with a romance novel and bore herself to sleep. The first three times she stayed there alone, she didn't express her feelings at the office about how she spent her time.

But when she faced the prospect of working late yet again, her dejection surfaced as she worked away on the mounds of paper on her desk. "Another fun night in the city . . . darn it," she said and groaned.

Steve looked up from the file he was studying and asked, "What's wrong with the city?"

"Oh, it's not the city. It's just that whenever I'm stranded here, my evening sucks," she said. Then she proceeded to describe the memorable routine of her evenings alone in New York.

"That really stinks," he said in a sympathetic tone. "I don't know if this'll interest you: A few of us go out most evenings for a quick bite and a couple brews—nothing fancy, Dutch treat. You're welcome to join us."

She was thrilled. "I'd love to. Are you sure your friends won't mind?"

"If they do, they'll let you know."

That evening she met his friends in a crammed and noisy Irish bar on the East Side.

When she was introduced to Don, he kissed the back of her hand and, opening his eyes wide, said, "I've got to say this: Damn you're gorgeous." Then, still holding her hand, he put his free arm around her and gave Steve a stern look. "Why have you been telling us your boss's daughter is a painfully plain blonde and an airhead? Care to explain?"

Everyone laughed. That was Erika's initiation into Steve's college crowd. From then on, her occasional stays in New York were anything but boring.

• • •

Sitting back in his chair, Steve was watching Erika clear her desk. The two financial specialists, who were standing just inside the office doorway, also watched.

As she closed the last desk drawer, she said, "Well, that's it; I'm out of here. Time to head back to Yale and hit the books. Picasso, Da Vinci and Jefferson await me."

"Let'em wait. Life's more fun among the living," Steve said, trying hard to mask his sinking spirits.

The financial specialists nodded, and one said, "We'll miss you."

Erika ran her hands through her hair and said in an appreciative tone, "I enjoyed working with every one of you. I really mean it." Then she squinted and continued, "This place is chaotic, but fun. I learned a lot about what it's like to work under pressure and . . . ah . . . earn a buck." She walked over to Steve's desk and looked at him. "You had to share your office with me; but you didn't have to share your friends. But I'm glad you did. Thanks."

He was flustered. "Oh, it was a lot of fun. It gave me a chance to see you in action outside work and you didn't disappoint. "

She walked around his desk and placed a hand on his shoulder. "I hope you'll allow me to return the favor. If you ever find yourself in the Yale area, promise you'll look me up, and we'll have a blast."

The touch of her hand felt like a mini electric jolt had gone through his body. He gave her arm a gentle squeeze and stood up. "It's a deal."

"So long." She hugged him and the financial specialists at the door, and was gone.

He sighed and returned to his work. The emptiness he felt told him that things were going to be dull without her.

• • •

December arrived, and so did frenzied activity and frayed nerves at Wolfe Financial Services. The rush to wrap up deals, complete proposals, and close books was a familiar year-end ritual. Everyone was putting in long, hard hours. Steve, without Don or someone else to help him, was drowning; but, he didn't complain.

Early one morning, he was tackling a heap of paper on his desk; he heard a familiar voice behind him.

"I'm back."

He was ecstatic. Grinning widely, he turned around and said, "She's back. Break out the champagne."

Erika put on a defiant mask. "Don't get smart. I'm here sacrificing my Christmas break because Dad said you need me to bail you out. So you better be nice."

Pointing to the mess on his desk, he said, "Boy, am I glad to see you. I'm swamped." He bounced up from his chair and hugged her.

Erika plunged right into work with the same high energy and zest he'd seen in the summer. He was no longer concerned about the day-before-Christmas-Eve deadline he had for completing his work on proposals. The two picked up where they'd left off in the summer. It was as if she'd never left.

• • •

Helmut Wolfe walked into the office wearing his hat and over-coat, and carrying his gloves. "Erika, it's six o'clock. Let's go home."

Erika pointed to the papers spread on her and Steve's desks and sighed. "I'd love to, Dad. But we still need a couple hours to complete these two reports by today's deadline." Then she returned to her attack on the paper.

Helmut studied the well-orchestrated, but hurried activity around the desks for a moment and said, "I called your mother this afternoon to tell her we'll be working until six."

"Dad, you go on. I'll just spend the night in the city."

Helmut tried one more time. "Your mother said she'd wait and have a late dinner with us."

Erika stopped working, dropped in her swivel chair and motioned him to leave. "In that case, you better hurry. Tell Mom I'll see her tomorrow afternoon. We'll enjoy Christmas Eve dinner together."

Helmut clasped his hands and addressed both of them. "Okay, you two. Make sure you close up this place tight." Then he walked over to Steve and shook his hand. "Young man, Merry Christmas; have a nice holiday with your family back home."

Steve nodded with a warm smile. "Thank you, Mister Wolfe. Merry Christmas to you and your family, too."

Helmut walked out of the office, pushing a hand into one of his gloves.

An hour and a half later the two reports were assembled, copied and arranged in stacks. Erika and Steve tied large, bright red ribbons and bows around them and placed them on the financial specialists' desks with notes reading: "Enjoy. Love, Santa."

"So, what are your plans for the evening?" Erika asked as she tidied her desk.

Steve said, "No plans. Everyone's gone home. I knew we'd have to work late, so I'm already packed for the flight home tomorrow morning." Then, as he stretched out his arms and twisted his torso in an attempt to get the kinks out, he asked, "Want to do something?"

She closed her eyes as if to visualize the evening she wanted. Swaying her head, she replied, "Yes. I want to wind down with a long, fun evening of fine dining, music and dancing."

He said, "Great. We could try this nice bar I—"

She interrupted, "No. No bar. This is on Dad. He owes his two lowly employees an evening out. We've worked our butts off today."

He was ambivalent. "Are you sure your dad won't mind?"

She shook her head and smiled. "This'll be our holiday celebration together."

He realized she was adamant, and he didn't stand a chance of changing her mind—and neither did he want to. He also felt she wanted to make decisions about the evening. So he said, "Count me in."

Her tone was impatient and firm. "Good. Let's get the hell out of here."

With the exception of a speeding car here and there, Wall Street was deserted. They did manage to hail a cab. Erika instructed the driver to take them to the Park Grill.

Steve had heard it was a lively, upscale restaurant in Central Park, New York's famous park in the heart of Manhattan; he was impressed. "Getting a table without reservations is going to be tough."

She shrugged. "So we'll wait."

He smiled at her and decided to relax and let the evening happen.

The restaurant was crowded with the holiday revelers. The *maître d'* informed them that they were in luck: He'd be able to seat them, but there'd be an hour's wait. They were more than happy to wait in the bar lounge, and started their evening with a bottle of *Dom Perignon*. The champagne flowed while they engaged in an effortless conversation. They were mellow and famished when they sat down to a candlelight dinner. Their sumptuous dining experience stretched into late evening. A six-member band in tuxedoes played soft background music and, as the evening progressed beyond dining, it switched to numbers with increased tempo and rhythm. The dance floor came alive.

When the waiter started to clear their table, Erika stood up as if on cue, held out her hand to Steve and said, "We're on."

He took her hand without hesitation, and guided her to the crowded dance floor. There, her instinctive response to the music inspired him, and he tried to keep up with her rhythmic gyrations. He also couldn't resist being infected by her spontaneous laughter and felt it was all a dream: *I'm having a marvelous time with this amazingly poised and beautiful woman.*

They'd been on the dance floor for about half an hour when a long jitterbug number ended. Both were breathing hard; He was sweating. The band started a slow number. He put his hand on Erika's shoulder and said, "Wait here." He walked over to their table, removed his jacket and put it on his chair, loosened his tie, unbuttoned his shirt-collar, and walked back. The wet shirt clung to his chest. "Might as well be comfortable," he said as he reached for her, and they started dancing.

Her cheeks were red from exertion; there was a hint of perspiration on her forehead. She was looking at him and smiling. He pressed his chest close to her; she pressed back. He could feel her firm, brassiere-free breasts and nipples digging into his chest through her silk dress and his wet shirt. For a brief moment, he studied Erika's face, the dainty mole on her left cheek, and her sensuous lips. He couldn't stop himself; he moved his head forward until their lips met. Their kiss lasted two brief seconds. When he moved his head back, Erika turned her head and rested it on his chest. They danced, chatted, joked, acted silly and drank right up to closing time.

Their cab left the restaurant and, after winding through the dark park, it neared the Wolfes' Park Avenue apartment.

Erika sighed and said, "I had a wonderful time."

Steve nodded. "Me too. Compliments of your father, we dropped a bundle tonight."

She put her hand on his. "No, no, no. I credit us for the great evening. What we spent was peanuts. Are you tired?"

"No, not really."

"Well then, let me show you the apartment Dad uses for entertaining friends and clients. It'll give you a good idea of what big money is."

"This I've got to see," he said with enthusiasm.

He settled with the cab driver and tipped the doorman who'd opened their cab door and was holding the eighteen-story building's glass entrance door ajar for them. They took the elevator to the penthouse floor. Erika unlocked the stout, cherry-stained door; he held his breath and followed her in.

She gave him a leisurely tour of the enormous and dazzling penthouse. In room after room he found himself surrounded with art treasures and overflowing elegance. Rembrandts, Van Goghs and Goyas were just a few originals he recognized.

He was awestruck. "Damn. So, your family owns Fort Knox."

She laughed. "Not quite."

She ended the tour in a spacious, multi-level room with velvety carpet, high ceiling, two skylights and a balcony. A couch, two loungers and a coffee table sat on the lowest level, facing a fireplace. The next level, one step up, had four chairs around a large, round table in a sitting area, separated from the outside balcony by sliding glass doors. The highest level—one more step up—held a twenty-foot wet bar with mirror wall panels. Erika walked to the fireplace and pressed a wall switch, starting a gas flame that gave the room a soft, golden glow. She ushered him to the couch. "Make yourself comfortable. I'll get drinks. What will you have? Sherry? Cognac? Green Chartreuse? Something else?"

"I don't know. Surprise me." He sat on the couch and stretched his legs out; a sense of relaxation overpowered him.

Erika returned, holding two large goblets; she gave one to him. "Here, try this."

He took a sip. "Cognac. Umm, nice."

She walked out of her shoes, sat down next to him and stared at the fire as she took a long sip.

He looked at her face a few seconds and blurted out, "Why don't you have a boyfriend?" His curiosity got the best of him; he had to know.

Looking surprised, she asked, "Does it show?"

He replied, "Lucky guess." Immediately, embarrassment set in: He felt he shouldn't have pried into her personal life, but it was too late.

"I'm not interested in *any* boyfriend and it's tough to find a good one."

"What are you, very picky or just snobbish?" he asked, while scouring his brain for a different topic.

She answered in a matter-of-fact tone, "Nothing of the sort. I simply detest jerks who grope on the first date; I don't care for egotistical bores in love with themselves; I don't respect guys who aren't confident enough to deal with a rich and smart woman; and I can't stand to be considered a meal ticket."

He chuckled. "Uh, oh, I bombed badly; you were my meal ticket today."

She laughed. "Dummy. That was different. I invited you."

He said without thinking, "I'm glad you did and I'm glad I kissed you—our first kiss."

Without waiting for an answer, he leaned forward, pulled her closer with his free hand and kissed her.

Her eyes were still closed when he stopped. He looked at her radiant face, and the irresistible attraction he felt for her intensified. He put down his glass on the coffee table, then took the glass from her hand and placed it next to his, and moved closer to her. They wrapped their arms around each other and kissed again. This time his tongue savored her sensual lips, which parted to invite it in. Their embraces and roaming hands heightened their passion. His desire became uncontrollable; he gently eased Erika down to the floor, on her back, and said, "You're so beautiful."

Both yielded eagerly to the urgent and untamed passion.

Afterward, as they lay in each other's arms savoring the moment, she said, "I've been in love with you from the first moment we met."

"I'd fallen for you, too. I was afraid to act on my feelings . . . afraid you might take offence." The lie was effortless for him; however, he felt a slight tug in his heart. It lasted for a fraction of a second, and then it was gone.

She sighed. "Each waiting for the other to make the first move."

"It'll sure be fun making up for the lost time," he said with a grin and sought her lips with his.

4
Opportunity

STEVE ZELLER CONTINUED to peruse financial data and analysis as he assembled documents to be presented to clients. Thus, he was able to spot an occasional typo or a more significant error that he'd bring to the attention of the financial specialists who were of course extremely grateful—and relieved. Also, he willingly accepted deadlines requiring long hours of work. Those were subtle, but effective, ploys at self-promotion that resulted in impressing Helmut and Victor, and translated into real money in his bank account. His much-improved financial position allowed him to move out of the postage-sized apartment in Greenwich Village and into an uptown, two-bedroom apartment overlooking the East River. He was finally able to indulge in an upscale wardrobe to complement his well-groomed appearance. Though Erika and the Wolfe Financial Services became the primary focus of his attention, he made sure he didn't ignore studies or his friends—especially Don, with whom he'd formed a special bond.

Early one Monday morning, Steve was shaking off the weekend with a cup of black coffee and trying to ease into his work when Victor Wolfe summoned him to his office. He found Victor sitting back in his chair and smiling. *Victor, smiling?* He thought that was odd because Victor seldom looked relaxed—let alone have a smile on his face. It was common knowledge that the office was his last place of choice; he was the happiest when he was working in his flower garden, playing the piano or taking in an opera at the Metropolitan.

"Hello." Victor motioned him to a chair across from his desk. "Take a seat. How about some coffee?"

He didn't want to prolong the meeting. "Just had a cup, Sir. Thanks anyway."

Victor sat up, put his elbows on the desk and clasped his hands. Then, still smiling, he said, "I've been looking forward to this chat very much—yes sir, very much, indeed. Let me start by saying I'm extremely happy with your performance so far—it's been simply outstanding. In the two and half years you've been with us, ah, your contributions have been noteworthy, at the very least. Also, ah, yes, I see in you a remarkable professional growth—great progress."

"Thank you. I enjoy my work." His curiosity was piqued by Victor's uncharacteristic behavior. *What's with this guy? He's too happy, too complimentary.*

Victor's voice remained upbeat. "That's quite obvious, and Helmut and I see a lot of potential in you. Thanks to Helmut's brilliance, the business's revenue has quadrupled, and so has its size. And, of course, the financial specialists have grown from two to nine."

He nodded. "There's an awful lot of work—even for nine."

"You're right. Okay, so now we want to increase the account executive positions. There will be three account executives: Helmut's two sons, Alan and Jack, and you. What do you think about that?"

Steve was stunned. Though he'd counted on snaring that position someday, he couldn't believe he'd succeeded so fast in penetrating the Wolfe family's perimeter defense.

Outwardly, he smiled and replied, "I'm very happy; I accept. Thank you . . . I thought the account executive position was for family members only."

"Yes, true. But in your case, Helmut and I made an exception; and I am absolutely sure you won't disappoint us."

"I won't," he said, betraying a mere fraction of the determination he felt.

Suddenly, Victor's face hardened. He leaned forward, looked straight in his eyes and spoke in a measured tone, "Good. Remember, the account executives report to me. I'll be relying on you much, much more than I do on the others. Are we clear on this?"

Steve maintained eye contact with him and nodded. "Yes. You can count on me." He understood what Victor meant. He knew Victor was in dire need of someone to cover for his lack of business sense and toughness—weaknesses he was reluctant to admit to his older brother Helmut. He was also well aware that Alan and Jack not only didn't help Victor, they found subtle ways to sabotage him, and then watch him squirm in front of their father. He detested the two brothers and their blatant victimization of Victor, but had decided on a hands-off posture: His priority was self-preservation, not shielding Victor from his callous nephews.

But now, he was being forced to take sides. While he considered Victor's veiled threat to be serious, he saw a potential to exploit the situation to his advantage.

Victor stood up and shook his hand. "Congratulations. Naturally, your salary and bonus will go up significantly. There'll be time to talk about that and other details later. Now, walk out with me and I'll let others in on your move up."

After Victor made the announcement, everyone complimented Steve on the promotion and shook his hand—that is, everyone except Alan and Jack. Their silent stares left no doubt that they resented sharing their turf with him, a lowly outsider, even though the only task they performed well as account executives was to entertain clients.

Alan pulled Steve aside and said in a low and condescending voice, "I know I should congratulate you; but I won't. What are they doing? This isn't fair to you. You know you're being asked to play in a league way beyond you. Of course, you'll fail; and, then what? You'll be out, that's what. Listen, be smart; tell them you'll be more comfortable in a financial specialist's role. And I promise you, with me and Jack guiding you, you'll do fine."

He looked Alan in the eyes and thought, *You incompetent bastard. You guide me? What a laugh.* But outwardly he smiled and said, "I really appreciate your concern; but I'll take my chances."

Alan persisted. "Look, if you're embarrassed to admit it to Dad and Victor, I'll speak to them and make them understand."

He shook his head and said, "No, Alan. I don't want you to do that."

Alan clenched his teeth. "Don't say I didn't warn you."

He watched the fuming Alan walk away. He knew he'd made an enemy—an enemy with direct access to Helmut; an enemy who wouldn't be satisfied with just waiting for him to stumble but rather actively create pitfalls to destroy him. He realized he'd just drawn a battle line with Alan making confrontation with him inevitable. He looked over at Victor. The idea of an alliance with Victor took on a new dimension and became even more appealing to him.

• • •

Steve was sitting with Erika in a cozy, oval booth in a neighborhood bar and grill on the East Side, close to his apartment. It was his favorite place to frequent after work and unwind; and it was also a place to enjoy zesty Cajun cuisine, which he loved. The subdued, indirect lighting gave the place a comfortable atmosphere and accentuated the glow from the candles on the tables.

Erika raised her champagne glass to him, looked into his eyes and squeezed his hand. "Congratulations, darling. Here's a toast to your promotion and continued success at Wolfe Financial Services."

He felt a surge of pride. He raised his glass to acknowledge her toast; both took a sip of champagne.

With a faint smile, he studied her face illuminated by the lighted candle. "Now, we can afford more and do more. But seriously, this Wolfe Financial Services is *really* something—I mean, it's been so good to me—you know . . . money, success and all that stuff. But it's given me something much more valuable and . . .er, more fantastic: It brought you into my life."

She looked at him with love-filled eyes. "You're so sweet."

He gently pushed away a few errant strands of hair from her face and said, "You know, it's been over a year since we first made love in your Park Avenue penthouse. A year! And I still can't get enough of you."

She blushed and lowered her eyes.

He continued, "I just don't know what I would've done without our weekends together."

She leaned toward him and, with a peck on his cheek, said in a low voice, "Thank God the commute between here and Yale isn't too bad. You know what? I can't wait for the weekends to come—to be with you. Every day, I imagine us together, making love."

He put his arm around her and pulled her closer. "We're lucky. Our parents have been great. My mother simply loves you; she approved of you from the moment she met you. And my dad, too."

"I think they're fantastic. My father keeps warning me not to let you get away; you know how fussy he is. I tell him I'll think about it," she said and laughed.

"Frankly, I thought Helmut would have a problem with our relationship."

"Well, you thought wrong. He approves totally. You'd already impressed him by sparing him the major embarrassment of a multi-million-dollar error. He still talks about it. Anyway, you cuddly oaf, what matters is I fell for you the moment I saw you."

"And, darling, so did I for you." His lie had become an integral part of their relationship. In truth, his first reaction to her had been a strong, physical attraction for a voluptuous and playful woman; and the insatiable lust for her and her father's power were the lures that had kept him around her long enough for his deeper emotions to blossom.

Erika looked at him with adoring eyes and kissed him.

He changed the subject. "By the way, Alan and Jack weren't too thrilled to hear about my promotion."

Erika raised her eyebrows and asked, "What happened? What did they say?"

"Not much. Alan told me the job was over my head. Everybody noticed they were pissed."

"I'll speak to Dad."

Steve was emphatic. "You'll do nothing of the sort. Don't say a word about it to Helmut or anyone else. I'll handle it my way."

"How? I'm afraid they'll make your life miserable. They know how to sway Dad—especially Alan," Erika said in a concerned voice.

"No, they won't. Just relax. I've two things going for me."

"What two things?"

"First, I know more about the business then they do."

"And the other?"

"I'm going to marry you."

"What?"

Steve put a small, blue velvet jewelry box in her hand.

Speechless, she opened it; a white gold ring sporting a dazzling, two-carat princess diamond stared at her. Her eyes widened and she exclaimed, "Oh, it is beautiful!"

He watched her reaction with deep satisfaction. Then, turning toward her, he dropped one knee to the ground and asked, "Will you marry me?"

Erika's eyes turned watery; her lips trembled. "Yes. Oh yes, yes I will."

She leaned toward him as he sat up and their lips met in a warm kiss.

After their long kiss, Erika sat back and said, "I'm so happy, but I have one request."

"Name it."

She ran a finger over his lips. "I'd like us both to graduate before we marry."

His eyes narrowed. "That's what, at least two years away?"

She looked in his eyes and nodded.

He knew the college degree was important to her. He thought a moment and then smiled at her. "Sure, darling. It makes sense." He looked at his watch and continued, "Look, it's six forty. Don will be here at seven. I wanted him to be the first to hear about my promotion and our engagement because he's responsible for everything that's happening to me—to us."

Her eyes lit up. "That's wonderful. I love that man. When do we tell the others about our engagement?"

He rubbed his chin. "How about Christmas, when my family's here too?"

Erika nodded. "That's fine. It's only a month away. Till then, it'll be our secret—and Don's." She reached for her champagne glass.

• • •

Steve's life at Wolfe Financial Services continued to be challenging. He'd learned from Victor that Alan and Jack had made their displeasure known to Helmut, who'd admonished them to concentrate on their jobs and be thankful the hardworking Steve would ease their workload. Also, he'd tried to mollify them by promising to pay close attention to Steve's performance.

Steve knew that wouldn't change anything: Alan and Jack would still undermine him. But he was also convinced he was smarter than they were and capable of countering their annoying attacks, as and when they happened.

And sure enough, the two brothers didn't disappoint him. Since they couldn't match his business acumen, work ethic or intellect, they took every opportunity to denigrate his cultural awareness and social graces—critical tools required in the world of high finances and high society, and in which their family's good fortune gave them a decided advantage. On more than one occasion, he became enraged enough to bloody their egos by reminding them their sister was going to marry him—a social lightweight. But he overcame the impulse to experience what would've been, at best, a short-lived gratification.

People in the office, including Helmut and Victor, were well aware of the brothers' vendetta against him. But the prevailing sentiment was not interfere because he managed to neutralize their shenanigans with restrained, yet adequate, response.

For his part, he stayed focused on doing his job and learning the subtleties of the business. He downplayed his skirmishes with Alan and Jack because he wasn't interested in escalating the feud between him and members of the Wolfe family. However, he did one thing: He went out of his way to shore up the hapless Victor. He did everything he could to make him come across as a strong and decisive executive. That was in keeping with his long-range strategy: He wanted Victor to be indebted to him—and very dependent on him.

• • •

Helmut Wolfe made sure Erika's graduation party and her wedding to Steve in June were extravagant affairs, and among the year's memorable social events in New York City. Steve's entire family, relatives and friends from Terryton traveled— all expenses paid by Helmut—to New York to be part of the celebration.

The two started their married life in Steve's apartment. Their honeymoon-like relationship continued unabated as they settled into their marital roles. Steve remained engrossed in business and, besides paying attention to Erika, showed little interest in other things. Erika, by default, ended up with responsibility for everything else needed to nurture their marriage, such as household decisions and finances, their social calendar and relationships with relatives. Of course, notwithstanding those time-consuming activities, she still managed to fulfill her unyielding commitment to social work and homeless children.

When their first child, Kathleen Margaret Zeller, arrived a year and a half later, Erika decided to hire a nanny, and Steve agreed with her. But he was unenthusiastic about participating in the selection process, and that neither surprised nor offended her.

She interviewed numerous candidates, including a middle-aged widow, Maria Gonzo. During the meeting with her, she asked, "How many children have you raised?"

"My own? Five—three boys and two girls. All grown up and gone on their own."

"That's nice. Have you worked as a nanny?"

"No, I haven't; but I sure worked like I was, and then some. I took care of my two nieces for two years —started when they were four and three. My sister came here from Turin—you know, Italy—no husband, and she needed help; so I help her. God bless her; she's okay now, and don't need me to take care of the children. Now, if you don't mind my asking, why you need a nanny?"

The question surprised her. "What do you—?"

"Paper says your daughter is one-month baby. Is she a problem for you? You know . . . messes, throws up, cries too much for you?"

Erika shot back, "Nothing of the sort."

But Maria persisted. "So why you want a nanny?"

She was irked. "Simple. I want a nanny so I can balance my personal and professional lives. I volunteer at social service agencies that help homeless families; I find shelters, homes for homeless kids; and I'm on the boards of several nonprofit agencies. All that takes a lot of time; but I have a passion for it. How's that for a reason?"

"Good. Don't get me wrong, Madam Zeller, but I don't want to work for anybody who's lazy. You know what I mean? Some women push out children, but don't want to take care of them. Anyway, what's your daughter's name?"

"Kathy."

"Can I see Kathy?"

"Sure." Erika left the room and returned with Kathy, who was struggling to wake up. She handed her to Maria.

"She's not so cute now, is she? But she will be later; it's the age. Mine were ugly, too; but all grew up beautiful."

Erika smiled; she was trying to get accustomed to Maria's bluntness. She watched how gentle Maria was with her daughter.

Maria was shaking Kathy's tiny hand. "Ah, yes, little girl, you will grow up beautiful, very beautiful."

Erika asked, "How do you feel about discipline?"

Maria shrugged and replied, "I feel fine." Then she laughed. "It's the kids who don't like it. So I tell them: I always love you; but, if you need it, I will punish you, too. What do you think?"

"Oh, I agree with you fully: Kids need both—love and discipline. I plan to be around a lot for my children and be a hands-on mother to them. It seems we share the same values and approach to raising children. So, when can you start, that is, if you want the job?"

"You won't find anybody better than me. I take the job."

"And, as the ad said, this job at some point would become a live-in position."

"That's okay. I start tomorrow."

From then on Maria Gonzo, a tiny woman of boundless energy, firm religious convictions, and ready humor, became a member of the Zeller family. Everyone called her Nanny.

• • •

For Steve and Erika, the first five years of blissful marriage went by in a flash. They remained in love— passionately and completely. By then, their family had started to take shape:

their daughter Kathy was three years old; their son Todd was one; and Erika was pregnant with their third child.

At Wolfe Financial Services, much to Alan and Jack's chagrin, Steve had built quite a reputation as a tough, polished negotiator and businessman. Clients, whose accounts he oversaw, were quite pleased with him and the results. Though he reported to Victor, he'd started to get additional sensitive assignments directly from Helmut; and Victor made it clear he didn't mind. As a matter of fact, Steve knew Victor was delighted to be spared impatient grilling by Helmut on those assignments.

The imperceptible result was what he'd hoped for: To become indispensable to Victor and Helmut.

• • •

It was close to eleven o'clock on a Monday morning. Steve was working at a feverish pace to polish an investment presentation for review by Helmut and Victor, as soon as they returned from a meeting with a client.

"Steve. Come into my office."

He looked up and saw Alan standing across from his desk. "Give me a few minutes." He went back to scribbling notes on the document he was working on.

"This can't wait. Come now." Alan's lips quivered and his voice was unusually somber.

He raised his eyebrows and studied Alan for a moment. *What mess has this idiot gotten himself into now and wants me to fix?* He put his pen down. "Okay, let's go," he said. There was a hint of irritation in his voice.

He followed Alan into his office. Jack was there, too; he looked pale.

Alan motioned and said, "Close the door."

He closed the door. "What's up?"

"Dad's suffered a heart attack."

"Jesus! When?" said the shocked Steve.

"Right after the meeting in Tierney's office. An ambulance is taking him to Saint Helen's; Victor's following in the limo. He just called."

"Damn." Until then, Steve had considered Helmut to be invincible.

Alan said, "Jack and I are heading to the hospital. You keep an eye on this place."

"Like hell I will. I'm going too," he shot back.

Alan was taken aback by his sharp reaction, but recovered quickly and countered through clenched teeth, "Dad'll be very upset if this place is left unattended."

Steve glared at him. "Screw you, Alan. You mean you'll be upset if I went to the hospital."

Alan and Jack looked at each other, speechless.

"I want to be there for Erika and Helmut. I'll tell the staff what's happened and put someone in charge." With that pointed statement, Steve walked out.

A minute later, Alan and Jack emerged from the office, and looked around the open area. People were solemn and quiet, two were in tears, and Steve was nowhere in sight. They rushed past everyone without saying a word.

• • •

Helmut Wolfe's uncanny moneymaking ability and seemingly boundless energy accomplished two things: the family business mushroomed and he drove himself into a debilitating heart attack. When he came out of the critical care unit, doctors warned him about the precarious condition of his heart, and ordered him to keep away from the exceedingly stressful business he'd created. They said if he didn't, he'd be dead in a month and that got his attention. He was released from the hospital after a two-week stay to convalesce at home under a strict regimen of drugs, diet and rest. He was home barely a week and still wheelchair bound when he invited Victor, Alan, Jack and Steve to a Saturday meeting at his house.

Erika and her mother joined the men for a leisurely lunch on the patio overlooking rolling lush meadows shimmering in the sun. After that, the men retired to the study with glasses of sherry. Helmut of course couldn't drink. His ordeal had aged him ten years—his cheeks were sunken and no longer rosy. So everyone seemed surprised at the energy with which he addressed them:

"Let me open by saying that my father, Otto, sweated for decades to save a small fortune; and we took that small fortune and built a family business, successful way beyond my wildest dreams. Every one of you in this room should feel very proud; I mean it. Without your loyalty, hard work and drive, the company couldn't have grown so dramatically. For that, I'm grateful to you.

"Now about me: I thought I was a superman and could continue the hectic pace forever. But God decided to give me, you know, a slight nudge . . . a small reminder that I'm not superman. And now, if I don't listen to His warning and slow down, my dear wife has promised to kill me."

There were smiles and laughter in the room.

He continued, "So. That brings us to the question: What are we going to do to keep Wolfe Financial Services prospering for us and our employees? Well, while I've been resting, I've been thinking. Here's what we're going to do: We'll make a few changes and reward everyone. First of all, every employee of the company will get a good-sized raise."

Everyone nodded.

Victor said, "I like that."

Helmut smiled at him. "Good. Second, we'll increase the financial specialists from nine to fifteen. We must eliminate the horrendous overtime work and strain we put on our poor employees. We should allow them to make a decent living and have a life, and not work them to death."

Everyone was attentive and looking at him.

He coughed and cleared his throat. He turned to Alan and Jack, who were sitting on the couch near his wheelchair, and said, "Third, you two have learned the business and proven your worth. Because the business is growing fast, you must be in more responsible positions and become part of the core management group, which now has only Victor and me. You're promoted to new positions. Jack, you become Vice-President of Business Operations; you'll manage the financial specialists, and office administration and support. Is that okay with you?"

Jack smiled and said, "Yes, Dad."

Helmut looked at Alan. "You'll become Vice-President of Marketing, and be in charge of the account executives and client relations. We'll hire five new account executives to report to you. What do you think about that?"

Alan narrowed his eyes, but smiled. "I think it'll be great."

"Excellent; you both will do just fine." Helmut then looked at Victor and grinned. "Victor, my dear brother, you'll move into my position: You'll be the president. But there'll be one change. Since the responsibilities of the position are growing and onerous, I don't want you to end up like me or, God forbid, worse. Okay? So, I want Steve to share responsibilities of the presidency with you. Over the years, Steve has demonstrated his value and loyalty. I'm absolutely sure you agree he'll be an asset to you; also, let's not forget he's now family."

Victor nodded with a smile. "It'll be great having Steve beside me. We work very well together." Then, looking at Steve asked, "Don't we Steve?"

Steve was flabbergasted. "Yes, yes we do. I enjoy working with you. Uh . . . I don't know what to say. Helmut, thank you."

Helmut smiled and nodded. "So now, to make my dear wife and doctors happy, I'll remove myself from the stress of daily grind, and become the chairman. You won't see me much at the office, but I'll be involved with business strategy and critical decision-making. That's all I have to say. What do you think? Questions? Comments?" He looked around the room.

Stunned silence prevailed for a few, long seconds.

Victor was the first to speak. "We . . . ah, everyone here is trying to digest your blueprint for the future—new, bigger organization and all that. I think the reorganization makes sense, but personally, ah . . . I'm not too crazy about your stepping aside. But it's for the best, and you must do what the doctors say—your health must come first. I know that, we all know that; and, we'll do our best."

Again there was silence. Alan and Jack didn't say a word. They just stared at Helmut.

Helmut rested his head on the chair and held his eyes closed with his hand. "Anything to add, sons?"

The unsmiling Alan shook his head. "Not really."

Jack's nervousness was obvious. "Me either."

Steve noticed that Helmut was getting weary. Without waiting further, he said, "I'll do anything I can to help."

Helmut smiled at him and then looked at everyone. "You four will make a great management team; I just know it. You'll keep the family enterprise strong and growing—no doubt about it. Victor, stop by tomorrow and we'll put together a reorganization notice. On Monday you can announce the reorganization at the office and to the newspapers. Now, I feel tired; I think I'll drive myself out of here and go lie down."

The meeting was over. A new era had begun for the Wolfe family and the Wolfe Financial Services.

• • •

Long Island lies to the east of New York City's borough of Manhattan and juts out over one hundred miles into the Atlantic Ocean. It's full of famous beaches, defunct whaling ports, colorful vineyards and farms, thriving towns, and opulence.

Sleek limousines and high-end cars navigate a tunnel, bridges and highways to whisk away the truly rich and famous from New York City's ferocious pace and clutter to their peaceful ornate homes and hideouts on Long Island. Its picturesque north shore, known as the Gold Coast, faces the Long Island Sound. F. Scott Fitzgerald used the striking estates of the north shore as a setting for his famous book, *The Great Gatsby*. On the ocean side, this island boasts some of the most sought-after property in Southampton, a quaint town settled in the seventeenth century by English colonists.

For a long time Steve had craved the prestige of a Southampton address; Erika loved the charm and serenity of the area. And, of course, money ceased to be an issue when Steve became the co-president of Wolfe Financial Services, and he single-handedly ran the business and the other co-president, Victor Helmut. So they bought a ten-acre, resort-like beachfront estate there and started enjoying a dream life.

Steve finally felt a sense of achievement—and entitlement. *It's all happening so very fast. But, I've worked like hell to get all this. Now I deserve to enjoy myself.*

Steve and Erika's life in Southampton chugged along on autopilot—smooth, comfortable, pleasurable and tranquil. While Steve's financial success got them there, it was Erika's charming and chameleon-like personality that established the Zeller family in its society. She was equally comfortable play-ing a gracious hostess to the Southampton's close-knit elite as she was rubbing elbows with the underprivileged people in soup kitchens.

She took pains to balance her professional and family lives; and, with proper planning, she was able to spend consid-erable time with her children.

Kathy had grown into a bright, quiet eight-year-old. She'd inherited Erika's oval face, high cheekbones and blond hair; and from Steve came her deep blue eyes. She had a ready smile, and everyone adored her. Steve called her "my kitten." Besides excelling as a student, she played drums in the school band and acted in plays. Todd was six and about to start school; Jeff was five. The two brothers looked like Steve did in his childhood photographs: athletic, with sharp features. And Erika's only contribution to them seemed to be blond hair. The brothers took swimming lessons and played in an informal baseball league. Erika made sure she was present at all her children's activities.

Steve was happy to see how loving a mother Erika was to their daughter and two sons. He admired her resolve to attend every event the children were involved in. As for himself, the fatherly responsibilities requiring his time clashed with his love for business combat and the exciting life. He tried to be a part of his children's lives, but those occasions turned out to be very few indeed. His kids stopped asking him to spend time with them, or to come to watch them participate in any activity. They looked to Erika alone to fill those needs.

Steve believed he and Erika had a good marriage, even though he'd reverted to discreet liaisons with other women, and convinced himself that his lust for casual sex didn't violate his covenant with Erika. His gut told him Erika was aware of his extramarital flings, but he wasn't sure. But there was something he was absolutely sure of: he loved her; and she loved him.

• • •

Steve made no attempt to hide his consternation at what he was being subjected to as he sat next to Erika. The long stretches of construction had created a massive bottleneck, turning the Long Island Expressway into a parking lot. Their limousine had been inching forward for over half an hour.

He couldn't control himself and said with a touch of irritation, "Damn. The traffic is awful. This expressway's been a mess for days. Why the hell did we take it?"

His long-time, dependable chauffeur, Eddie Weiss, eyed him through the rearview mirror with a sheepish look on his face and replied, "Sorry, Sir, I should've checked. I thought the construction ended yesterday."

Steve didn't say anything; he turned his face to once again gaze at the sea of cars sharing their fate.

Erika looked at her wristwatch. She appeared anxious. "I've tried Don's cell phone to tell him we'll be late; but he doesn't answer. I can't even leave a message. Strange. It's already five. I hope he's in a patient mood today."

Still looking at the cars, Steve said, "I wouldn't bet on it."

They arrived at Don's apartment building at six twenty, fifty minutes late. Eddie jumped out of the limousine and disappeared into the building. He returned minutes later; he looked crestfallen. "There was no answer. I buzzed Mister

McCoy's apartment three times," he said and got back into his seat.

Steve had, by then, resigned himself to the unfolding misadventure, and didn't react overtly to Eddie's news. He surmised that Don being Don had waited only until five thirty-five; after that, he'd placed a phone call to them and couldn't get through, not realizing his phone was acting up; then, left with his date for God knows where.

Disappointment was written all over Erika's face; a groan escaped her lips. "This isn't turning out as I'd planned."

Steve felt sorry for her. She'd tried to give him exactly what he wanted: a quiet birthday celebration. He'd gone along with her suggestion to invite Don with a companion to join them for dinner at an exclusive spot in Manhattan. His irritation dissolved completely; he put his arm around her and gave her a loving peck on her cheek. Then he said in a soothing voice, "Honey, let's go and dine by—"

She interrupted, shaking her head, "No, no. Let's just go home, please. We'll celebrate your birthday tomorrow. Would you mind?"

He saw a very dejected Erika looking into his eyes, and thought it'd be best not to press the point about going ahead with their plans without Don. He pulled her closer and nodded with a smile. "You're right. A relaxed evening at home with you and the children sounds wonderful."

They rode back in silence. When their limousine turned onto the long brick driveway and proceeded toward the house, Steve had his head resting back on the seat and was listening to soft music with his eyes closed. He heard Erika's voice:

"We're home."

He opened his eyes and sat up. He saw rows and rows of limousines and cars parked on their lawn. Stunned, he opened his mouth to speak, but Erika silenced him by pressing her finger to his lips. By then the limousine had reached the house; the front doors flung open. He sat there wide-eyed and watched a stream of people flowing out of his house; among them were his children, their nanny, his parents from Terryton, his in-laws, and Don. There were shouts of "Surprise!" and "Happy Birthday." He looked at Erika with a faint smile and shook his head; she smiled back at him with bright, mischievous eyes. Eddie, with a wide grin on his face, opened the door for him. The crowd applauded as he stepped out of the limousine. He waved; Erika grabbed his hand and, followed by the boisterous throng, led him to the back of the house to a large table. On the table sat a pyramid of three chocolate cakes with elaborate decorations; thirty-three lighted candles stood on the top cake. The crowd gathered around the table and chanted:

"Happy birthday to you. Happy birthday to you. Happy birthday dear . . . ."

Steve smiled and looked on, enjoying the loud singing and the applause that followed. Then, puffing up his chest, he blew out the candles. Out of breath, he said, "Too many candles . . . growing old."

The crowd laughed and applauded some more.

He bent down to allow his children standing on both sides of him to put their arms around his neck and kiss him. He kissed them back. Then, he put a silver knife into the cake as a symbolic gesture, and walked away to the side of the table where Erika was standing. That signaled the people to disperse and resume partying.

Steve put his arm around Erika's waist and looked into her loving eyes. He hugged her and said, "Great surprise, honey. Thank you." Then he gave her a long kiss.

She pulled back after a few moments; she was blushing. "Wow, you're welcome, birthday boy. I'm so glad everyone showed up, especially your parents."

He nodded and his eyes narrowed. "The limo ride to Don's was a nice touch."

"Darn it, I can't take credit for that. It was Don's idea—had to get you dressed and away from the house somehow. Snarled traffic and all—it was perfect. But frankly, the ride was the longest of my life. And poor Eddie, that sweet, sweet man took all the heat from you. I wouldn't do that to him again for anything."

Both laughed and kissed again.

He marveled at Erika's accomplishment: *Damn! I can't believe she pulled off this elaborate, surprise birthday celebration for me . . . in our own home, under my very nose. She's one hell of a woman.* He took in with great satisfaction the festive scene around him and glittering bright lights. He saw two hundred plus guests enjoying flowing champagne and elegant dining, pleasing music and dancing under the stars, and the visual pleasure of the estate's magnificent, park-like oceanfront setting.

Steve was holding Erika in a playful embrace when she got into a conversation with a couple standing next to them. So he walked over to his mother. Marge was sitting alone at a table, watching her husband Stan and her granddaughter Kathy's brave, but awkward, attempts to move to the music on the dance floor. He sat down next to her and rested his arm on the back of her chair. Then, joining her in watching Stan and Kathy laughing and swaying on the dance floor, he said, "Dad isn't so tough around his granddaughter. She's got his number, doesn't she?"

Marge nodded. "Nobody else can get him to dance."

He thought it was a perfect time for small talk with his mother. He asked, "What's new in Terryton?"

Her response was slow and pleasant. "Not much. Well... the new school is just about built. And, your brothers and sisters are talking about a clan get-together this fall. They wanted me to be sure to invite you and your family. So, consider yourself invited. Let me see, what else? Ah yes, your uncle Jim has started repairs on his house—that house sure needs them; and, before I forget, your aunt Amy told me to remind you to send fifteen thousand dollars you promised them."

Steve couldn't believe what he was hearing. Annoyance surged inside him: He didn't like the turn the conversation had taken. The only evidence of turmoil within him was a mild emphasis in his voice. "Ma. I promised them nothing."

"She says you did; that's why they let the contractor start work," Marge said looking surprised.

He shook his head. His annoyance was turning to anger. But he kept his tone even. "No way, Ma. Months ago Uncle Jim asked me if I'd consider helping him with some improvements Amy wanted. And all I said was I'll consider it. That's it. Those people are nuts."

"You can afford to help them," she said in her usual undemanding tone.

"You know what? I can afford to help a lot of people—you, Dad, other people I love . . . care about; but not those who made my lunchtime hell when I was a kid." He clenched his teeth; the hurtful, years-old memories returned, as fresh and vivid as if they were a day old.

"Steve, listen to me: You've avoided helping every relative—even your brothers and sisters. You shouldn't be like that," she said with raised eyebrows.

Holding back his anger, he said through clenched teeth, "They don't deserve my help."

Marge shifted her position to get closer to him. She placed her hands on his cheeks and, looking into his eyes, spoke in a soft voice, "The help they asked for, time and time again, was peanuts for you. Son, God's made you rich, very rich, and the proof of your wealth is all around here. You could have saved a lot of pain and suffering to many in our family."

He pulled back, but maintained eye contact with her. He knew he was losing the debate. "What about the pain and suffering they put me through? Huh? At least I didn't *cause* their pain and suffering." At that moment, he felt the way he used to as a stubborn twelve-year-old, arguing his case with his mother.

"You must decide to be a better person than those who hurt you. Steve, please soften your heart a bit; let the childhood grudges go. Please do it for me." Her voice was quivering; she seemed to be on the verge of crying.

He realized he was hurting his loving mother. He looked at her for a long moment before saying, "Okay, Ma. I'll think about it." Then, looking toward the dance floor, he added, "Hey, here comes Dad with his swinging dance partner." He got up and, waving to Stan and Kathy who were returning to the table, walked to the bar for a drink.

Steve felt a tinge of guilt as he walked away. He knew his mother was right. He'd been paying back his brothers and sisters for all the misery they'd subjected him to when they were kids. As soon as he became successful, they'd tried to form a closer, warmer family relationship with him, but he'd turned them down in such a crass fashion that they looked completely pathetic and humiliated. After that, at one time or another, they'd come to him because they needed him: two after long illnesses; one after the loss of a lucrative business; and one after a messy marriage and abandonment. The common denominator was they all needed money; and, he had money. But they didn't get a penny because he chose not to forgive.

The thoughts of facing his mother with a response also swirled in his mind. *How will I tell her how I really feel about Amy's sticky fingers reaching into my wallet, and not hurt her? Will I be able to watch as my words hurt her?* He stopped walking for a moment and shut his eyes tight. *Damn it. Stop worrying about it now. You can't let Amy—that conniving broad—still make you miserable; don't let her spoil a wonderful evening and your birthday.*

After getting a cognac at the bar, Steve wandered over to join Helmut and Don standing together and chatting.

"Hi. Enjoying the party?" Steve asked.

"Boy, I've got to have a word with Erika. She's way too good to you. This is quite a celebration," Don said.

Steve laughed. "I understand you were a part of the conspiracy."

Don looked around and gestured. "Everyone was part of the conspiracy." Pointing to Helmut, he added, "Even you; right, Helmut?"

"I'm having a great time," Helmut said with a smile, avoiding a direct answer.

Their small talk continued for a few more minutes when a tanned, petite redhead appeared behind Don. She waved to Steve. "Happy birthday, Steve."

He waved back in acknowledgement.

She tapped Don on the shoulder and said in an exaggerated husky voice, "Come on, darling, let's check out the band."

Don's tone was laced with feigned earnestness. "Anything you say, dear; whatever you want."

She laughed. "I'll remember that, lover boy."

"I guess I walked into that one. Excuse me, gentlemen, duty calls." Don put his arm around the woman's waist and both headed to the dance floor.

Helmut studied the departing couple and asked, "Is he serious about that beautiful woman?"

"He sure is—this week," Steve replied with a chuckle.

Helmut laughed and changed the subject. "What's the latest on Centomat?"

Steve said, "We met with Carl Wyler, the new CEO, and his management team. We told them the company needed to become more viable; I explained the additional monitoring systems and cost cuts we wanted."

"Were they receptive?"

Steve grimaced and replied, "I'm not too sure. I thought the management team understood our rationale. But everyone waited for a cue from the new boss, who didn't seem too excited about the suggestions. He said he'll study them and get back to us." Steve took a sip of cognac.

"When?" Helmut asked as he took in the party scene.

"In a few days, maybe a week. He wasn't specific," Steve replied.

"Huh. What's your impression of the deal?" Helmut asked in a slightly emphatic tone.

Steve rubbed his chin and thought for a moment before answering. "The company's a keeper; but that Carl's another thing. He's smart, arrogant and very interested in making a name for himself. He doesn't seem too concerned about the long-term health of Centomat."

"If he's not the right man, then you must act quickly," Helmut said with a smile.

Steve had already decided on the approach he was going to take. "I'll give him some time to settle down."

Even though age was taking its toll on the frail-looking Helmut, his dark, penetrating eyes betrayed a sharp mind. He trained those eyes on Steve and, still smiling, asked, "Tell me, do you know how cancer works?"

"Huh?" Steve was surprised at the question.

Helmut didn't repeat the question. "I'll tell you. If a single cancer cell living in a healthy body is given enough time, it can multiply and spread and kill the very body it feeds on. It doesn't matter to that stupid cell that, when the body dies, it dies too." Helmut paused and took a sip of his drink.

Steve didn't speak; he was trying to absorb the full impact of what Helmut was telling him.

Helmut continued, "That's why, where cancer's concerned, time's your enemy. So, as soon as cancer is detected, what do you do? The reaction has to be swift—surgery, chemo-therapy, radiation, whatever—to remove and kill the cancer. Then, and only then, the body can avoid or limit serious dam-age, and even prevent death.

"So you see, you must decide about that CEO and act quickly, before he settles down to do some serious damage to Centomat. This is a major capital-formation attempt by Zeller Enterprises. A wrong or untimely move here would be a disas-ter for the company, and also reflect poorly on you and your leadership. Failure of this magnitude will also have negative spillover effect on the reputation of Wolfe Financial Services. Don't you agree?"

Steve was well aware of the stakes involved in the Centomat deal. They were extremely high, especially for him. Two years ago, he'd talked Helmut into taking a big, risky step: Investing the company funds—not investors' money—to buy and sell whole companies. Helmut decided to keep the new business separate; so he formed a subsidiary, made Steve its president, named it Zeller Enterprises, and moved it into separate offices on Fifth Avenue. Steve also retained his responsibilities and position as the co-president of Wolfe Financial Services. Centomat was the first significant candidate Steve selected for acquisition. The deal was to be in the neighborhood of fifty million dollars. Helmut's informal—but pointed—chat was bringing the stakes into sharp focus for him.

He nodded. "I see what you mean. I'll remember your advice. The deal will be a success. You have my word."

Helmut's voice remained calm. "I'm not concerned, just giving you my two cents worth." Then, looking in the direction of Steve's parents, he added with a smile, "Look, your parents are hogging my grandchildren. I think I'll join them."

Steve laughed and said, "You do that."

Helmut grabbed his arm. "Oh, by the way, my sons ran into the new Centomat guy—Carl, is it?—at the yacht club, and they think he's pleasant and smart. He told them you impressed him as someone who lacks, er, strategic thinking. Just be aware. Take it for what it's worth." He shrugged and walked away.

Steve froze. He felt as if Helmut had placed a hundred-pound weight on his chest. A film of perspiration appeared on his forehead. He emptied the glass of cognac and muttered, "Goddamn Alan and Jack. I must do something soon about those shitheads." Then he clenched his teeth and stared past the boisterous and swinging party toward the pitch dark ocean.

• • •

Steve's birthday celebration continued deep into the night. Early the next morning, his sleep-deprived parents were ready to return to Terryton. They'd completed the goodbye hugs and kisses. Eddie was busy loading their luggage into the limousine.

With Stan standing beside her, Marge expressed their appreciation to Erika and Steve. "Thank you for inviting us. We thoroughly enjoyed the party, you and our grandchildren. Oh, and Nanny was so wonderful to us."

Erika put her arm around Marge and said, "Thank you for coming. It was a pleasure to have you here."

Marge looked into Erika's eyes. "Stan and I think you're simply adorable, and so are your children. I must ask you to do one thing for me: Make sure Steve doesn't have any excuse for not coming to Terryton in the fall. I'm counting on you, dear."

"Don't worry, Marge, the whole family will be there. And as for him, he'll be there even if I have to drag him," Erika said, as she tweaked Steve's ear.

Steve, with face contorted, cried out in mock pain.

Everyone laughed.

His parents were already in the limousine when he handed Marge an envelope and said, "This is for Aunt Amy and Uncle Jim."

She took the envelope, folded it and eased it into her purse. She looked at her son and pressed his hand; her voice crackled with emotion. "Bless you, son. I'm so proud of you."

Steve said with a serious face, "One more thing for Aunt Amy: Tell her I'll definitely attend the big party she'll be throwing for me this fall; and I'll be very hungry, and will eat at least a second helping of everything—especially desserts." He gave her a light kiss.

Both laughed—Amy's antics were still fresh in their minds.

As he closed the door, he heard Stan ask Marge, "Why did Steve say that?"

He smiled and watched the limousine pull away. He knew his father wouldn't get a truthful answer—if he got one at all. But he felt good: He'd made his mother happy.

• • •

"Yes, Joan?" Steve spoke into the intercom.

"Barney's on the phone. He says he has good news. Should I connect him?" Joan Winters asked.

Steve had met Barney Williams three years ago. Barney was then a junior attorney toiling away unappreciated in a mega law firm retained by Wolfe Financial Services. During their occasional brief encounters, he noticed Barney's brilliance and, more importantly, his hunger for action. He decided he could use Barney's ambition to his advantage and added him to the Zeller Enterprise's team.

"Sure, go ahead." He picked up the receiver. "Hi, Barney. What's new?"

Barney laughed and said, "What's new? You know damn well what's new." He added, "Yes, the Centomat stock's sold. The board of directors and CEO's investors agreed to our price. They signed the papers and their lawyer just dropped them off; the electronic transfer of funds to Zeller Enterprises is taking place as we speak. You've made a cool seventeen-million-dollar profit. Whew!"

"That's good. Now let's sit back and watch the company crumble."

"Good company, but it doesn't stand a chance with that Carl Wyler as its CEO. What an egomaniac."

Steve's words were more direct. "It takes more than blowing smoke up the directors' butts to run a company. That jerk's history; he just doesn't know it. Let's get together someday soon to discuss how we'll move in to pick up the pieces. Okay?"

"Sure thing."

"Centomat will prosper when I'm in full control of it," he said as he tapped on the desk with a pencil.

"Can't argue with that. But really, Steve, I've got to tell you, you're one hell of a poker-faced bullshit artist."

"Thanks. But let's face it, I couldn't have done it without your solid legal mumbo jumbo."

Both laughed.

Barney said, "I'll call Joan in two weeks to see when you're free for a meeting. Is there anything else we need to discuss?"

He rubbed his forehead. "Nope, not at the moment. Nice work, Barney. Talk to you soon. Bye."

"Bye."

He eased out of his comfortable leather chair and walked over to his well-stocked bar. He had a tight-lipped, faint grin on his tanned face as he poured himself a cognac. With cocky satisfaction he stared at his drink for a few seconds and then finished it in one gulp. He was ecstatic: He'd come out way ahead in the very first business deal of his new venture. He went to his desk and dialed Helmut's phone number.

Helmut answered.

"Hello, Helmut. This is Steve. Remember our conversation about Centomat? It was about two months ago, on my birthday."

"Centomat . . . your birthday? Yes, yes I do."

"I just wanted to tell you that the first phase is complete and we've come out ahead by seventeen million."

"Seventeen million? Wonderful. What can I say? Good for you."

"No, Helmut, good for us, and our companies. Now, Alan and Jack can breathe easy, because I have things under control."

"Forget about them. You make me very proud."

Helmut's blunt comment made him smile with pride: Once again, he'd neutralized Alan and Jack's assault on him. But, while he continued to make them irrelevant to his business, he knew he had to postpone the pleasure of defanging them to an appropriate time. "Look, I've got to run. I'll fill you in on the details later. Bye."

"Okay Steve, bye."

He hung up and pressed a button on the intercom, and said, "Joan, get Erika on the phone."

"Right away, Mister Zeller."

Moments later he was on the phone hearing his wife's familiar, soft voice. "Hello, darling. Why don't you join the kids and me at the pool? It's a beautiful day to soak in the sun."

"Hi, Erika. Boy, I sure wish I could. But you know this damn business won't let me. Hey, guess what? I just divested the Centomat stock at a substantial profit."

"That's wonderful. All those long, hard hours you put in paid off."

"Yep. But it's freed up a lot of cash that's got to be put to use, and that's why I've called you. I'm getting ready to leave on a trip to take a closer look at some of the hot investment opportunities that'll disappear fast."

Her voice turned glum. "Darn. How long will you be gone?"

"Four long days—should be back on Saturday. I know it stinks. But when I return, how about going away for a couple days, just the two of us?"

Erika ignored the invitation. She said, "Oh, come on, you know you love your business deals; I know they're your life-blood. So, where are you off to?"

"At least New Hampshire, Colorado and California. After that, I'm not sure. We may end up going to Texas also."

"We? Who's we?"

"Joan and I—"

"It figures," Erika interjected.

He said, "I'll need her to keep the mass of paperwork organized on different proposals, and—"

"I understand, dear. I just hope her fiancé's as understanding as I am."

Though she spoke in an even tone, he felt defensive. "He'd better understand the business world and the obligations of an executive secretary. If not, he isn't right for her anyway."

Erika said in a deliberate, but soothing voice, "Honey, I did *not* say he was jealous; I just hoped he wasn't. That's all."

Steve shed his defensive posture. "You know what? Let them sort it out if it's a problem for him. Give my love to the kids; I'll bring them something. Why don't you decide where we should go when I return?"

"Okay, but don't work too hard. Call me."

"Yes, I'll try. Goodbye."

"Bye." He hung up and pushed the intercom button. "Joan, please come in."

Joan Winters, a brunette in her thirties, entered the office and stood in front of the desk poised with pen and pad to take notes.

He sat back in his chair and, with an almost imperceptible smile, looked at her. "Send Erika three dozen roses. Call the main office to let Victor and the others know we're going on a business trip. Tell them we'll keep in touch daily."

Joan maintained her business-like demeanor. "How long will we be gone?"

"Four days. We'll return Saturday."

Joan shook her head. "Saturday's bad for me."

"Okay, three days then. But, tell the others four. Charter a jet for the trip. We're going to the condo in the Bahamas to celebrate today's success. How long do you need to get ready?"

"I'm ready, Steve. We can leave in a few minutes, as soon as I make the calls," replied Joan. Her formal façade was gone.

● ● ●

After Erika ended the phone conversation with Steve, she put the receiver down and stared at the sun's glare shivering in the pool water. The children had left the pool only minutes earlier and could be heard creating a ruckus in the house, despite Nanny's authoritative voice ordering them to stop.

Teary eyes were the only evidence of Erika's concealed emotions. *So, now it's Joan Winters. He's off for four days of sex with that damn secretary...mature, efficient, soon-to-be-married . . . that slut . . . I should've known.* She bit her lip.

To prevent her mind from dwelling on vivid images of Steve and Joan entwined in passionate embraces, she tried to immerse herself in the things she'd invested a lot of herself: the cause of homeless children, her three children, and her marriage.

She'd been in love with Steve for a long time; perhaps she still was, but she wasn't sure. Over the years she'd come to understand him better than he understood himself. She knew he loved her; but he was a slave to his craving for wealth, and his insatiable urge for casual sex. Of course, she had confidence in herself: She knew she was beautiful, desirable and smart. And she'd concluded she was pitted against the demons inside Steve, and not some gold-digging floozy or a vivacious, conniving home-wrecker. That understanding gave her an edge in their relationship and marriage.

Erika learned to feign ignorance whenever Steve was involved in a liaison with another woman; but, in return, she controlled the rest of their relationship. She made sure her every need was met to live in style and luxury, enjoy mother-hood to the fullest, be respected in society, satisfy her pro-fessional objectives, have a stable family life for her children, and enjoy the love and security of a husband. She'd decided to dismiss the white lies he told to mask his sexual escapades. But try as she might, those conversations with him and his lies always hurt; perhaps she was still in love with him after all.

Three days later, on Friday afternoon, she was working on a speech she was slated to give at an upcoming fund-raising event when the phone rang. She picked up the receiver. "Hello."

"Hi, Erika. I'm back."

She was surprised. "Steve. What . . . where are you?"

"I'm in New York—in the office."

Her surprise turned to concern. "What happened? You said you'll be back on Saturday."

"Oh yeah, but we finished a day early. How are you?"

She relaxed. "Fine."

"And the kids?"

"They're fine too," she said and then admonished, "You better have some goodies for them. You promised."

"I didn't forget the three munchkins—or you."

"Oh boy, now I can't wait to see you." She managed a light response.

"Listen, I've come back to a lot of work; I'll have to work late, and I'm tired. I think I'll sack out in the city—stay at the apartment, or hang out at Don's, whatever."

She said in a resigned tone, "In that case, I'll plan on you being home for lunch tomorrow."

"Absolutely. By the way, have you planned our getaway?"

Thinking of what she had planned cheered her a bit. "Yes. I'll tell you all about it when I see you tomorrow."

"Okay, honey. Bye."

"Say hello to Don if you see him."

"I sure will. Bye."

"Bye."

A tear trickled down Erika's cheek. She kissed the receiver softly and put it down. She was happy to hear his voice. The anguish of him being in the arms of another woman and not hearing from him for three days simply melted away.

5
The Question

GROWING UP IN a house of highly successful and social, but absent, parents had a corrosive effect on Don McCoy. He became an unmotivated and aimless young man. Though he excelled in school, he was devoid of passion for anything. That is, until he entered New York University. Since he'd arrived there without a preference for a specific major, he embarked on an arbitrary process of elimination and narrowed his choice to two: philosophy or undeclared. He opted for philosophy. He thought, *Why not philosophy? At the very least it'll make me focus on something. And, if it's a drag, big deal, I'll try something else.*

As it turned out, philosophy immediately captivated his logic-biased brain and excited his imagination. He immersed himself in the study of life, and other related disciplines— theology and science. Of late, he'd started to devote considerable energy and time to poring over ideas of the world's greatest minds. Also, in an uncharacteristic move, he cut back on social activities.

One early spring afternoon, he and Steve were sitting on a bench in Washington Square and soaking up the sun. They had a class in an hour. Steve sat with his arms and legs crossed as he watched people walk by or gather around the offerings of hawkers and artists. Don was sprawled on the bench with eyes closed and his head resting on the back of the bench. The two friends were engaged in sporadic, lazy chat.

Steve broke a long stretch of comfortable silence without interrupting his people-gazing activity. "When are you going to return to work?"

"No. I've quit for good."

"Say what? You're kidding."

Don opened his eyes and glanced at Steve. "No I'm not. That's it, man—adios, goodbye to Wolfe Financial Services."

Steve said with unmistakable sarcasm, "Why? What happened to all that talk about independence from good old Fred, you know, the crap you've yapped about? Ever since I've known you, your biggest bitch's been your dad's generosity."

He smiled at Steve's reaction. He knew he had it coming—thanks to his big mouth, Steve was aware of the strained relationship he had with Fred, his over-achieving father, and the contempt he felt for his financial support. Remaining in his semi-prone position, he said, "Guess I'll need Dad's help. Hey, it's peanuts for him, and I don't like it. But, I'm serious about my major; I want to graduate with a degree in philosophy."

Steve asked, "So what? Are earning a buck and graduating in philosophy mutually exclusive? They're not, you know."

"Man, I know that, but—"

Steve interrupted, "But nothing. Take the long-term view, dummy. You've got a good thing going at Wolfe Financial Services. Helmut likes you and will look after you; you'd make it big. Don't blow it."

He said, "But I *am* looking ahead—way ahead."

Steve shook his head and said sharply, "You don't know shit about long term. To you, it's deciding which broad you're going to date this weekend."

He couldn't argue with Steve's assessment, so he shrugged. "Philosophy's intriguing. It's super and I'm drawn to it . . . I don't know, but it's hard to explain. I want to spend as much time as I can to study it."

"Is that why you haven't been goofing around with the gang, not showing up in bars and things like that?"

Don replied, "Yeah. That's helped. But, see, I need more time." Then he thought, *Hell, you'd never really understand my motivation anyway. And I've no intention of selling you on my values, because I know your values revolve only around money and financial success.*

Steve interrupted his people-watching activity and looked at him. "To hell with studying life, Don, just live it."

He raised his eyebrows and said with emphasis, "Why not live—and study—life? You know, a lot of gurus of physical and metaphysical sciences did exactly that."

"Gurus? Like who?" Steve asked.

He said with slight impatience, "Come on, you know, gurus like Plato, Socrates, Confucius, Aristotle—you want more? Darwin, Galileo, Einstein, Emerson, Thoreau, Sartre. Enough gurus for you?"

Steve squinted and said, "Damn, you're diving really deep into this scientific and philosophical stuff, aren't you? We've argued . . . in general, I mean. But now these . . . are you picking the brains of all those dead guys?"

"Somewhat," he replied. "But I'm concentrating on my favorites."

"Your favorites? And who are they?"

"Aristotle, Thoreau, Darwin and Einstein."

"But of course. Now tell me why you picked them?" Steve was obviously attempting to keep the conversation going.

"I'm more attuned to their thinking, I guess," he said with a nonchalant expression on his face.

That didn't seem to satisfy Steve. "Yeah? How? Tell me what attracts you to these guys?"

"Oh super. You can't be serious?" He knew it would be a waste of time.

"Really, Don, I do want to know, for example, why you feel a bond with Aristotle. Because he was logical? Right? Maybe he was too logical, and, like you, he probably irritated the hell out of everybody," Steve said as he watched two approaching female joggers in skin-tight shorts and bouncing sweatshirts.

Steve's ogling of the shapely joggers amused Don. He had no doubt Steve was concerned with his decision to quit working; and he was equally certain that, at that moment, Steve had little interest in anything that was being said, and even less in engaging in the intellectual and spiritual discourse involving the great minds of the past. But they had time to kill before the next class. So he thought he might as well go along and engage in a futile exercise to enlighten him.

He responded to Steve's snide remark. "Small minds found Aristotle irritating; and now, small minds find me irritating. I'll tell you what attracted me to this guy—I mean besides his single-minded drive to know the truth. This was the guy who developed the actual theory of logic. What does that tell you about his intellectual capacity, and ability to organize thoughts?"

Steve answered with a question, "Was he Greek?"

"He was from Macedonia, a kingdom located north of Greece. He lived about three centuries before Christ. And guess what?"

"What?"

"He taught a Macedonian prince who later became the famous Alexander the Great. You didn't know that, did you?"

Steve smiled. "No, I didn't. Fascinating tidbit, though. I'm sure there's more you like about this guy."

"Well, he got into so many things. For example, he opted for common sense instead of mysticism popular at the time.

What else? He was quite a humorous guy; well-versed in a variety of disciplines, and wrote a lot about them; had enormous effect on a bunch of philosophies and religions of the world."

"Huh. Okay, what about the Thoreau bird? Why did he make your list of must-study minds?" Steve asked, his eyes still wandering.

Chuckling at Steve's feeble attempt to remain interested, Don said, "Uncomplicated free-spirit, in a nutshell. Henry David Thoreau believed in shunning material possessions and being self-reliant. He preached living simply. It makes a lot of sense to me."

"Yeah, that would make sense to you."

"You know what this nineteenth-century American philosopher did? He built a sparse cottage by himself on the edge of a secluded pond in Concord, Mass. and lived there for two years."

Steve asked, "Why the hermit life?"

"He just wanted to be as self-sufficient and close to nature as possible, you know—"

Steve interrupted, "But why?"

"Oh, to read, introspect and write—basically, that's why. He documented his experience in a super essay, *Walden*, titled after the pond's name. You might want to read him; makes a compelling case to simplify life in order to gain spiritual insight."

Steve's flippancy was evident. "Well, maybe someday, when the hermit in me wants to come out. But I can see how you'd feel affinity for a guy like that." Then he added with a grin, "Now talk to me about the evolution guy."

Don said, "Charles Robert Darwin was a nineteenth-century naturalist—"

Steve interjected, "And an Englishman. I know he researched nature all over the world . . . er, in places like South

America, Pacific Islands, Australia and then came up with the evolution theory. Right?"

"Super. Then I'm sure you also know he wrote a very massive and controversial book, *The Origin of Species.*"

"Yes, I most certainly do," Steve said with mock smugness.

Don smiled and continued, "And that it permeated a vast number of disciplines—science, theology, sociology and such."

Steve nodded. "Well, I know enough about the uncovering of evolution by this guy to be impressed. But what made you fall in love with him?"

"What amazed me were his stamina and mental fortitude in deriving the theory from excruciatingly detailed evidence— all empirical—and observations of the creatures on islands, and everywhere."

"And that brings us to your last character, relatively speaking, of course," Steve said with a straight face.

Don shook his head and said, "Couldn't resist it, could you? Let's see. You do know that Albert Einstein, a science and mathematics genius, was born into a poor Jewish family in Germany."

Steve nodded.

Don continued, "But do you know the school teachers considered young Einstein mentally backward?"

"Really? Why was that?" The surprise in Steve's tone was genuine.

"It had something to do with languages and memorizing stuff; they weren't his thing. Anyway, after the Nazis took over Germany, he came to the US and became a citizen, and Princeton University offered him a job."

Steve gawked at two more shapely female bodies jogging by. "He had to be superhuman to come up with the concepts he did in his theory of relativity."

"Yeah. And he did it without experimentation—just used his brain, that's it—and conceived interrelationships of mass, gravity, motion and time and then tied that into a neat mass-energy conservation concept—"

Steve jumped in, "Yes, I know; he tied all that into the famous e=mc². Absolutely fantastic."

"And because of him we took a quantum leap in understanding the universe; that's why I picked him." Don stopped talking.

Silence reigned for a few minutes. Then Steve looked at his wristwatch and said, "Let's go. Class starts in seven minutes."

The two gathered their books and walked away.

● ● ●

Deep in his heart, Don wanted faith; he wanted to believe. But thanks to his well-meaning nanny, routine and rigorous exposure to Catholicism had been a required part of his childhood—like eating vegetables or brushing his teeth. That forced-feeding of religious rituals etched in him a feeling of ambivalence that followed him into adulthood.

Therefore it was no accident he was attracted to philosophy at New York University, because its in-depth discourse needed dialogue on religion. He spent a lot of time studying the impact of theology on life and humans; and he delved into the precepts of the world's largest religions: Christianity, Islam, Hinduism, Buddhism and Judaism. As he expected, he found striking differences among their teachings and concepts of life, earth, universe and God. But he also appreciated the principles at their very foundation that transcended them and were professed by them: love toward others, rules and discipline for living on the earth, allegiance to at least one divine authority, and belief in some form of Judgment.

The broad and prolonged study of theology crystallized in him a fresh understanding of the purpose and role of religion. It was different from what he'd learned in church and Sunday school, and that perspective made a lot of sense to him. He continued to mold his new thinking; for him there was no turning back to previous concepts and beliefs.

Just before he got his degree, Don made fruitless attempts to get one of the scarce positions teaching philosophy. Except for a brief working stint at Wolfe Financial Services, he'd devoted his time and energy to studies. Therefore, he wasn't qualified as the graduates who'd worked as assistants to professors during their college years. He began to regret the hardheaded decision he'd made as a sophomore to devote all his time solely to the study of philosophy. That commitment had not only forced him to submit to even more financial shackles of his father, Fred, whom he couldn't stand, it was responsible for his current untenable position. His younger brother Les who, unlike him, had made peace with Fred and was enjoying a secure career at Wolfe Financial Services—compliments of Helmut Wolfe, Fred's long-time business associate and friend.

Of course, Don had his own contact at Wolfe Financial Services: his friend, Steve Zeller. But he'd concluded the world of finance wasn't for him, and he must focus on finding a position in some other area in the corporate world. His job search, again, resulted in endless rejections: Few employers were interested in hiring someone with a philosophy major.

It was soon evident to him that his prospects of being employed were indeed bleak. His frustration was at its peak when he accepted a dinner invitation from his parents—something he'd avoided for quite a while.

At the dinner table, Jessica McCoy was talkative as usual, but a bit more flighty; and she announced she'd decided to devote more time to charities because it was the thing to do for a woman of her stature.

Fred McCoy smiled and nodded. He was his same old sociable and combative self. He never argued with his wife. But, with his sons—well, that was a different matter entirely. The three were engaged in a pleasant chat, and their main course had been served.

Fred was spreading butter on a piece of roll. He looked at Don and asked, "So what's happening on the job front?"

Don was taking a sip of red wine. He put his glass down and replied, "I've got my résumé out."

Fred smiled. "You've had the résumé out for what now . . . a year? Maybe less? Have you had any interviews?"

"If there had been a nibble, I'd have already mentioned it."

Fred shrugged. "Maybe. But you're not around much and, you know . . . when you're here you don't talk about your job hunting. I ask your mother, and she doesn't know anything either. That's fine, really. But, sounds like the philosophy degree isn't doing a damn thing for your résumé, now is it?"

Fred's belittling comment irritated him. "All right, Dad. Tell me something I don't know." He released his fork; it hit his plate with a loud noise. He sat back with his arms folded and glared at Fred. "Guess what? I'm still glad I studied philosophy."

Jessica's nervous eyes darted from Fred to Don to Fred again. She put her hands up and said, "Okay, you two. That's enough. Let's have a nice dinner, without fighting."

They ignored her. She opened her mouth again as if to speak. But she seemed to change her mind and went back to eating.

Fred looked into Don's eyes and said, "Well, let me see. Here's something you don't seem to know: You need an attitude adjustment—and fast."

Don's defiance in his raised voice was unmistakable. "Oh, yeah?"

With a cold stare, Fred answered, "Yeah. Getting you a job's no problem, no problem at all. The problem is your attitude toward authority, toward responsibility, toward work. No employer's going to put up with that; I know, I wouldn't."

Don realized his father, in his own way, was offering to come to his rescue once again. He hated that thought; but he knew he could use his help. "I'll change." The rough edge in his tone was gone.

Fred said in a stern voice, "You have no choice."

Don nodded. "I understand, Dad. I said I'll change." He kept his irritation well hidden.

The expression on Fred's face softened and he smiled. "Excellent. Now, I want to help. You want to see what I can do?"

"Okay, Dad," Don replied and put a piece of roll into his mouth. But deep inside him it wasn't okay. He was still bristling at having to continue to accept help from Fred. He thought, maybe—just maybe—the financial success will eventually translate into the control he craved to pursue his own interests and destiny.

• • •

A month later, Don was employed. Thanks to Fred's few well-placed phone calls, he landed an assistant buyer's job with a major wholesaler of designer apparel in New York. He decided to become a true corporate soldier and go as high as he could in the company's hierarchy to achieve financial success. In order to play his role correctly, he even moved into a tastefully-furnished two-bedroom apartment in a prestigious building on Fifth Avenue—compliments of Fred, of course.

But from the very beginning, he started paying a price: He felt a nonstop, draining stress. In time, he was able to trace the cause of stress to his lack of "the killer instinct" essential to surviving in some corporations.

He realized his firm rewarded those who worshipped greed and played subtle self-preservation games involving under-handed tactics such as backstabbing and deceit. Uncovering this tidbit probably wouldn't have come as a surprise to some-one other than Don. He rightfully concluded he had to be on constant guard. *I'm surrounded by people who'd eat me alive if they had the chance. I can't afford to make any mistakes with these goddamn cannibals around me.* Even though he was successful in keeping one eye on his enemies, he'd forget to keep the other on his "friends," sometimes with unpleasant consequences.

After surviving eight years of distasteful office politics and advancing to the position of vice-president of marketing, he decided his sanity and destiny lay elsewhere, and turned in his resignation. For him, leaving the corporate world proved to be painful in more than one way.

As a budding marketing executive, he'd met Kim Roper, a seductively charming brunette buyer for a chain of garment stores. On their first date, he realized she was a smart, ambi-tious and sophisticated woman with expensive tastes. He was surprised at how comfortable she became with his pas-sion for philosophy: She spent hours discussing works of the likes of Sartre, Jung and Plato, over dinner or while enjoying a glass of wine in his apartment. He fell in love with her. Kim had been honest with him: She admitted that, besides him personally, she was attracted to his ability to support her high-maintenance life style. Nonetheless, he married her; and, when he removed himself from the corporate arena, she divorced him. Their childless marriage lasted six years and left him heart-broken—and broke.

That wasn't all: Fred McCoy was incensed with Don for throwing away a promising career. The chasm in their relationship grew wider and deeper.

Don gave up his Fifth Avenue suite and moved into a modest, one-bedroom studio near Columbia University. It was an old apartment with a high white ceiling, drab blue walls and creaky floors. The expensive furniture and furnishings he brought from his upscale residence looked incongruous in it. Three locks secured its front door, and its windows offered a view of the mildewed brick wall of the adjacent building.

Once he was settled in his new surroundings, his mother Jessica relayed Fred's message to him: Financial support was his, whenever he wanted it. He didn't admit to her, but he was grateful—and relieved—for Fred's grudging generosity.

Things were getting back to the way they were over eight years ago. Once again he felt a sense of peace, something he'd misplaced while he chased wealth. He rediscovered his brilliance that people in the past had found blinding and painful; and he also reverted to his much-feared, biting, impatient candor during intellectual sparring. It was time for a fresh start.

One thing, however, remained constant for him: A strong bond of friendship with Steve Zeller. They'd met fourteen years ago and for him Steve was the closest thing to a true friend. They were about the same age, but that's where the similarity ended; and it wasn't the similarities that mattered. Steve appeared to be at ease with him because he wasn't his competitor or his underling—he was his equal. He was content, had mastered his ambition and was therefore not compelled to look up to the likes of Steve. Furthermore, he'd proven himself to be sincere, non-judgmental and safe: Not once had he questioned Steve's methods or motives. He never visited Steve uninvited, and his visits were rare. Steve, on the other hand, stopped in at Don's apartment—uninvited and unannounced—whenever it seemed he needed to get away to a safe haven and a no-nonsense soul. During those visits they'd catch up on each other's lives and lose themselves in relaxed and, sometimes, spirited conversations with no regard for time.

• • •

The buzzer rang.

Don got up from the couch and walked over to the intercom. "Yes? Who is it?"

Steve's voice crackled, "Hi, Don. Want some company?"

"Sure, Steve, come on up." He pressed the button to open the building door.

Then he walked back; dropped to his knees; started to pick up crumpled papers laying around a coffee table and stuff them into a wastebasket.

He heard a knock on his apartment door and said aloud, "It's unlocked."

Steve opened the creaky door and looked at him busy on the floor. "Hi. What's with all the paper? Is this a bad time to be barging in?"

He waved to Steve and replied, "Nope. I was just scribbling. Let me get rid of the paper. Help yourself to a beer from the fridge. Beer's all I have."

"Beer's all I want."

"Bullshit. What you want is cognac or a perfect martini."

Steve laughed. "You're right, you broke bastard."

Steve opened the fridge. "A beer for you, too?"

"Yeah, of course," he answered as he dropped the wastebasket in the corner of the room.

Steve walked over with two open beer cans. A lounger, a beanbag and a couch shared the coffee table in front of a television. He took a sip from one can and placed the other on the coffee table for Don. While he was making himself comfortable on the lounger, he said, "Haven't seen you in a quite a while."

"Yeah. Couple months, at least . . . since your birthday bash." Don flung himself onto the beanbag opposite Steve's lounger. He noticed something was odd about Steve, who'd made a habit of marching into his apartment looking stressed: *This guy's already decompressed—too damn relaxed. What gives?* He reached for his beer can, took two deep gulps and burped. "That felt great," he said, as he stretched out his feet and arms in a semi-prone position. A faint smile played on his creased, bearded face. His eyes were focused on Steve, and the beer can dangled from his hand.

"Yeah, great." Steve was lying on the cozy and fully stretched lounger, and staring at a cobweb hanging from the ceiling. "So, what you've been up to? Last time I saw you, you were mulling over an advertising job."

Don said, "I was."

"So, what happened?"

"Nothing. It just died."

Steve grinned. "Jobs don't die; you kill 'em. Good thing, Fred loves you."

He sighed. "If you say so."

Steve asked, "What's with all the papers on the floor?"

"I'm writing a book—correction, scribbling thoughts for a book before getting on the computer."

"A book? That's a surprise. What kind?"

"I don't know. I'm not there yet; I'm still trying to develop the idea." He was being evasive because he wasn't quite ready to talk about it.

Steve said, "Must be hot stuff. Let me guess: It's about the confessions of a divorced man. No, no, wait. It's a how-to book on exterminating divorce lawyers. Yes, that's it." It was obvious Steve wanted to keep the conversation light.

He was amused. "Interesting topic, but no. Right now, only jumbled thoughts are swirling in my head—thoughts I've wrestled with from time to time. I imagine, so have you."

Steve shrugged and said, "I give up. What's the topic?"

"It's heavy stuff—you know, quite dry. I don't know if you have time for all that. Let's do this another time," he said, watching Steve yawn and rub his forehead.

Steve was adamant. "Damn it, will you quit stalling? I've got all the time in the world."

"How come you have all this free time?" he asked, taking the opening to satisfy his curiosity about Steve's uncharacteristic demeanor.

Steve sighed. "I've just returned from heaven: Spent three days with Joan—"

Surprised, he interrupted, "Three days with Joan? Joan Winters? That cold, stiff secretary of yours? No!"

"Yes. Out of the office, she's one hell of a woman; very liberated. Umm . . . massaged every kink out of every part of my body," Steve said.

"Joan, a sexpot? That's hard to believe." He thought, *This guy's totally drained—that explains why he's so relaxed.* But he was still curious about what had really transpired with Steve. *Screwing Joan's one thing, but it's out of character for this moneymaking machine to spend so much time away from his business.* So he asked, "Why three days? What was the occasion?"

There was a hint of pride in Steve's voice. "Pulled off a critical business deal. A tough nut—something I'd been working for a long time. And hear this: I crushed those Wolfe punks, Alan and Jack, in the process—at least for now."

"Good to hear that." He was well aware of the misery Alan and Jack caused Steve: He'd vented about them on several occasions.

Steve smiled and said, "So I took off with Joan to celebrate. Since I wasn't in a mood to return home today, I called Erika and told her I'd spend the evening with you and see her tomorrow."

"It's simply super. I wasn't getting anywhere with organizing my thoughts, and needed a break anyway." He was pleased at the prospect of spending a long, lazy evening with Steve.

Steve adjusted his body in the lounger. "Ahh. Let's just relax, booze up and shoot the crap. So what's your book about?"

"Topic's anything but relaxing," he warned.

"Aw come on; I'll be the judge," Steve insisted.

Don knew he couldn't brush him off. "All right, what the hell? Let me get us a couple more beers before we start." He got up from the beanbag.

Steve asked, "Are your parents back from Europe?"

"Nope. They're still hopscotching—Italy, Spain, England, Ireland, and God knows where else. How're Marge and Stan?" He was at the fridge, pulling tabs off the cans.

"Well, Ma's convinced she's got *Alzheimer's*. Forgets things, that's all . . . but, she's rational, functional, and all that. So, we don't know; they're running some tests."

"Huh? And how's the tough old man Stan?"

"Like a rock, hasn't changed. He's great, and always there for Mom."

Don handed Steve a fresh beer and settled back in the comfortable beanbag. He let his beer can ease out of his hand onto the floor and focused his eyes on Steve. "Now, about my book—remember, my scrambled thoughts are still in embryonic stage. Okay? So, first tell me, do you ever wonder: 'Who am I? Why am I here? Why is anything here? How did it all begin? What happens after death? Who is God?'"

"Yes, every day, right after tackling mergers, acquisitions and mindless CEO's," Steve responded with a straight face.

He smiled. "There's hope for you yet. But seriously, I've decided to take on the big, the basic, the age-old questions most people wonder about at one time or another in their lives." He paused for Steve's reaction.

Steve remained quiet.

He continued, "For ages, humans have been trying various approaches to find answers to those questions; you know—to get a glimpse of the unknown. They've tried everything: They've attempted to rationalize; use logic; do a lot of soul searching; seek help from deities, ghosts, sciences, and nature. But they couldn't arrive at satisfactory answers—none. And that was a totally unacceptable situation for them. They craved some sort of closure, any closure, which would mitigate their anxiety about the unknown. So what did they do? Any idea, Steve?"

"No, what?"

"Well, they ended up in one of the three camps: One, most of them decided to believe in someone or something powerful and called themselves religious; two, a few decided to believe there was nothing before life and nothing after life—no God, nothing—and called themselves atheists; and three, the rest decided to remain undecided and called themselves agnostics."

"And where do you come out in all this?" Steve asked, then placed his hand on his mouth and burped.

Don rubbed his chin and said, "As I said before, I've done my share of thinking about these subjects at different times in my life. But you see, unfortunately, I haven't been able to convince myself of any of the explanations I've heard or come up with myself so far. And damn it, I'm just not prepared to force-fit myself into a religious, agnostic or atheist category." Then he shook his head and added, "It just doesn't feel right."

Looking pensive, Steve said, "Come to think of it, I've never really thought about what I am. I don't go to church regularly; but I do go, especially on religious occasions. I've no qualms about Catholicism's teachings or anything like that. To be honest, I've taken religion for granted—it's just been there; and all I can say is I'm fine with Christ and God. So I guess I'm religious."

"Sounds like you are," he said. "You know, my brother and I grew up religious. But now I'm just not sure I can classify myself so neatly."

Steve ran his hand through his hair. "What made you pick this subject?"

His eyes narrowed. "I've thought about writing for quite some time, and scrounged ideas for over a year for something fresh or some new twist. You know what I mean? But nothing seemed to click. Then, just recently it dawned on me: Why not tackle the unknown beyond as a subject of my book."

"The revelation came to you just like that?" Steve snapped his fingers.

That made him smile. "Hell no. A while back, I was so damn frustrated at failing to come up with a topic, I blurted out without thinking that I should bribe God to help me, like I used to as a kid. And, just like that, the questions that used to plague us in the philosophy classes at NYU resurrected in my head. I couldn't shake them, and finally it occurred to me that tackling them might be a super exercise that may turn into a book. The more I thought about it, the more I liked it."

Steve raised his hands for emphasis. "Wait a minute, Einstein. It's already been done, countless times. You yourself said you wanted a fresh topic or something with a new twist. So, why go after stale questions millions have already hashed out?"

He nodded. "Right you are about the questions being stale. But, the new twist is the approach I've decided to use in my thinking about the unknown."

"Ah, yes, don't tell me. You're going to do the bribe trick, and God will let you in on His little secret," Steve said with a serious face.

He grinned. "Hey, moron. Suck on your beer and listen; you might learn something. Here's the scoop: Instead of bouncing around on all the frustrating and interrelated questions—you know, about God, life, death and the universe—I thought I'd gain better understanding and increase the odds of success by perhaps focusing on one question: Why? Why are we all here? Well, settling on the question to tackle was the easy part. What comes next is tough: The task of how to tackle it." He paused and took a sip of his beer.

Steve said in a voice that was no longer flippant, "How did you pick that question versus, say, who is God?"

"I'm a human and there's lot more information available on humans than God: history, habits, motivation, progress— things like that. I can use my brain and all the senses to study them, and myself."

"Jeez, Don, you've thought about this a lot, haven't you?"

He nodded. "Yes, but I've barely got a rough framework of how to proceed—"

"Oh, sure. I know you: You wouldn't be sniffing around a challenge unless you felt you had a chance to meet it," Steve said and, pointing a finger at him, he continued, "If you say you have a new angle on this worn subject, then you have a new angle and I believe you. You know what I think?"

"No. Is there something I said that makes you think I'm a mind reader?"

Steve smiled. "I think you need my help."

"Yeah?"

"Yeah. The subject has universal appeal. That's good, but... still remains a mystery, without an answer. You'll need a brutally honest critic with a quick and pragmatic mind to help you examine your creativity and new thinking. Without that your ideas and work could very well bomb. What's more, my service is free. No charge," Steve said with mock smugness.

"Now, why didn't I think of that?" He was thrilled. He knew Steve's offer was sincere. He stroked his beard and said with enthusiasm, "Super. Buddy, you're on."

"Tell me how you intend to answer the question: Why are we all here?"

He was very aware of Steve's penchant for the bottom line; but he wasn't ready to oblige. "Before I tackle that question, let's talk a bit about the brain and the mind. Actually, for the purposes of this discussion, the distinction between the two isn't important; it doesn't matter. So, let's refer to them collectively as the brain."

Steve said, "Okay. Let's."

"Now, what are some of the things we know about the brain?"

Steve answered without hesitation, "It soaks up knowledge."

He nodded. "Yes, at an exponential rate. Just think about the short time it took to go from believing the earth to be flat to rushing to solve the mysteries of life and the universe. There's another thing we know about the brain, don't we?"

Steve squinted. "We do? What?" He took a sip of beer.

"We can use different faculties of our brain to accomplish different things. Right? In some cases, we've used feelings, prejudices, emotions and imagination to unleash powerful forces and achieve immense success, without ever using or being able to use our faculty of reason. Religion's a great case in point. I remember an expression I heard from a high school teacher: 'Where reason ends, faith begins.' Then, there are other cases, where we've used only reason, logic and imagination. This approach, too, has yielded super benefits in things like, let's see . . . like scientific research, material advances, and creature comforts. This use of the brain made it possible for us to explore and hypothesize about the nature and origins of planets, stars and the universe as a whole. Simply incredible. Don't you think?"

"This is the right-brain, left-brain stuff psychologists carry on about. Right?" Steve asked.

He nodded and continued, "We don't need to get too clinical, philosophical or technical to talk about the brain. We all know that this is a very, er . . . one of the most complex organs; has the ability to interpret feelings and emotions, to imagine, to reason, to employ logic, and to extrapolate—all at the same time when it's addressing a . . . some process, activity or thought." He paused.

Steve looked at him in silence.

His throat felt dry. He took a sip of beer and continued, "What happens when the whole brain—not just the right or the left brain—approach is used to address a challenge? The results are generally superior to those that are derived from using only a part of the brain. As an example, our use of reason, logic, intuition, imagination, science and extrapolation, coupled with attributes such as perseverance, have opened up the space frontier to mankind. The examples are endless and phenomenal. So I asked myself: Why not use the 'whole brain' approach to figure out why we're here? Why not, indeed. And, that completed the new twist I was searching for and decided to run with it. Steve, does all this make any sense to you?" He wanted to make sure Steve was keeping up with him.

Steve replied, "So far it does."

Encouraged, he said, "Good. Now, let's put human beings in perspective—"

Steve interjected, "What do you mean?"

He welcomed the interruption. He paused and rubbed his hands together; his eyes took on a faraway look because his mind was creating an image of his response. "I'm telling you. Let's imagine a field the size of one thousand football fields, two thousand football fields, three thousand; pick a large number. Let's say this enormous field represents two dimensions of the universe, and spread all over this field are stones and pebbles. Then, a golf-sized stone might be the sun, and a pea-sized pebble the earth. Let's say that pebble is covered with tiny specks of dirt, which represent all life on earth. Then, one tiny speck might represent all the human beings. So, in a sense, the question we're trying to address is: Why is that one tiny speck sitting on a pea-sized pebble suspended in a humongous space?"

Steve scowled. "Boy, you couldn't make humans look more insignificant if you tried."

He shook his head. "No, I'm not. Just trying to make sure the stage's set correctly," he said with emphasis and added, "Also, let's clear up one more thing: God's gender. It has absolutely no bearing on what we're talking about, none at all; I for one think God's genderless, but let's simply use the conventional, masculine gender when referring to God. Do you have a problem with that?"

"I think God's not genderless. But, if it makes no difference to your book, then use what you want," Steve said.

"Super. Phew. That was easy. And now we come to the 'why' question." He emptied his beer can and crumpled it. Then, pointing to Steve's empty can, he said. "We both could use more beer. I'll get it." He got up from the beanbag with an exaggerated motion and a grunt to hunt down fresh beer.

• • •

Steve felt Don needed a rest from expounding his thoughts. Even though he was intrigued by the topic and what Don was saying, he surmised he needed time to mull the subject over in his own mind before he could play a meaningful role in his friend's attempt to write a book. So, when Don returned with the beer, he asked, "Where the hell are you getting these ideas from—from your wino friends on skid row?"

Don answered with a straight face, "Of course, and if I were you I wouldn't knock those winos. Some of those guys, besides being well lubricated, are well connected. At least one's a personal friend of Moses; he says he almost bought it when the breach in the Red Sea closed behind him prematurely. Poor fellow still has nightmares."

Both laughed.

Steve said, "Hey, let's drop the book talk. Next time I'm stranded in the city, we'll get together and pick up where we left off today. That'll give me time to chew on what you've told me so far and, of course, give me a chance to prepare my ammunition to blast holes in your theories. Sounds okay to you?"

Don nodded. "Sounds okay to me."

He yawned and stretched. "By the way, since Erika knows I'm meeting you today, she'd expect me to know if you're seeing someone special. Frankly, I'm curious too. Well, are you?"

Don replied, "Hell, no. There isn't going to be a special someone—ever. I mean it—ever. I don't intend to get sucked into another 'special relationship.' Life's finally good, so why mess with it? Tell Erika I'm having a ball."

He looked at Don with amusement. "Don't ever say 'ever.' Second marriage doesn't necessarily mean second divorce. You're not a rookie anymore."

They continued chatting.

6
The Answer

IT WAS FRIDAY, a week after Steve had heard about Don's idea for a potential book. A hectic work schedule that day made the long commute to East Hampton unappealing to him. So, he decided to spend the night at the Park Avenue penthouse and requested Erika to come into the city the next day to join him for their planned theater and dinner date. He of course invited Don to visit him that evening and was glad to have an opportunity to spend time with him again so soon. The enthusiasm with which Don had discussed his thoughts about life on the earth was something he hadn't seen in him for years; that's why he was excited for him and had demanded to help him with the book. The topic wasn't something he'd ever pondered; but now he couldn't stop thinking about it. He suspected that Don's passion for the subject may have influenced his mindset.

• • •

Don and Steve sat in oversized loungers in front of the fireplace in the Park Avenue penthouse. They'd finished a succulent Maine lobster dinner, and Steve had shown the caterer and server out. He'd brought two snifters and a bottle of cognac from the bar, and both were sipping brandy and expressing their ire at the hapless New York Yankees.

After exhausting his thoughts on how to turn around his favorite ball club, Don changed the subject. "By the way, how was the romantic getaway with your charming wife?"

"Perfect, simply perfect. Erika took care of every detail and made it a memorable trip—boy, she's really something. I just can't describe how wonderful she is."

"You're one lucky bum," he said, marveling at him for cheating on Erika one week and showering love and adulation on her the next.

Steve nodded and cleared his throat. "You know Erika worries about you. She wasn't pleased to hear you've sworn off serious relationships, but felt time will take care of that madness. I told her about your book. And guess what? She liked the idea; she thinks you may have found your niche—writing."

Erika's validation pleased him. But he felt he must address a glaring disparity between his thinking and that of Steve. "Let me set something straight right here and now. Regarding the book . . . in baseball jargon, ah, I see myself at bat at the home plate, trying desperately to connect with the ball. You, on the other hand, seem to see me running after I've hit the ball, and rounding second base on my way to third."

Steve's eye's narrowed. "Huh?"

He continued with emphasis, "No book, Steve—not yet; maybe never—only thoughts, and at best they're still rudimentary and disorganized."

Steve lifted his hands and put on a look of someone duly chastened. "I stand corrected. So, let's talk about them."

He squinted and strained to remember. "Where the hell did we stop last time?"

Steve said, "In your own long-winded way you were finally going to tell me why we're on this planet."

"Ah...yes, now I remember. As a first step in hoping to zero in on the answer, I've made a list of broad possibilities or dogmas suggested or preached by countless people, religions and other institutions. Let me just tell you what they are before we jump into discussing any of them. First: There's no God; it doesn't matter in any scheme of things why we're here. Second: We're here because of God's will and plan, and to serve Him; He'll judge us and send us to heaven or hell based on our actions on earth. Third: We're here to complete a cycle of self-cleansing, and to pay for our sins before attaining a place with God. To this list, I've added three other possibilities—"

Steve interrupted, "You came up with the next three?"

He shrugged. "Yes, I did some free thinking and there they were. So here's the fourth: We're robots and are here undergoing the process of being perfected. Fifth: The evolution of God is stymied and we're looking for clues to get it going. And lastly, the sixth possibility: The evolution of God is complete but not successful, and we're here retracing the evolutionary path to find and correct past mistakes." He paused and then smiled at the quiet Steve. "Come to think of it, this is the first time I've seen you so attentive to a subject other than money. I know I'm good and make a lot of sense, but I haven't succeeded in overwhelming you, have I?"

Steve smirked and replied, "Hell no. I'm loose and enjoying the booze. But, just try spouting off nonsense and you'll see what happens to my patience."

He laughed. "I have an inkling—"

Steve interjected, "Why don't you walk through your thoughts in layman's terms on each one? That'll help my understanding and, at the same time, probably clarify and organize your thinking too."

Don thought, *Boy, he's really getting into it. That's super.* He said, "Okay, but I'll also whittle down the options by giving you my rationale for rejecting them. Then we'll get into the meat of what's left."

Steve shrugged and said, "That's fine with me." He emptied his snifter and poured more cognac into it.

Don took a sip and placed his glass on the table. "Okay. Let's take the first possibility why we're here: No purpose, no God. Basically, this claims there was nothing before the universe began and there will be nothing when it ends, and we were nothing before we were born and will be nothing after death. This scenario makes no sense and atheists, agnostics and believers alike have discussed it to death. My argument against it is simple: I'm here, you're here, the earth's here, and the stars are here. We were, somehow, created. Something or someone nudged something or put some thought into bringing this whole thing about. This effort to create—even if it's only creating an event that promotes or sets off a chain reaction resulting in such things as the universe and life—implies purpose. Enough said on that, unless you've something to add." He paused.

Steve shook his head and said, "I can't argue with the premise that you can't get something from nothing."

"Super. You got it," he said and continued, "Second possibility: We're here because of God's will and plan, and to serve Him." He took a sip of his cognac and continued, "And He'll judge our actions on this earth to send us to heaven or hell. I'm afraid this assertion makes absolutely no sense to me." He waited for Steve to react.

Steve took his time to speak. "Let me get this straight: You haven't the slightest idea of God's plan. No one does, right? And yet, here you are, dismissing one of the most widely held premises."

Don moved the snifter in his hand in a circular motion and watched the brandy swirl. "This scenario's asking us to believe that God, who's perfect, loving, everlasting, and wants for nothing, creates imperfect humans to serve Him on this earth. Then, when He gets less than stellar service and actions from some, what does He do? He sentences those puny, powerless minions to eternal hell. Now you tell me, does that make any sense? I mean really, if He does want humans for whatever purpose, why not simply create perfect, permanent ones that wouldn't mess up? I can't accept this premise as a reason for us being here." He paused and proceeded to refill Steve's snifter with cognac. "And get this: People think God responds to praise and prayers."

Steve shot back, "There's nothing wrong with people praising God and praying to Him—after all, He created us. What's the matter with you?"

His tone was deliberate. "Use your brain, Steve. I know you have it; just think it through. Why would God want humans to do that? If He's swayed by praise or prayers, it tells me that either He hasn't thought through his so-called plan or He has an ego problem. That demeans Him; I can't buy that." He looked at Steve to assess his reaction. He saw grudging nods from him.

He continued, "The third possibility is another widely touted, but erroneous, claim that we're here to complete the cycle of self-cleansing and paying for our sins before reaching God."

"What the hell's wrong with that? God had enough sense to give us free will. Guess what? That makes us responsible for our actions. So, if we screw up, we pay; and then we ask and receive forgiveness, and move on. I can relate to that. You should too; you're no stranger to screwing up," Steve said and took a sip of cognac.

Don's voice became sardonic. "Free will. Ah yes, the cornerstone of our psyche." He smiled and added, "But the issue isn't free will; and Steve, it isn't rocket science. Look, God's perfect and can do anything, right? So why the hell would He create human beings prone to mistakes and sins, and then put them through a wringer on this earth—once, or a number of times, depending on your belief—to improve and atone? He does all that before He accepts them into his fold, and I ask why? Why go through all that? It just doesn't jibe. I think He's quite capable of making perfect human beings without involving the use of the earth or other transitory things. There's got to be a better reason why we're here."

Steve thought for a moment and said, "I'm sure He has a good reason—"

"Hold it. That's accepting only on faith; and, in that case, this whole subject's over before we start. No, that's not good enough; my whole brain says the answer lies elsewhere."

Steve frowned, but said nothing.

Don was exhilarated: *He's showing a lot of interest. He's questioning, objecting and all that. Man, this is super. I've got a tenacious critic in him; if my arguments are weak, this sharpshooter will pick 'em off.*

Steve was lying back on the comfortable chair. He lifted his head and said, "Guess what? On the plus side, I'm following your logic and gut feelings. The negative is . . . somehow, er, there's something disturbing about what you're saying. Sorry, Don, but the way I see it, in a few short minutes you've decimated countless theologians, scholars and centuries-old beliefs and precepts that are, ah, at the very foundation of religion. Now—be honest—are you down on religion?"

He remained thoughtful and gave a matter-of-fact response: "Quite the contrary, damn it. You know me better than that. I think religion has played, and will continue to play in some form, an absolutely crucial part in the development of humanity. It's permeated everything, and molded everything mankind has: values, social order, institutions, creativity, stupendous progress, uh . . . undying thirst for knowledge and truth, and—"

Steve interrupted, "You really feel that way? You could've fooled me."

He said, "You're easily fooled. Look, I'm doing what the religions teach the world over: I'm trying to understand myself by using my own tiny brain to think through life's questions. The only difference is I'm doing it as objectively as I can—without relying on what others have to say about them." He wasn't sure Steve believed what he was saying, but he continued, "When the thoughts of every human brain—including yours and mine—are shared, they produce a collective and on-going change in humanity. This change, eventually, results in the collective progress of humanity. Therefore, I'm not knocking religion; I'm merely trying to express my half-baked thoughts and intuition. I don't know yet if all this makes any sense even to me. But I feel I must explore this as far as my brain can take me."

"That and the fact your brain has nothing else to do," Steve said with a smirk.

He was amused. "True. But right now, I don't want it to do anything else, either. Everything else is too mundane, and I leave that to you and other small minds. My brain can't be bothered with it; it has to be uncluttered and focused to tackle this fascinating mystery."

Steve smiled and, once again, put his head back and closed his eyes.

Don gave his beard a few deliberate strokes to get his thoughts refocused. "Now let's see . . . the next possibility—"

Steve cut in, "It's possible we're robots and are here under-going debugging, er, the process of being perfected."

He rubbed his cheek. "Yup, that's it. It's a possibility, but unlikely. First of all, it suggests that whoever made us and devised this elaborate and intricate universe can't design a robot with right specifications. That's ridiculous. Second, our life-and-death cycle is designed to progressively debug us. That too doesn't make sense."

"And why not?"

"Steve, think. Hell, if our destiny's to be perfect robots, then our minds and consciousness would somehow be linked together so any improvement or learning by one of us is instantly shared by us all to achieve perfection expeditiously. But that's not the case, is it? Your brain isn't connected to mine. So there. Nope, I don't believe we're robots running around and dying to be perfected."

Without lifting his head or opening his eyes, Steve said, "Your . . . logic . . . is . . . correct . . . we . . . are . . . not . . . robots . . . thank . . . God."

He laughed at Steve's attempt to mimic a robot. "Before we go further, let me get a beer; I've had enough cognac. How about you?"

"Beer sounds good." Steve yawned, and stretched his arms and legs.

Don had walked up to the long, well-lit bar, and was remov-ing the caps from two bottles of beer. "Overall, Steve, what's your assessment of the stuff I've thrown at you so far?"

Steve pondered a moment and then said, "My assess-ment so far? Now let's see: I've followed the scenarios you've developed and you've done a good job of listing the possibili-ties why we're on this earth, and . . . ah yes, you've kept your discussion focused on that question. Er . . . I have a bunch of questions, but not pertinent to the points you've been making. And that's okay. I'm sure I'll get a chance to ask them soon enough."

"Make sure you do. The more questions you ask, the more opportunity I have to test the substance in my thinking," he said as he walked down with the beer bottles. He handed one to Steve and settled back in his chair. "Okay. We're down to the last two possibilities on the list: The evolution of our God is stymied, and we're here looking for clues to get it going; and, the evolution of God is complete but unsuccessful, and we're retracing the evolutionary path to find and correct mistakes. For me, these two are the most tantalizing and plausible scenarios."

"Because?" Steve asked.

"Because they don't trivialize us, our hopes, our sufferings, our accomplishments, our life and death, and, above all, our God."

"So, now God needs our help. That's funny—very funny. What happened to 'He's omnipotent and perfect?' Huh? That *is* the argument you've been using, until now," Steve said in a sarcastic voice.

He gestured with indignation. "Aw, come on, Steve, that's not quite right. In prior scenarios I took a stab at assessing possible common beliefs concerning why we're here and who created us, and drew some conclusions. Basically, I concluded that something or someone created everything and us, and if our creator was an omnipotent and perfect God, He wouldn't put us on this earth as His personal servants, admirers, entertainers, or robots. Isn't that right?"

Steve gave him a pensive look for a moment and nodded.

He felt he could finally proceed with his point. "All right then, the two possibilities we're discussing now require a fresh look at a number of difficult questions, and the nature of God's one of them. We'll get to them soon."

Steve appeared to relent. "Okay, God needs help—if you say so."

He placed his fists on his back and pushed forward to get the kinks out. "Yes, I say so. Both scenarios claim we're here to help God. And for me, that's the key. But damn it, once I reached this point, my thought process got stuck, and for a long time I couldn't figure out how to move forward. Then, during a long and irritatingly exhausting session of generating ideas—any ideas—it came to me: Perhaps, I'm not using the right disciplines to examine the subject of helping God; I must draw on different disciplines."

"For example?" Steve asked.

He replied, "For example, I relied on philosophy and logic to reconfirm the argument supporting the existence of a God or something; and I turned to science for insight into such things as the evolution of mankind and the universe, and the mass-energy conversion and conservation. Then, I took the assertions that mankind was made to evolve, that it was evolving to achieve a purpose, and that it wasn't simply evolving for itself, and used logic to surmise that God was looking for something specific in mankind's evolution."

"Simply brilliant. What astonishing move did you make next?"

Don feigned annoyance. "Mock away," he said and added, "But trust me, all this has been a mind-numbing exercise—downright masochistic. The next step was tricky too, nothing was easy anymore. This time science and logic came to my rescue."

"How's that?"

Don gestured and said, "A mountain of scientific data, records and observations indicate life and the universe are in constant flux and movement of some sort. Also, although the physical and natural laws are in place, a random process and a shotgun approach seem to be operating where life and death are concerned. You can help me illustrate by answering this: How many sperms are needed to fertilize an egg?"

"This is a trick question, right?"

"No."

"Okay, normally just one."

"Super, you're correct. One will do the job. However, you also know literally millions of sperms are released to compete and die for the opportunity to penetrate an egg. Likewise, consider the birth and extinction of countless stars and planets, not to mention natural disasters like earthquakes and droughts killing people and animals by the thousands and millions. Such examples are many."

Steve asked in an impatient tone, "And your point is?"

He was in no hurry. He took a gulp of beer and put the bottle down on the coffee table. Then, he spoke with controlled excitement, "Don't you see? This whole thing mimics a scientific experiment that's trying—empirically trying—to systematically and expeditiously optimize a previous result or discover something new." He stopped speaking and waited for some reaction from Steve.

Steve remained quiet, but Don could see he was concentrating.

He continued, "In most experiments, a vast majority of trials fail, don't they, wasting tremendous resources? But that's expected, and the work then continues on a few trials that show promise or can be modified. Eventually, what happens? One trial may succeed, making everything worthwhile; or every trial may fail, requiring the experiment to be rethought and redone, or simply terminated." He felt very good about how well his thoughts were flowing and the way he was presenting them, even though he was starting to feel mental fatigue.

Steve bounced out of his chair. "This discussion is inspiring, but it'll go better with munchies. I'll see what's in the fridge." He marched up the steps to the bar.

Don welcomed the break. "Super," he said, then left his chair and stretched out on the couch.

Steve returned with a tray holding a plate full of crackers and cheese, a bottle of Tabasco sauce, a bowl of caviar and a knife, and placed it on the table. "This should do the job."

Don found the snacks less than appealing. "Beluga caviar, top shelf; hot sauce . . . interesting."

Steve said, "Try a drop of Tabasco on cheese or caviar or the combination—gives it just the right zap. Don't get up. I'll fix a couple crackers for us."

He grimaced. "Hot's not my thing. Then again, neither's caviar. What the heck, I'll give both a try."

They bit into the combinations on crackers thrown together by Steve.

Steve sighed. "Umm. Perfect."

Don's voice had a touch of hoarseness caused by the spreading sting of hot peppers. "I'm wide awake now."

Both laughed.

"Back to your book." Steve put a second cracker in his mouth and asked, "How did you decide God wants to evolve?"

He took a gulp of soothing beer. Then, taking a deep breath, he replied, "That deduction was . . . sort of a leap of faith . . . almost a . . . a revelation. You see, once the experiment model fit—and I was convinced that, you know, we were helping God find something—I was stumped for the longest time: What was that something? Out of desperation, I took a step back. I relied on philosophy and logic, and a hefty dose of intuition, to reexamine the broad picture." He stopped because his mouth was still burning. He sipped more beer.

Steve nodded. "Smart of you to take a step back."

He continued, "That's when my attention kept going to the progress over time, and evolution of human beings. Why are we evolving? Why does God want us to evolve? Why does He need it? What's He looking for? More important, why doesn't He know already? And that triggered the thought that, maybe, He doesn't know everything and, just maybe, our evolution has some connection to Him . . . His evolution. After that, more things started to fall into place, and I came up with the two more possibilities."

"That was quite a leap." Steve's tone betrayed grudging admiration.

He nodded and said, "For now, it's of small consequence to us to know which of the two scenarios is correct, or what the difference is between the two. The most important thing is that God needed to create life, earth and the universe. All—"

Steve waved his hands and interrupted, "Not so fast, Don boy. Let's not skim over that one. I do want to know what you think the difference is between the two situations God may be facing."

He eyed Steve with controlled irritation that lasted only a moment. Then he sighed and said with an air of resignation, "Okay, I'll try. But, before I tackle that distinction, let me pull together my thoughts that are common to the two situations. Also, I have to make a very significant point before we go too much further."

Steve put a pained look on his face. "Must you digress again?"

He shrugged. "Sorry, but I have to. We'd be insane to try to come to grips with this topic without first confronting a broad but absolutely crucial concept I'm about to lay on you. Play along, will you? See if it makes any sense to you."

Steve rubbed his chin. "Okay, out with it."

He looked at him. "In my opinion, the universe and everything in it, including you and me, is an experiment designed by God to help God. The envelope of the experiment contains within it a constant and convertible amount of physical matter and energy. And all the living creatures, including humans, are part of that completely efficient mass-energy conservation equation we've known about for a long time. The only external input into this envelope is what gives each of us life when we're born, and what leaves the experiment when we die. And that external phenomenon or power is what we call 'soul.' And the goal of the experiment is what I've said: Find a new path or provide a course-correction for the successful evolution of God to a state He desires or needs."

By the time he finished speaking, Steve was sitting on the edge of his chair. It was obvious he was irritated and couldn't contain himself. "Come now, this is worse than the ramblings of some wacko. It's very clear to me that you've cogitated a lot about this life-death-God thing. But, believe me, your assertions stink. In my view, the very idea that the omnipotent God's still evolving and needs help is just plain ludicrous, outlandish—even for a nut like you."

He remained calm as he defended himself. "I unloaded on you too fast, didn't I? But, like I told you at the start, my thinking hasn't crystallized, and for all I know it may never."

Steve smiled. "If I were you, I wouldn't try too hard to crystallize this thinking."

He said, "Look, I know my ideas sound a bit—okay, a lot—weird to you. But, before you take pot shots, let me make a couple other key points."

"Oh, you have more key points? I can't wait to hear them."

He was starting to feel tired, both physically and mentally. But he saw Steve in a remarkably attentive mood and very willing to participate. Therefore, he was determined to carry the discussion of critical concepts as far as he possibly could. "A very useful feature of this experiment is that each one of the billions of human beings is self-contained and independent, and that each human is powering his or her own brain. Each brain is free to explore, imagine; feel emotions such as fear, love and hate; interpret physical and visual sensations; and, hypothesize and create without bounds. And what does that do? Plenty, as I see it. It allows virtually unlimited degrees of freedom in creative thinking and uncovering a variety of avenues to explore and pursue. Do you find that's true of us humans?"

Steve didn't reply to his direct question; but he seemed pensive. "Go on."

He said, "Compare that scenario with the one in which billions of human minds are linked with one another and powered to create and develop collective thoughts. What do you think would happen?" He paused.

Steve remained quiet and looked at him.

He tried to read Steve's face. He decided Steve's lack of response meant he didn't object to his line of thinking. So, he continued, "I'll tell you what would happen. This collective thinking would produce a far less variety of options and paths to pursue change in a given time. Not a very efficient approach, by any means—not if you're hoping for a minute change or a slightly different nuance to put you on a path to success. Right?"

Steve made a non-committal sound. "Huh."

Both took a gulp of beer.

Don, energized by the fact his assertions were finally being presented to someone else, didn't want to lose momentum by pressing Steve for more reaction. Knowing Steve, he was sure there'll be plenty of that later. "Now here's another crucial factor you'll definitely appreciate: The communication of independent thinking among humans. This factor's responsible for the overall progress of humanity toward its goal. People have an instinctive desire to communicate. Don't we know it, huh? And, boy they communicate: You see verbal and written diarrhea about everything all the time—every incident and every emotion, large and small, important and unimportant, exciting and boring. Isn't that so?"

"You mean like what you're doing now?" Steve asked.

"Pretty much," he answered. He liked Steve's attempt to be humorous. It meant he was listening. "The objective is to not lose potentially valuable experiences that could move us in the direction of our goal. You see, in the final analysis, it's this instinctive communication that enables the sharing of independent thinking to bring about change in humanity. The change could be readily discernible or subtle. Sometimes it could be slow—dragged out over months, years, even centuries— and sometimes instantaneous. Again, it might be unifying or divisive, positive or negative and who knows what else. That change, my friend, is the evolution of humanity."

He stopped talking and looked at Steve; he could see frustration on his face.

Steve shook his head and, after a long pause, said, "In the speech you just gave, you said 'as you see' and 'you'll agree.' Well, I've got news for you: I don't see, and I don't agree. Let me tell you why I—"

He raised his hand to signal him to stop talking. He felt he was losing the battle with drowsiness, and he'd burdened Steve's brain enough for one night. "I'm sorry to cut you off, Steve. I can barely keep my eyes open; too much wine, cognac and beer. I suggest we continue this at some other time. We've got plenty to talk about."

Steve nodded. "I'm tired too. Look, why don't you sack out here? I'll drop you off at your place before I go to work in the morning."

He was delighted at his suggestion; he gave out a loud yawn and said, "Super. Point me to a bed."

• • •

It was a crisp and sunny fall Saturday morning.

"Kathy, it's time to leave. We don't want to waste this gorgeous day. Make sure you have your coat *and* hat on," Erika called out as she stood in the spacious foyer of her home, buttoning her mauve cashmere jacket and eyeing the hallway at the top of the stairs.

Kathy appeared almost immediately. "I'm coming, Mom," she said aloud with a big smile and hurried down the stairs.

Soon, they were in their limousine and heading for Manhattan.

Erika was glad when her sons, Todd and Jeff, received a rare invitation to sleep over at a friend's house the night before, and weren't expected to return until late afternoon. She decided to take advantage of that opportunity to have some fun time in the city alone with her nine-year-old daughter; a few hours of shopping and lunch—something she hadn't done with Kathy before—appealed to her. Then she planned to meet Steve, who'd spent the Friday night in the city listening to Don McCoy's idea for a book and had to work in the office until late that afternoon. She was looking forward to an elegant and romantic evening.

During the limousine ride, a thought of getting Steve a gift occurred to her. Lately, he'd been giving her jewelry that wasn't prompted by special occasions, and she'd accepted his offerings without pressing him for reasons. She decided since she was out shopping anyway, she'd surprise him with a present that evening.

It was about ten thirty when their limousine pulled up to the curb in front of Dreams on Fifth Avenue. Erika had decided to get a wristwatch for Steve and give Kathy a glimpse of that famous jewelry and gift store. The chauffeur, a gray-haired black man stooping from old age, held the door open for them.

"Thank you, Nick." Erika smiled at him.

Nick nodded and smiled back. "You're very welcome, ma'am."

Erika and Kathy exited the limousine, laughing and chatting. As they approached the store's door hand-in-hand, it flew open and two persons in leather jackets and ski masks backed out of the store. The next instant, gunfire erupted. Erika heard Kathy shriek and felt her hand being pulled back. She turned her head and looked at Kathy, who fell backward to the ground. Horrified, she spun around and cried out, "Kathy!" As she dropped to her knees to shield her motionless daughter, Erika's head snapped forward with violent force. She slumped on top of her daughter.

● ● ●

Joan Winters rushed into Steve's office, startling him. She was shaking and had tears in her eyes. "Steve, there's been a horrible accident. It's . . . it's Erika and Kathy; they've been shot."

Steve sprang out of his chair, knocking his half-full coffee mug over the papers on the desk. He screamed, "My God! How? Are they okay?"

"They're being taken to NYC Medical Center. They were in front of Dreams when shooting started . . . robbery or something. Nick's on the phone; but that's all he knows. Steve, I'm so sorry."

He regained his composure and fought hard to hold back his tears. As he raced out of his office, he said to Joan, "Call Erika's parents. Don't mention the shooting. Tell them Erika and Kathy have been in an accident, and ask them to come to the hospital. Then, stay put right here until I call you."

Joan called out after him, "You're limo's waiting in front of the building."

For Steve the limousine ride was the longest of his life; he thought it'd never end. Myriad thoughts and ghastly scenes played havoc with his mind. But he kept willing himself to remain in control of his emotions: The situation demanded it. When he arrived at the hospital he found Nick and a man waiting for him at the emergency registration counter.

Nick had been Erika's chauffeur for over three years. She was very fond of him and treated him like family. His eyes were red and swollen from crying. The chauffeur's hat he was holding close to his chest shook in unison with his hands as he sobbed. "Sir, there was nothing I could do—nothing. It all happened so fast. I'm sorry."

Steve patted him on the back and said, "I want to see Erika and Kathy."

The short, muscular young man with a clean-shaven face, rumpled tan suit and loose tie cleared his throat. Then he stepped closer to Steve and said in a polite and respectful voice, "Mister Zeller, I'm Detective Gomez of the NYPD. Ah, there are some things you should know before you see your wife and child. It's best if we and the doctor speak in his office; he's expecting us there. Please follow me."

He hesitated. *What's he trying to tell me?*

Just then Nick nudged him. "Please, Sir, go with him. I'll wait here."

His eyes locked with Nick's. His heart was racing; he was desperate for any news. He nodded and followed the detective down a crowded hallway, toward a closed door. When they entered the office, he saw a balding, thin elderly man in a green smock sitting behind a desk.

The doctor pointed to two chairs in front of his desk and spoke in a somber voice, "Gentlemen. Please sit down. Mister Zeller, I'm Doctor Sweeney, a surgeon. I'm afraid I have bad news for you. Your wife's in a coma. She's suffered head trauma; the bullet, well, it's damaged some of her brain tissue."

Steve felt like someone had dropped a massive boulder on his chest. His breathing became labored, and his vision blurred from tears. His words were a whisper. "Oh my God. And Kathy? How's my daughter?"

"Your daughter is dead."

Steve cried out, "No, no, God, no! Not Kathy. Not my kitten. Not my dear, sweet kitten." His voice trailed off to a whimper.

Steve, the powerful business genius with nerves of steel, had never before experienced a feeling of total devastation and loss. He sat there, feeling helpless and overcome with excruciating grief.

Doctor Sweeney said in a comforting tone, "Mister Zeller, this is a terrible tragedy. I'm sorry." He pushed a box of tissue toward him.

He was unable to control his crying. He was bent over; his head was buried in his hands, and tears dripped from his fingers. "Oh God, God, what have you done to my family? How could you allow my beautiful and innocent Erika and Kitten to get shot? Why? This . . . this makes no sense . . . no sense at all. Damn, damn, damn it all."

Doctor Sweeney and Detective Gomez sat in silence, obviously allowing a husband and father to absorb the shock of his loss.

Long seconds went by without any conversation; Steve's sobbing was the only sound that filled the office. Then, he felt numb and couldn't cry any more. He straightened up, took some tissue and asked in a calm voice, "What happened?"

Gomez cleared his throat and responded, "Preliminary conclusion is robbery gone bad. Two masked thugs burst into Dreams with semi-automatic weapons. They ordered everyone in the store to lie face down on the floor, then grabbed a bunch of jewelry and were leaving the store. Just as they backed out of the store's door they saw security guards from inside the store rushing toward them, and they apparently opened up with the semi-automatics. Guards returned the fire and one of their bullets went right through your daughter's heart."

At that point Sweeney said, "What happened was horrible. But her death was quick—she didn't suffer."

Steve nodded. "And my wife?"

Gomez answered, "Apparently, as your wife was kneeling over your daughter, a bullet struck her head. All this happened in a matter of seconds."

Sweeney added, "She's in CCU, the critical care unit. Our neurosurgeon is evaluating and monitoring her. As I said before, she's in a coma."

Steve dabbed his eyes and asked, "And the masked men?"

"They escaped in a getaway car driven by an accomplice." Gomez lowered his eyes from Steve to the ground.

Steve momentarily clenched his teeth and shook his head. Then he became anxious to do the next thing. "I want to see my wife and daughter."

Sweeney got up. "Of course, Mister Zeller, please follow me."

As he walked between Sweeney and Gomez through the wide, brightly lit hallways, he felt his legs becoming heavy and wobbly. His mouth was dry. He hadn't come to terms with what was happening: It was as if he was watching a movie plot unfold. When they reached the CCU, Gomez stopped at the nurses' station, allowing Steve and Sweeney to proceed into Erika's room. Steve stopped at the foot of Erika's bed. There were wires, instruments, beeping monitors, IV bags and tubes all around her. Her head and most of her ears were covered with bulky bandages; the dark bloodstains on the bandages were a stark evidence of what had transpired. Her eyes were closed; her beautiful face was peaceful.

He asked in a whisper, "Can she hear?"

Sweeney replied in an encouraging voice, "Don't know ... it's hard to tell. But, it wouldn't hurt a bit to talk to her. Your voice may trigger a response from her. I'll be outside. Take your time." Then he eased out of the room.

Steve sat on the bed beside Erika. He held her hand between his hands and stared at her. Lingering seconds passed; his shocked brain refused to process words. He bent down and kissed her on the lips. Then finally, slowly, softly, painfully, the words came out. "Have I told you lately I love you, huh? Have I mentioned you grow more beautiful each day? Have I? Well, I should have. How about waking up now? Please open your eyes. Could you do that for me? Don't forget we have a date tonight. We're going to have a great time. I'll be very disappointed if you don't show up." He again lost control and broke down. His hands trembled as he sobbed, "Oh, Erika, darling. God's taken away our daughter. My kitten's gone . . . gone. I'm scared, really scared; I need you now . . . more than ever. Erika, darling, please, please help me . . . wake up."

He fought to compose himself. He took a deep breath, and let it escape slowly. He looked with loving eyes at Erika for some time while he rubbed her hand. Then he said in a soft voice, "Dear, you rest here while I go and check on our daughter." He leaned forward, kissed her on the forehead, and backed out of the room.

As he emerged from Erika's room, Sweeney asked, "Are you okay?"

"Please take me to my daughter." He was emotionally drained and empty; he knew what awaited him.

• • •

After the tragedy, Steve visited the comatose Erika every morning in the hospital and spoke to her for hours. He'd reminisce about all the good times and love they'd shared in painstaking detail. Often, before leaving, with tears trickling down his cheeks, he'd plead with her to indicate she'd heard him by giving him a sign: a flicker of an eye, a movement of a finger, a whisper—anything. The controlled appearance he managed to present in public belied the recurrent wild mood swings he underwent in private. When he was alone in his house, he'd go from gut-wrenching sorrow at the vision of Erika and Kathy getting shot to unbridled guilt for not being there to save them to seething rage at the perpetrators getting away scot-free—all in a matter of minutes. Then, totally spent, he'd walk the cold beach next to his estate and gaze with tearful eyes at the ocean. He'd frequently feel the urge to rush into the water and swim aggressively out to the ocean. He didn't know why he felt that urge, and knew even less why he didn't act on it. He'd remain on the beach until Nanny or someone would come looking for him. He didn't eat much, and drank himself into oblivion every night; his appearance became unkempt, a sharp contrast to the crisp, clean-shaven and smartly-dressed look he'd cultivated with deliberate care as one of his key personal traits. Nanny took over the management of the household, in addition to looking after the boys and him. He kept away from the office, refusing to discuss any business matters. Victor Wolfe, somehow, kept things under control at the office; and Helmut Wolfe, frail and confined to a wheelchair, increased his phone conferences with Victor.

Kathy's funeral was held on Wednesday, four days after the bullet took her life. With Erika in a coma and Steve overcome with grief, Erika's parents stepped in to make the final arrangements for their departed granddaughter. In his in-laws, Steve saw the inner strength and dignity he hadn't noticed before. They got his permission to hold Kathy's funeral in their church in Westport and to lay her to rest in their family's burial plot. They also honored his request to limit attendance to only the family and close friends. Seeing his daughter, barely nine years old, lying in a casket tore his heart. She seemed like she was asleep, and would wake up any minute. The finality of the moment sunk into him as he saw his daughter's casket ease into the ground.

At the solemn gathering afterward at his in-laws' house, he was polite and spoke to everyone—even those he'd hated. He felt strange: When he looked at the people he despised such as his brothers, sisters and Aunt Amy, he didn't—couldn't—feel the usual revulsion. It was as if his heart had purged itself of the hatred of the past to make room for the grief and anger at what had happened to his family.

Marge Zeller saw him hug and kiss his brothers and sisters—something she'd not seen before. Watching him with a melancholy smile, she walked up to him. "God is with you, son." She put her hands on his shoulders, pulled him down, and gave him a soft, lingering kiss on his forehead. Then, both put arms around each other and wept in silence.

• • •

It was eight o'clock on a Thursday evening; a talk show, with volume set at barely audible level, was in progress on the television. In front of it, Don McCoy was lying on the carpeted floor with his head resting on a beanbag. He was deep in thought, and jotting notes on a pad.

The door buzzer rang.

He stopped writing and looked at his wristwatch. *Who the hell can it be?* He was annoyed at the disruption of his concentration. When he spoke into the speakerphone, a familiar and welcome voice answered him. His scowl and irritation evaporated. A minute later he opened the door to Steve Zeller, who was holding a case of beer with a pizza box sitting on top.

"Are you hungry?" Steve asked with a weak smile.

He couldn't help wincing at the incongruous sight: Standing before him was his dear friend with unshaven stubs of two or three days, unkempt hair and mismatched clothes. He'd expected Steve to stop by a lot sooner; it had been two weeks since Kathy's funeral. He longed for the neat, impeccably dressed Steve he'd known. Time, he reasoned, would bring him back. He moved aside from the door and replied, "Always. Come on in."

Steve walked past him and put the beer and pizza down on the kitchen table. "I'll put some cans in the fridge."

"Good. Get a couple of cold ones already in there. I'll get paper plates," he said and thought, *Good grief, he's a mess. Is he still in a mental sinkhole?* He eyed Steve for any clues as to his mental state; but he couldn't tell.

They settled down with food and drinks in front of the television that he'd turned off. Steve had eased into the lounger, and he'd let himself down on the beanbag across from him.

Chomping on a big bite of pizza, he asked, "How's Erika?"

"She's about the same—lost some weight since you saw her . . . when was it? A couple weeks ago? Life support's barely keeping her alive." Steve took an unenthusiastic bite of a pizza slice.

"How are Jeff and Todd doing?" He hoped his gentle prodding would pry open Steve's locked-up emotions.

Steve appeared to be straining to think—to visualize. "They're fine, thanks to Nanny. I tell you she's . . . she's doing one heck of a job with them, with me, with everything. They haven't really grasped the impact of what's happened—too young. But they miss Erika . . . and Kitten. I spend a lot of time with them; I didn't do that before, you know. Nice father I was, huh? I'm starting to get better acquainted with them, their personalities. God, they're different! Todd's sensitive like Erika, and plays the big brother; Jeff's aggressive, carefree. Anyway, they seem to enjoy my company and attention. We're, you might say, bonding."

Don decided to be more direct. "That's super. But, how are you personally coming along?"

Steve took a big swig of beer and rested his head on the lounger. After a brief pause, he replied, "Not so good. Don, I can't shake the grief and . . . this, this smoldering anger. I just can't."

Don nodded. "Perfectly understandable." He was encouraged by Steve's willingness to share his feelings.

Steve let out a deep sigh. "You know, at Kathy's funeral the priest kept talking about God's mysterious plan and the will of God. All that made absolutely no sense to me." His voice quivered, and he shook his head. "My kitten's death was violent and meaningless. God allowed a child's life to be cut short by a couple maggots, you know. And my Erika, she lies in the hospital in limbo. She's being cheated out of her life, unable to care for her children, be a wife to me, and work for her cause—the homeless children. What a waste of a loving and talented human. How the hell does that help God or His plan? How does violence help Him? I don't have a damn clue, do you?" He stopped talking.

He could feel Steve's suffering and anger; and his noticeable agitation concerned him. He said in a calm voice, "That's a tough question for anyone to answer." He knew it was imperative for Steve to express and work through those powerful emotions, before they did irreparable damage to him; but he wasn't sure Steve had, or even cared to have, the resolve to tame those destructive feelings. He was determined to do his utmost to help Steve pull through the consuming moroseness and hatred, while respecting his need to mourn.

Steve looked pensive as he said, "Sure it's a tough question. That's why you never hear an answer, only bullshit platitudes." He paused. Then, with a long, intent gaze at him, he continued, "Last time we talked about your book, remember? Well, you seemed to have all the answers—"

He interrupted, "No, Steve, you're wrong. A lot of deductive thoughts? Yes. Intuition and guesswork? Definitely. But, answers? Nope, sorry."

Steve acknowledged his clarification with a nod, and then said, "But that's not where I'm headed. You claimed we're part of a sort of universal mega-experiment designed by God to help Himself—"

He cut him off again. "Right. I feel it's a reasonable proposition. I remember the evening when we were discussing it. That's the time we boozed up and had to quit so we could pass out and . . . that happened before I could complete my thought about the experiment."

Pushing the last piece of pizza slice into his mouth, Steve said, "This is as good a time as any to complete it."

He was pleased to see the interested look in Steve's eyes. He coughed to dislodge a bit of pizza from his throat and took a sip of his beer. "Super idea. I think I talked about the experiment being closed and self-contained. But did I say that the only external thing entering or leaving the experiment was a power or phenomenon we call soul?"

Steve replied, "Yes, you did."

He put the beer can down on the coffee table and sat back on the beanbag. He raised his arms and clasped his hands behind his head; then said in a slow and thoughtful voice, "I've been playing with another idea. I tell you, it's wild. But I'm suspecting that the external power is God Himself, and I'm guessing—no, it's my warped intuition—that each one of us is a god. You think I'm ready for the funny farm, don't you? But, Jesus Christ, it all fits."

Steve had stopped munching and was scowling. "Are you for real?"

He ignored him and continued, "There's an outside chance, a miniscule one, that we've designed the experiment for our own benefit. I suspect each of us is born into a human body not by some grand plan or selection process but by random chance occurrence. We've—"

"Ha. Me, a god; and you, a god. Do you really expect me to believe that?" Steve asked, sitting up and raising his eyebrows.

He smiled and replied, "Yes, only as a theory."

Steve was incredulous. "As a theory? Damn right it's only a theory—and a crummy one at that. If it were true, how come I—a god—don't know a thing about all this? And, as for you—again, a god—why are you struggling with guesswork, intuition and crap like that?"

He got defensive and responded in an impatient voice, "I don't know; but I have a guess. Now, do you want to hear it?"

Steve threw up his hands. "Might as well."

He could feel Steve's degree of frustration rising. "It's possible we've designed the experiment in such a way that, when we enter it as humans, we somehow suppress our awareness that we're gods and designers of the experiment. It's almost like . . . we sort of undergo a separation process."

Disbelief was written all over Steve's face. "Separation process? How are you dreaming up all this—grass, LSD? Okay, let's skip it for now. First, tell me why . . . why all the violence? I'm going crazy thinking about what the violence did to Kathy and Erika. If, as you say, we're gods, why the hell have we set up an experiment with a shitload of violence?"

Don opened his mouth to speak.

Steve put a finger on his own lips and said, "Don't answer yet. I'm not quite finished. Why do millions of us gods enter this experiment only to return after a brief, but often agonizing, existence here without adding anything to, as you say, our evolution? I'm talking about those who die as babies and children, and those who die in famines, floods and wars all over the world without voicing or recording any of their thoughts? It's as if they never existed. In World War II alone, over sixty million innocent and guilty perished. Why do we massacre one another? What's the point of pestilence and disease? Why do we, the gods, often compete and cheerfully bring misery, cruelty, tragedy and even death to one another? What possible public service was performed when Erika and Kathy were gunned down? And now, Mister God, your explanations are?" Steve fell back on the chair.

When Steve started to speak about violence—an intensely emotional subject for him—his voice had been calm. But as he proceeded to spew out questions, his voice grew in decibels, his speech speeded up and his hands trembled perceptibly.

He found Steve's escalating emotional state to be deeply worrisome; he strained to think of a way to tone the conversation down. "Explanations? I can offer none. At least, not any good ones; they're more like far-fetched conjectures."

"After all the wild . . . weird scenarios you've painted so far, what difference will a few more make?" Steve's tone was a bit subdued as he made the light comment.

He displayed mock indignation. "Wild scenarios? I resent that characterization. Okay, fine. But they were thoughtful, logical and intuitive, weren't they?"

Steve grinned. "Yeah, right, and very entertaining."

He was relieved to see Steve was no longer angry. He smiled and said, "Let's get back to violence. Now bear with me—I know that's tough for you to do. But, perhaps, just perhaps, the seemingly gratuitous, indiscriminate and sense-less death and destruction are designed into the experiment to accelerate renewal and hence to complete the past evolu-tion process and experiment quickly. The rationale being, the sooner we're armed with new knowledge, the sooner we can resume our journey forward, you know—toward our destiny."

Steve said, "Good guess. Damn, why didn't I think of it?"

He ignored his comment. "Another possibility may be to excite emotions in us powerful enough to inspire us to action and change—both mentally and physically."

"You mean violence evokes fear and anger?"

"Yeah, sure, among other emotions—sorrow comes to mind. And yet another reason may be that this is one of the many diversionary tools designed into the experiment to keep us separated long enough to successfully conclude the experiment, and put ourselves on the right path." He waited for Steve's reaction.

Steve rubbed his forehead. "I think I'm following you. Continue."

He nodded. "Super. You've been paying attention. See if you can go for this: The unknown after death, and linking vio-lence to death, heightens the fear of dying, which motivates us to cling to the known, the life. This fear makes us want to remain and participate in the experiment as long as we possibly can." He paused and took another swig of beer.

Steve looked thoughtful and said nothing.

He decided to finish his speculative thoughts. "It's quite possible that dying itself may serve to advance knowledge. How? Try this: Those who die leave behind in the experiment the knowledge they've gained and shared with others. I'm talking about all the thoughts they shared, their creativity, and their accomplishments in a variety of fields. That reservoir of knowledge is given a fresh look by the newcomers in the experiment; then it's added to, molded and refined to keep knowledge growing and moving ahead." He gulped down the remaining beer.

Steve asked, "So, you believe knowledge is the key product of the experiment, and that knowledge will point us in the right direction?"

Don twisted and crushed the empty can. "You bet. To me the evidence is pretty strong: Every physical entity in the universe—stars, planets, you name it—is born, lives, dies, and is recycled. The only thing that survives is the knowledge, period. As I said before, it doesn't merely survive, it grows. Don't you agree?" He jumped up from the beanbag to chase down fresh beer.

"I don't know about the rest of the universe, but what you say about knowledge seems to apply here on earth," Steve answered. "Look, I distracted you from finishing your brilliant thoughts on death and violence—"

"I was almost done except for one observation," he said, as he walked back with two open beer cans. "It's occurred to me that maybe death's also a way to balance and optimize limited resources in the experiment. In that respect, death may be one of the underlying aspects of the renewal process critical to our progress toward the final destination. That's it. Right now, this is as far as my mind can speculate on death and the violent nature of our experiment." He handed a beer can to Steve and, once again, sat down on the beanbag.

Steve's tone betrayed his skepticism. "I'm not sure I thoroughly understand everything you said; and that's okay. However, I do know one thing: The violent and premature death of my innocent kitten made her life meaningless and insignificant . . . made her insignificant."

He again detected anger rising in Steve's voice. He thought, *Poor guy's been doing super so far; it'd be a shame for him to get dragged back into an emotional whirlpool now. I can't let that happen.* He said, "I understand your sentiments completely; but I can't agree with your conclusion that Kathy, her short life, and even her violent death were insignificant or meaningless. In my opinion, nothing's insignificant. Nothing."

Steve gave him an appreciative look. "Thanks for being a friend."

He shook his head. *No, no. This guy's taking it all wrong.* He said, "Look. A seemingly insignificant event took place about four hundred years ago: A bunch of seemingly insignificant people—mostly those who were fed up with religious oppression, a few adventurers, and not-so-few scoundrels—set sail from England to the New World in search of a better life. Who'd have thought then that that minor event would lead to the creation of the United States of America, the mightiest nation and superpower on this earth? So, you see, the lives of those pioneers didn't turn out to be so insignificant after all. Again, I say nothing's insignificant; it's just that the significance simply isn't obvious to us."

Steve's voice was somber, but free of anger. "You've no idea how much I want to believe that. I want my daughter's life to have mattered, to have meant something. I want her to be remembered."

He stroked his beard, and said, "You know, an idea just popped into my head about that. No . . . no, just forget it."

Steve's voice was insistent. "What is it? Spit it out."

He was castigating himself for blabbing without thinking, but it was too late. "Oh, it just occurred to me that, perhaps, you could perpetuate her name by making an endowment in her memory to whatever, a university or something. You know, it could be used to further the studies of criminal justice or psychiatry; or, as another option, it could go to a church. I'm sure there are number of things you could fund. But it'll require some thought. I don't know; I'm talking without thinking."

"Huh, you may have something there," Steve said, looking interested.

"Super, but nothing you have to do right away. Let me know if I can help." He noticed the moroseness had left Steve. That was in stark contrast to when Steve arrived at his apartment. He also felt pleased with himself: He'd succeeded in planting at least one tiny seed of concrete and productive thinking in Steve's grieving mind. He thought if Steve could be kept talking and venting, he may start to undergo a catharsis and become himself again.

Steve looked and sounded animated. "If I remember correctly, the last time we chatted about your bizarre concepts, like the evolution of God, I told you I'd need more explanation. Today, you've compounded the situation with notions of 'we're gods,' 'gods undergoing separation,' et cetera. This definitely calls for time out and some clarification. Right?" His raised eyebrows creased his forehead.

"Right." Don washed down with beer the pizza he was chewing.

Speaking in a deliberate tone, Steve said, "All right then, I'll recap your separation concept to see if I've got it straight. We, the human beings, are gods and this is our experiment and we're starring in it. But, while we're in the experiment, we don't know we're gods and we don't know we're in it. And, all that magically happens because of this . . . this unbelievably sophisticated separation process we've devised to block out our memory of everything that happened to us before we're born as humans. Correct?"

He was smiling as he listened to Steve. He felt a warm sense of satisfaction; he'd been able to provoke Steve into concentrating on something else besides his recent tragedy. He nodded and replied, "Super. That's good. Just think about it: The experiment wouldn't be much of an experiment if we, as subjects, knew everything right from the start, now would it? Of course not. Our thinking would be biased, not fresh. Without fresh thoughts and virgin ideas, there can't be creativity or advancement of knowledge; and new chain reactions to actions would be forced—not spontaneous—thereby limiting new paths open to us. Can you see that?"

Steve opened his eyes wide and said, "Yes, I can."

He laughed. "The idea is that through understanding of new knowledge, a path would emerge that'll take us where we must go."

Steve just nodded.

Don paused to study the can in his hand and then took a big gulp of beer. "Look, Steve, I know all this is tough to follow. Even I don't have much of a handle on it, and I've been at it for a while. So, let me share with you an analogy I made up to clarify things for myself. Okay?"

Steve gave him an intent look and said, "Go ahead."

He sat up straight and gesticulated. "Okay then, imagine a blob of matter—a gelatinous mass—suspended in empty space. Imagine this blob's undergoing constant change in its shape and motion. Also, picture a light source, miles away in space, to be the destination of the blob. Can you do that?"

Steve by then was stretched out on the lounger and had his eyes closed. He replied, "Done. I'm picturing a large, dark space; floating around in it is a baseball-size, thick and gooey blob. It's changing shape constantly and slowly moving toward a distant bright light. Now what?"

He pointed a finger at him. "Just hold on to that image. Now, let's take a closer look at the blob: It's made up of billions of individual living cells called human beings, gods or whatever. Each of these cells has unlimited degrees of freedom of movement, and moves any which way. This movement results from either its own action or from reaction to other cells' actions. Are you okay so far?"

Steve replied, "I'm with you."

He felt encouraged. "Super. Let's say that these cells must act or react until they die, and new cells take their place. Billions of actions, interactions and reactions by these cells give the blob its shape, and result in a net force that gives the blob its motion. The magnitude and direction of the force determines how fast and where the blob will go. Now, at any instant, the blob may move up, down, sideways, backward or forward; it may move toward the light, its destination, or move away from it, all depending on the behavior of its cells. How are you doing so far?" He wanted to make sure Steve remained involved.

Steve shrugged and said, "Never thought of myself being a part of a blob; but I'm keeping up with you. Go on." He lifted his head and swallowed some more beer. Then he put his head back on the lounger, wiggled his frame, and once again closed his eyes.

Don didn't want to rush the explanation; he waited for Steve to get comfortable. "All right then, with the help of that visualization, you can see that so long as the blob, er, the humanity, is moving, and so long as the overall trend of its movement is toward its destination, the experiment is accomplishing its objective."

Steve asked, "What about other possibilities? Let's say the blob moves away from the light, or simply stops moving."

He ran a hand slowly over his beard. "Both of those situations would be extremely serious. Let's talk about a motionless blob. What does that mean? It means the blob is internally or externally static; that's to say, either all its cells are dead, or the actions, interactions and reactions of all its cells completely counteract one another to produce a net force of zero and, hence, no motion. That's another way of saying that humanity's maintaining status quo; it's neither progressing nor regressing—a totally unacceptable condition in the experiment. Now, let's take the situation where the net force acting on the blob makes it externally dynamic, but the direction of that force continually moves the blob farther away from the light. That's a clear sign that humanity has, somehow, settled on a completely wrong path and, therefore, would never reach its objective." He settled back on the beanbag and waited for Steve to speak.

Steve sat up. "So let's say our experiment's in trouble. Then what . . . what do we do to salvage it? Or, can it be salvaged?"

Don yawned and burrowed deeper into the beanbag to find a comfortable position. "If the experiment starts to go awry, it may require physical upheaval to essentially restart it, or it may require some tweaking in the form of—how shall I put it?— the introduction of a semi-separated god on the earth."

Steve rolled his eyes. "You're making things up as you go along, aren't you?"

He grinned. "You really believe I'm that good?"

Steve's tone was measured. "Okay, what's a semi-separated god?"

"A semi-separated god, like all other gods, gives up awareness of entering the experiment. But he's different in one way: He intuitively feels very powerful and driven to initiate and lead change for purposes even he might not understand, ah . . . purposes that are definitely not influenced by any mortal or earthly gratification."

Steve said, "Give me an example."

He got up from the beanbag, stretched his arms, and sat on the arm of the sofa. "Example? Um . . . sure, Jesus Christ's a super example; and there are others, of course. You see, a semi-separated god's mission is to excite the emotions and minds of the masses of humans into taking a different direction, hopefully toward the final destination. You've heard people talk about divine intervention? Well, consider this tweaking to be a form of divine intervention. *Now* do you comprehend the concept?"

Steve's eyes narrowed. "Tell me something: Are you semi-separated?"

He put his head back and laughed out loud. "Hell no, not by a long shot. All this I'm doing is with a book in mind, and money, of course. Remember? You can't have a more earthly motive than that."

Steve nodded. "Huh. Are all great persons semi-separated gods?"

He scowled as he mulled over Steve's question for a while. "Umm . . . I don't think so. I think the semi-separated gods are extremely rare events. Christ, as I mentioned before, is one example. To me, it seems reasonable to believe that the semi-separated gods are planned, not random, events designed to keep the experiment viable. They fix major glitches brought on by humans, or the experiment's design, or whatever. Beyond that, the results and progress of the experiment are up to the fully-separated gods, randomly born on this earth, like Socrates, Lincoln, the Pope, Mother Theresa, Einstein, you, me—"

Steve smiled. "You're lumping us with great minds and distinguished people."

"I'm lumping them with the rest of humanity. I've already theorized we're all gods, remember?"

"How can I forget?" Notwithstanding his skepticism, it was obvious that Steve remained interested. "Last time we chatted about this subject, you avoided explaining God's most likely motive for the experiment and human evolution."

He'd hoped he wouldn't have to tackle that subject; he simply couldn't come up with more insightful thoughts to pinpoint God's motive for human evolution. But realizing Steve would keep pestering him about it, he acceded. "Like I've tried to get through your thick head, I don't think it matters much at this point. But hell, I'll take a stab at guessing the reason—"

Steve seemed to be enjoying his discomfort. "As I recall, you laid out two possibilities."

"Yes, I did," he agreed. "In both cases I believe that we, the gods, have achieved a spiritual level that's extremely close to, but not the same as, the ultimate level or state we're seeking. One possibility I offer is that the evolution of gods is stymied, and we're here looking for clues to get it going. In this scenario, we, the gods, reached a point in our evolution where only one path should've remained for us to continue on to reach the desired ultimate state. But that isn't what happened; we found we still had multiple paths to choose from.

That implied that an aspect or nuance of our evolution hadn't been dealt with correctly or completely."

"For example?" Steve's rapid question barely allowed him to complete his sentence.

"Oh come on, Steve." He wasn't thrilled with the questions Steve was throwing at him. He felt his neck muscles tighten as he fought to control his defensiveness. He knew Steve was only doing his job to help him—and doing it, perhaps, too well. So, uncomfortable or not, he was going to answer. He scratched his forehead and allowed his thoughts to flow. "What would be a good example? Well . . . how about this: Very early in our evolution, we the gods may have adopted a biased view that fairness and justice are inherent traits; or, we may have eradicated an apparently undesirable emotion such as anger without fully understanding its implications to our evolution." Then he raised his hands in a gesture of disclaimer and continued, "Again, I don't even pretend to know what it might be. The only thing I can surmise is that somewhere along the line there was a misstep." He paused with his eyebrows raised.

Steve asked, "And that's why we set up this universe and experiment?"

"Sure. Why not? Once we realized that our evolution was flawed, moving forward was not an option; the flaw had to be corrected in order to pick the right path to move forward on. We decided to find and correct the flaw via an experiment that would mimic our evolution on a vastly scaled down and accelerated basis."

"Okay," Steve said in a tone laced with doubt, "now the next premise—"

He interrupted, "No, not the next premise. It's *the* last possibility—the very last. My brain can conjure up only one more possibility. That's it."

Steve smiled and nodded. "Okay, okay, you're right. So tell me about the *very* last possibility."

Exasperated, he rolled his eyes. *Damn it, I've got to corral this subject and put a quick end to it.* He thought for a long moment about how to accomplish that and then said, "It's quite possible our evolution was complete but unsuccessful. Before you ask how can that be, I tell you it's quite simple. I can say that now, of course, after months of abusing my brain with this subject. Anyway, in this scenario, we, the gods, reached a point where we found that the only path in front of us was the one we were already on. In other words, we were no longer evolving, and worst of all, we hadn't evolved to the ultimate state we desired. All that says is that it was pointless to continue on that path. So we set up an experiment to retrace our evolution to find and correct mistakes. We loaded the experiment with more variables and degrees of freedom to dramatically increase the number of potential evolutionary paths and hoped that this expanded choice of paths would help us to end up on a different path that leads, of course, to our desired state."

Steve bullied the lounger into an upright position. With an attentive look on his face, he asked, "What kinds of variables create more options or paths?"

Again, he took his time to answer. "Um . . . what would be good examples? I got it: it's possible our original evolution didn't have an emotion such as fear, or traits such as greed and selfishness. So, now we've added them to our experiment, thinking they might be important in some way to the success of our evolution. But, once again Steve, I really haven't given this much thought because the key point in both scenarios is simply this: We're in an experiment looking for the right answer, the right evolutionary path. You see? And really, man, I'm fighting not to muddy up my thinking and overwhelm my tiny brain with topics that are related to our discussion only in a peripheral way. Trust me, I know they're all significant topics, but right now they're a waste of time."

Steve said, "Fair enough. What else don't you want to tackle now?"

He was happy to oblige. "Oh, let's not dwell on questions like: Is the human-earth experiment one of a kind in the universe, or is it one of many? Are humans just one phase of a multi-phased experiment involving the whole universe? Is the growing decoupling of sex and procreation a passing fad or a natural progression of our evolution? Will our human body someday evolve to a point where it's resistant to all diseases? Questions like that." He stopped talking. He stretched his arms over his head and yawned and waited for Steve's reaction.

Steve said in a relaxed voice, "I'm afraid there's one small, related point you must tackle now."

He cringed. He knew his admonishment had been in vain: Steve was tenacious. So, he asked with resignation, "And what's that?"

Steve replied, "The universal belief is that God's all-knowing and omnipotent; we agree on that. Hell, even your arguments have been based on that premise. But at the same time, if I'm hearing you correctly, you're also claiming that God—gods, whatever—doesn't know everything, and has set up an experiment to find information. That implies there's an entity higher than God. See what I mean? How do you reconcile the two positions?"

Don was frustrated, and it showed. He put his hands up and said, "Super question, and I wish I had an answer, but I don't. I've focused on that issue quite a few times and found myself going around in circles. Er . . . I honestly don't have a good answer for you. All I can say is when I examine the reason why we're on this earth, I end up with us as gods look-ing for answers in an experiment. It's ... ah ... disconcerting as hell to think that there may be something higher than the God we've believed in for the longest time to be *the* Supreme Being. Look at it this way: Tackling this subject has been very much like fighting a giant octopus in murky waters."

"Octopus ... murky waters?"

"Yeah, just when you think you've subdued that bastard and contained its tentacles, a tentacle appears from nowhere to whack you or grab you. Man, I have these gaping holes and disconnects in my thinking, and I tell you that's irritating as hell."

Steve lowered the beer can from his mouth and said, "Hate to do this to you, Don, but here's another tentacle for you. If, as you say, we're gods—excuse me, gods who've undergone the separation process—then every one of us is equal, and equally important, in the experiment. So, let's see what hap-pens if we take this one step further: A murderer, a beggar, an average Joe or Mary, a pedophile, a mobster, a tiny fetus, President of the United States, the Pope, and Moses are all equally important."

Where the hell's he headed now? The disconcerted Don asked, "So?"

Steve answered, "So, being gods, we obviously can't be judged based on our actions and behaviors on the earth, how-ever good or evil they may be. Actually, according to your line of thinking, we're not judged at all; there *is* no judgment, period. Is that right?" Steve's eyes narrowed; he seemed to be trying to absorb the shock of his own words.

He gave Steve a long, probing look. *This guy's going to keep coming at me; might as well face his prodding. It's kind of enjoyable. Got to hand it to him, zeroing in on "judgment,"—no, rather "lack of judgment"—outside the experiment.* He managed a faint smile and replied, "Correct. Super observation. Sounds like there'll be no judgment in the afterlife—"

Steve interjected, "I don't buy it."

He understood his feelings. "I know it's a tough concept to swallow. Your skepticism's well placed. As a matter of fact, I too have a hard time stomaching this and would love to agree with you. But hey, don't fret, you're in good company. A vast majority of people, including thought leaders and celebrities like the Pope, can't fathom afterlife without judgment. For them, judgment, or rather the fear of judgment, plays an important part in moving people away from evil thoughts and actions—a sort of incentive to do good and lead a virtuous, religious, loving life. And you know what? There isn't a damn thing wrong with that view. But, unless we missed something in what we've talked about, I'm afraid the judgment scenario doesn't seem to fit too well."

Steve'd been reclining on the lounger. He sat up and appeared to be annoyed. "Oh hell, Don. Just think of the nonsense oozing out of your mouth. How can you sit there and imply that the maggots that were responsible for killing Kathy and putting Erika in a coma aren't going to be judged and punished? Huh? How can God excuse punks like that, or . . . or some cowards who beat up or knife an old woman trying to hang onto her purse? And how about the spineless lowlife who kidnaps, molests and dismembers a defenseless child? Or, how about a mobster who snuffs out innocent lives, but lives to a ripe old age in luxury and comfort? Should I go on?" His voice cracked with emotion.

The last thing he wanted was to awaken Steve's raw feelings. He also noticed Steve had reverted to referring to God in a traditional sense. He said in a calm and measured voice, "Steve, I'm not arguing—just trying to follow the reasoning wherever it leads. Tell me, do you see any evidence of justice, compassion or judgment in nature—anywhere in nature?"

Steve countered, "I don't know and don't care. Anyway, what has that got to do with what we're talking about?"

"Only that it may help us gain better insight into the experiment's design. The weak and defenseless are easy prey for the strong. Take an animal, say a gazelle. While older, sure-footed gazelles speed away, a gangly youngster becomes an easy meal for a stalking powerful lion. Or, take a tornado ripping through a small town in, say, Kansas. It hits a church with a full congregation praying in it. It obliterates the hell out of the church, and most men, women and children inside the church are killed mercilessly; but some walk away unscathed. Now, can you tell me on what basis were the few lucky ones spared? Where's justice, compassion or judgment in all this? Do you see any of those things?"

Steve shook his head.

He said, "Super. I don't either. The only dictum in our experiment seems to be evolution through renewal. Justice, compassion and judgment probably are lofty human concepts and behaviors that have evolved on this earth, very much like the unsavory concepts and behaviors such as avarice, selfishness and ego."

Steve sat stone-faced and listened. Then, shaking a finger at him, he said with emphasis, "Let me tell you something: I've been ticked off at God for what He's allowed to happen to my family. I blame Him and Him alone. Now a schmuck like you is telling me that judgment isn't His concept at all, and it's something He doesn't get involved in. Shit, I'm getting more pissed now."

He could feel Steve's anger rising—definitely not a good sign. *This guy's ready to blow; I've got to calm him down by keeping the conversation in the intellectual arena.* "Okay, okay, Steve. No need to get more pissed. Now you've got to remember that all this is my conjecture. Just do me a favor, will you? Let's together walk through the consequences of judgment by God in light of how the experiment is set up and see where we end up. But let me get more beer before we start." With that, without waiting for Steve's response, he got up and headed for the refrigerator.

Steve's face softened and he appeared to visibly calm down. "I'm sorry, man. I lost my cool on your hypotheticals."

He waved his hand. "Forget it." He was encouraged by how quickly Steve regained control over his anger.

Steve took a deep breath and settled back in the lounger. He seemed to be in deep thought when Don nudged him to hand him a cold beer can. As soon as Don lowered himself into his comfortable beanbag, Steve said, "Go ahead and talk about the rationale why God doesn't judge."

He took a long gulp of beer. He wanted to slow the pace down to allow himself time to think and keep things logical, rational—for Steve's sake. "Let's see how we can approach this . . . umm . . . we've agreed that we arrive on this earth in a random fashion. I mean, there isn't some grand plan that slated me to be born healthy and rich in Connecticut, and you to be born smart and athletic to loving parents in a peaceful, small town in Illinois. Right? It's purely a chance occurrence for someone, anyone, to be born rich, poor, sickly, healthy, blind, dumb, intelligent, mentally retarded, whatever. In short, we all aren't born with the same faculties, senses and advantages. Do you disagree with anything I've said so far?"

"Nope. Continue."

"Super. Let's take someone who's a bit slow mentally. Let's stipulate further that, from birth, he was surrounded by crime, degradation and depravation. This guy dies a hardened criminal. Now let's take someone else who was blessed with all the physical and mental faculties and grew up in an affluent, religious, stimulating environment. He dies an accomplished musician. Let's consider yet another person whose life was short and unremarkable because of a degenerative congenital disease that destroyed his muscles. He drowns in his own phlegm. On what basis should these three be judged? They didn't have a choice in the roles they played on earth; they weren't aware of the rules of the game—their memory before birth is a complete blank. So, why would God take three entities, put them into wildly unequal situations on earth, and then judge their actions to dispatch them to heaven or hell? Do you see any kind of logic in that?"

Steve's right index finger tapped on the lounger's arm, and his voice was animated. "Just stop and think of what you're expounding: No judgment. *No* judgment. If that's true and people start believing it, what's going to happen? I tell you what's going to happen: Hell will break loose. I mean, come on, 'no judgment' sounds like a license to do whatever comes to mind—good or evil. And guess what? No consequences—none. Why should people make sacrifices to do good in this world when they're going to get the same treatment the killers, the rapists and the like are going to get?" He shook his head and added, "That makes no sense to me, no sense at all."

Don leaned forward in the beanbag. "I'm having a problem with that, too. But we mustn't separate the concept of 'no judgment' from the assertion that we're all gods. Taken together, the two complement each other and strengthen each other. Let me throw this at you: Once we start to suspect we're gods, we'll be less and less inclined to act irresponsibly; a number of our phobias and anxieties would vanish, including, of course, the fear of judgment; we'll become tolerant and supportive of one another; and avarice and hunger for power would be replaced with a collective desire and effort to find out what we're seeking."

Steve didn't sound convinced. "Even if logic dictates that God can't be judgmental toward humans, there's got to be a down side to all this."

He nodded. Even he felt unsure of his own arguments. But he was following the fragile thread of his thoughts on impulse in the presence of his emotional friend. "Of course, there's a serious negative potential to all this. We have to face the fact that the new awareness will alter human interactions in a drastic way. One possibility is that a greater focus on what we're looking for may push us into selecting a wrong direction. That could end up in a disastrous detour, and that may require a major correction or interference in the experiment. However, that possibility, I think, is unlikely." He paused.

"What's likely to happen?"

He scratched his chin through the beard. "It's more likely that this new awareness is one of the natural consequences of the experiment's design, and the concept that we're gods was to be stumbled upon like millions of other concepts. Whether or not this concept has any merit, who knows? But that's beside the point, anyway."

Steve teased, "It's beside the point because it's a bad concept."

He ignored Steve's comment. "The only point is that this concept gelled in my brain, and we're discussing it. Whether or not it's accepted, even if it's true, is also beside the point. What counts is that it's born, and it'll get some form of hearing on this earth. I prefer to think of this as an outgrowth of the process that's to lead us to the end of the search. How this'll play out, only time will tell."

Steve's eyes narrowed. "How sold are you on all this?"

He scowled. "You mean, do I believe my own speculation? My honest answer is: I don't know."

The intense intellectual sparring between two friends continued. Steve was finally acting like he'd cut through the veil of grief and was more than happy to engage in a lively conversation with Don.

7
Legacy

TWO WEEKS LATER, Erika passed away without regaining consciousness. She'd grown thinner at a steady pace; the exquisite features of her high-cheek-boned face had given way to a gaunt, gray look; and the mole on her left cheek was creased. She was withering and the doctors concluded her situation was hopeless. They advised the family to allow them to remove the life support systems keeping her alive.

Steve was an emotional wreck; the doctors could barely understand the words he uttered in a hoarse whisper: "Let her go with dignity. I know she would want that." He looked in the direction of his weeping in-laws. Both nodded.

He, Todd, Jeff and Erika's parents were there when her heart stopped beating. The heartbroken Steve held her hands, and everyone watched through their tears as she was pronounced dead.

● ● ●

Erika's funeral was a private affair—as had been her daughter Kathy's—open only to the family and close friends. She was laid to rest next to Kathy, and afterward everyone was invited to her parents' house.

With a glass of red wine in his hand, Don McCoy sat in a comfortable light blue chair in the corner of the spacious living room that exuded elegance. His mood was somber as he observed Erika's grieving loved ones commiserate and comfort one another. He was again a part of the group that had attended the heart-rending funeral of the young Kathy only a month ago. But this time, despite the solemn atmosphere with obvious signs of sorrow, a sense of peace—almost relief—prevailed.

Steve waved to him from across the room and started to walk toward him. After he took a few steps, he wound up in front of his young son Jeff who was using his shirt sleeve to soak up his tears while talking to Aunt Amy. He stopped and pulled Jeff close to him and gave him a warm hug; then, he kissed his forehead and said in a reassuring voice, "Your Mother's fine now—she's just fine. You know, the very best doctors couldn't do anything for her. But God can, and now she's with Him and . . . and He's taking care of her. You understand? She's in heaven, and wide awake—no coma and no brain damage; and, she's happy. I'm sure she misses us a lot, just as you and the rest of us miss her. But son, we must be happy for her, even though she's not here with us. Okay? Also, you know how your mother is: If she suspects we're unhappy even a tiny bit, she'll feel very sad. And we don't want that, do we?"

Jeff shook his head. "I don't want Mom to be sad. But Dad, she's gone and I won't see her again . . . I'll try to stop crying." He wiped his tears again; but more appeared.

"I know you will, son, I know you will. I love you," Steve said in a quivering voice.

Amy, with eyes red from crying, put her arm around Jeff's shoulders and said, "Jeff, honey, please walk with me to the kitchen and help me find a tea bag. I see only a coffee pot; but I don't drink coffee." She steered him away from the room.

Steve watched them disappear into the kitchen. He closed his eyes, gently rubbed his eyelids and then walked over to Don and sat down on the ottoman. "Have you had anything to eat?"

"Not yet. I'll get something shortly. How are you holding up?" Don was concerned about his fragile emotional state.

Steve nodded, rather unconvincingly, and appeared to search for words. "You know, as well as I can be . . . no, I'm fine . . . really."

Don saw his friend was uncomfortably self-conscious, so he decided to change the thrust of his conversation. "I see Jeff's having a hard time."

"He's going to be all right . . . just needs a little time. He was very close to Erika. She was such a great mother."

"I don't see Todd around. How's he?" he asked, looking around the room.

Steve gestured and replied, "He's busy helping out with some chores. That's his way of handling grief. Both kids just need time."

He found Steve's response heartening; he put his hand on his shoulder and squeezed it. "You need time, too."

Steve gave him a faint smile. "I'm okay, really. I've been more prepared to let Erika go than I was when Kathy left. The doctors had warned me that the Erika I knew died the moment the bullet pierced her skull and damaged her brain. If by some miracle she'd come out of the coma, she would've been a cripple for life; and, in all probability, she would've been unaware of the life she'd lived. The doctors knew she'd be disabled, mentally and physically; the only question was how severely. I know Erika wouldn't have wanted the life the doctors were describing—no way. I'm sad and glad at the same time that she's passed away. Tell me, is it wrong for me to feel that way?" It was obvious Steve had these painful and ambivalent feelings bottled-up inside him and desperately wanted to share them with someone he could trust.

He patted Steve's knee and said in an empathetic tone, "No. Your feelings are perfectly natural. You wanted her misery to end, but that also required her life to end. This is going to sound horrible, but I think that everyone including me, who loved Erika, must feel she was blessed to have been spared a prolonged, vegetative existence." It was gut-wrenching for him to say that: He had a special affection and respect for Erika and was having a difficult time hiding his emotions.

Steve was watching his melancholy face. "It's comforting to hear you say that. Thank you."

Don struggled to keep tears at bay; he managed a weak smile and nodded.

There was a moment of silence. Then Steve straightened his posture and said, "Hey, there's something I have to ask you."

"What is it?"

"Would you be willing to take care of Todd and Jeff if I'm not around . . . if I die?"

The question alarmed him. "What kind of talk is that?"

Steve raised his hands and shook his head. "Relax, just planning, that's all. I'm saying I'd like you to be the guardian and estate executor for my sons until they reach the age of, say, thirty-five. My parents and Erika's parents are old, and besides them, I think you're the best person to guide my sons if I'm gone. Do you mind taking on that responsibility?" Steve said, looking into his eyes.

He lost it: Tears welled from his eyes. He answered in a proud, crackling voice, "Oh, this is super. I'm honored. I consider Todd and Jeff to be the sons I never had; of course I'll take care of them. You have my word."

Relief was written all over Steve's face. He took a deep breath and shook Don's hand. "Good. I knew I could count on you. You've no idea what this means to me. It's settled then: In the next couple days you'll get a confirmation and some papers from my lawyer, Barney Williams. Now, there's one other thing we need to discuss."

His eyes narrowed. "I'm listening."

Steve shook his head. "Not here. This gathering's going to start breaking up soon. Why don't you grab a bite and then meet me in Helmut's study in about half an hour?"

"And where's Helmut's study?"

"Oh, it's in a separate wing behind the kitchen. You can't miss it."

"Okay, in half an hour then," he replied as he got up from the chair.

Steve also stood up. "Good. Now I better go check on Jeff." He walked away in the direction of the kitchen.

His eyes followed Steve in amazement. *This guy's drowning in grief; and yet, he manages to concentrate on the business of living.* He started to mingle and make his way to the food.

•   •   •

The fireplace, vaulted ceiling, traditional furniture and maple-paneled walls displaying Van Gogh landscapes made Helmut's study a very warm and inviting part of the mansion.

Steve heard a knock and saw the door open.

"Hi, Don. Come in and make yourself comfortable," he said with a smile and motioned to him to take a seat. He was enjoying the guarded and quizzical look on his face.

"Hi, Helmut, Victor, Dad," greeted Don. After exchanging nods with them he looked at Steve with raised eyebrows.

Steve laughed and put his hands up. "Sorry, I didn't tell you they were part of the chat we're going to have. Just bear with me. Okay?"

Don shrugged but his scowl indicated he didn't appreciate his intentional omission.

"Remember the last time we discussed your book?" Steve asked.

Don looked at him as if questioning why he was bringing up the book in the presence of those people. With apparent defensiveness, he replied "Yes. Couple weeks ago in my apartment."

"Do you remember the suggestion you made when I was struggling with Kathy's life being cut short and made insignificant?"

Don's eyes narrowed. "You mean making an endowment in her name to a university, church, or something like that?"

Steve nodded. "The minute you mentioned a way to perpetuate Kitten's memory, I was sold on it. For the next few days the only question I wrestled with was to which entity and what area should the funds go? I felt that funds should go to an apolitical institution—to advance the knowledge of a subject that's been ignored but is, or could be, of immense value to everyone. Suddenly it occurred to me that your book's subject would be a perfect candidate. Why not study the reason for human beings' birth-life-death and evolution? The more I thought about it, the more I liked it. The other thing I wanted to assure was that the subject would receive a completely unbiased treatment and that meant a non-affiliated, freestanding institution. I also knew the right person to head that effort would be you." He paused to see Don's reaction.

Don looked at him in silence.

He continued, "But, before I spoke of my proposal to you and assessed its feasibility, I wanted to make sure I knew the maximum initial endowment we could count on. So, after I decided to personally gift five million dollars, I shared my thoughts with Helmut and Victor. They liked the idea and each one offered to contribute five million dollars. Then Helmut mentioned it to your father, who also pledged the same amount if you participated. Yesterday, I decided to contribute another five million dollars in the memory of Erika. The Wolfes are doing the same thing. So what do we have? Well, we have to set up a foundation that'll start out with thirty-five million dollars. Don, now you know everything, including why the other three are in the room. What do you have to say?" He was beaming with pride and excitement.

Don looked around the room, obviously trying to stall for time to think. All eyes, full of anticipation, were on him. He had trouble speaking. "This is amazing, unbelievable . . . simply super . . . thirty-five million . . . wow."

Steve grinned and asked, "Will you do it?"

Don seemed to be recovering from the shock. "You don't mess around, do you? Damn. Let's talk some more before I commit myself. I'll need help—lots of it. For starters, I don't know the first thing about the workings of endowments, trusts and foundations."

Helmut, who until then had been content to listen, said, "That's what attorneys and accountants are for. We already have those for you. Steve has a lot of faith in you and your ability to lead the foundation. The subject, I understand, is of great interest to you. This generously-funded foundation provides you a lifelong opportunity to pursue your desire for the knowledge of mankind's mission."

Don nodded to Helmut, then turned to Fred and said, "You're putting down a lot of money, Dad. The studies may go nowhere."

Fred looked at him with a loving smile. "It's important to me and your mother to support you in whatever you want to do; it's taken me a long time to realize that. I believe you'll make this foundation a resounding success."

Appreciation was visible on Don's face. "Thanks, Dad," and hesitatingly added, "I love you."

Fred said softly, "I've always loved you."

Steve was touched by the remarkable transformation he was witnessing in Don and Fred's relationship. He felt encouraged about getting a commitment from Don. So, to reassure him, he said, "Let's go over how the foundation would work—in broad terms, of course. First of all, there'll be a board of trustees, which will include a member of each family giving a substantial endowment to the foundation. The board's job will be to manage the investments, and give you what you need to pursue the stated mission. We'll work out details such as how a chairperson will be named. But you'll be a permanent member of the board, because you'll be the president of the foundation. The board will make sure you get all the administrative, legal and business support, and whatever facilities you need. So don't worry; you'd get loads of high-powered support. Get the picture?"

Don nodded, his eyes focused at him in a thoughtful stare.

He continued, "You alone will have the authority to determine the size and composition of the think tank you'll need. You'll decide the disciplines and qualifications of the visionary candidates you hire, the creative consultants you'll require, and the joint undertakings with other institutions such as universities or churches that could benefit your work. No one here will interfere with you. To get things started, the foundation will rent offices near Zeller Enterprises. I'll be the first chairperson of the board. Helmut and I'll work closely with you to get this thing off the ground. Does this help you make up your mind?"

Relief covered Don's face; his pensive look gave way to a broad smile. "Super. I'm in. Let's do it. What will the foundation be called?"

Steve replied, "We haven't thought that far."

Don said without hesitation, "Let's call it the Zeller Foundation, Center for the Study of Humanity."

Helmut said, "Excellent suggestion. You're already off to a good start."

Everyone looked at Don with approval.

Fred started subdued clapping; but it was catching and others joined in. He said in a proud tone, "Congratulations, son."

Steve was excited at how well things had turned out. He got up from his chair, walked over to Don, and patted him on the shoulder. "Thanks, buddy. You've come through once again." Then, turning to the others, he added, "The five of us in this room have decided to create something meaningful in memory of Erika and Kathy. I think it's time to tell others what we're going to do. Shall we do it now?"

All verbalized their whole-hearted agreement.

Helmut in his wheelchair, Victor and Fred started to leave the room.

Don called out after them, "I want a word with Steve. We'll be right out." Then he grabbed Steve's hand and motioned him to sit in a chair next to him. "I saw your hands shaking, trembling a bit."

Steve made a nonchalant gesture. "Just excited, you know—"

"Cut the bull. That's a hell of a front you're putting on, old friend. You're hurting bad; just not letting on—not even to yourself."

"I'm okay, really," he replied, feeling uncomfortable and defensive.

"I want you to listen to this." Don picked up a phone sitting on the table and started dialing.

He asked, "What is it?"

Don signaled to him to be quiet, and held the receiver to his ear.

He heard the familiar recorded message:

This is the Zeller residence. Please leave your name, phone number and a brief message. We'll be happy to call you back.

It was Erika's voice. Steve said nothing; he grabbed the receiver and put it back on the cradle.

"Steve, you've got to let go. Please, you've got to mean it, not just say it." Don was plainly pleading.

His voice was hoarse with emotion. "I love to hear her voice . . . I couldn't erase it . . . her beautiful voice, I keep listening to it . . . it's the only thing I have to make me feel close to her."

Don whispered, "She's gone, Steve—gone."

"Yes, she's gone, I know."

"Erase the tape. Promise me."

"I'll erase the tape."

The two friends hugged each other and wept.

• • •

Don couldn't stop worrying about Steve.

It'd been over a week since he'd confronted Steve about the depth of his dangerous depression. Steve had promised to stop listening to Erika's recorded phone greeting, erase it and get on with his life. He decided it was time to check on his grieving friend.

He called Steve at his home in the afternoon knowing he'd be at the office. He was in luck: Neither Nanny nor one of the kids picked up the phone. He heard a recorded message; the voice was Steve's, not Erika's. He relaxed and hung up.

He said to himself, "Nice going, Steve. You took the first, crucial step."

He picked up the phone again and this time he dialed Steve's office number. Joan Winters, the secretary, exchanged brief pleasantries with him and put him right through.

Steve's voice was warm. "Hi, Don. How are you doing?"

"Couldn't be better. Just called to see if you—"

"Are you calling about the guardianship papers? Barney said he's already sent them to you."

"Yes he did. But I'm—"

Steve interrupted him again. "Is there something wrong with them?"

He said with exaggerated exasperation, "No, the papers are just fine and Barney's done a good job. But that's not what I'm calling about. Just shut up a minute and let me speak, will you? I'm calling because I've been cooped up with the computer since early this morning and feel the walls of my apartment are closing in on me. I need a break. How about joining me for drinks and a bite to eat somewhere? My treat."

Steve laughed and said, "I've got a better idea. You're coming to the house and spending the night there. We'll enjoy the beach and Nanny's great cooking. It'll also give you a chance to see the boys, too. I'll pick you up at four thirty."

"Super. I'll be ready. Bye." He hung up the phone and leaned back on the beanbag with hands clasped behind his neck. He couldn't be happier with the way things had turned out: He'd have ample time to not only assess Steve's healing but also that of Todd and Jeff. It would give him an opportunity to observe their home environment and see how the three were readjusting as a family unit without Erika and Kathy.

* * *

The bright sun with increasing reddish hue was descending lazily in the cloudless sky: It was taking its time to prepare to disappear behind Steve's oceanfront Southampton estate.

A deeply-tanned, middle-aged couple was jogging along the edge of foaming water. They waved to Steve and Don who acknowledged by raising their wine glasses. The two friends were about thirty yards from the water on soft, silky sand, sitting back on loungers with a low, round glass table between them. On the table was an ice bucket with two bottles of Chardonnay, a bowl of barbequed shrimps and a plate full of Nanny's signature tomato bruschetta.

The picturesque setting enhanced by a cool ocean breeze paced their conversation.

"Those schmucks sure are a pain in the neck for you. But they're Helmut's sons and not going anywhere. So just ignore them." Don didn't want Steve's anger at Alan and Jack's latest attempt to irritate him to get the best of him.

"Ignore them? Not a chance. That'll just encourage these punks. I'll shut them down. You'll see ... just a matter of time. As far as Helmut's concerned, they lost a lot of credibility with him a long time ago. You know that."

Don didn't say anything.

Steve looked at the wine in his glass and slowly swirled it. "I'll take Alan down—hard. Then the spineless Jack will find himself alone, unprotected. From then on, he'll be afraid— very afraid — and that'll be the end of it. When the time comes, I'll be merciless"

He said light-heartedly, "Well, super, if that's the way you want to be."

Steve clenched his teeth. "Yes, that's the way I want to be."

He took a sip of wine and, with a faint smile, gazed at the ocean. He was heartened to see that his old friend was back: Besides being clean-shaven and dressed sharply, Steve sounded as if he'd regained his confidence and, once again, was ready to fight the power battles.

He noticed an encouraging new wrinkle: Steve had increased interaction with his sons, Todd and Jeff. That behavior was in stark contrast to his hands off attitude toward them before the tragedy struck. Don also had a chance to chat with the kids and play ball with them and Steve before Nanny called the boys in for dinner. There was little doubt left in his mind that Steve and the boys were doing exceptionally well.

Steve poked at a shrimp with his fork and said, "So tell me. Besides brainstorming about the foundation and wearing out the computer, have you made any progress with the book?"

"Nope. I haven't given it much thought," Don replied with his gaze locked on the distant horizon. He took another bite of the bruschetta he'd been working on and added, "Boy. I could eat this all day."

Steve nodded. "Nanny makes the best. But, how about your thoughts? Anything new?"

"No, absolutely nothing. I've taken a hiatus from the book—writing, thinking … everything. I'll get back to it soon enough." He hoped that declaring complete lack of attention and progress would put an end to that subject; he reached for another palate-pleasing piece of bruschetta.

Steve sat up and poured wine from the bottle into his empty glass. "I'm just wondering. Let's see … so far, in our

previous conversations about the book, you made some outlandish claims about why we're gods, why we're evolving here
on the earth in an experiment, and on and on—"

He grimaced and shook his head. "Jesus, Steve. You've
committed millions of dollars to my premises and ideas. At
least try to get it right, will you? They're not outlandish claims.
Can you get it through your head that they're my thoughts,
not claims; based on my observations of life and nature; my
logic—"

Steve raised his free hand and interrupted. "Okay, okay.
But even you've admitted there's gobs of imagination involved
in this."

He nodded. "Of course there's imagination; there's no
denying it. And there's also extrapolation—absolutely critical
and essential to advancing discussions or arriving at results.
Actually I insist on using every faculty. Remember? My whole
brain's involved. It has to be."

Steve raised his eyebrows. "Ah yes, we mustn't forget the
complete involvement of your whole brain." He took a sip of
wine and continued, "We both know I'm skeptical about your
so-called conclusions. Perhaps your work at the foundation
will shed more light on the subject and then maybe— only
maybe— it'll help change my mind."

He said, "Super. I think that's quite decent of you to
patiently wait to satisfy your curiosity and see the light about
the ultimate truth."

Steve shrugged and reached for a shrimp. "I'm patient
about certain things—up to a point. But there's one thing I'm
very curious about right now." He bit the tail off the shrimp in
his mouth and tossed it into a bowl on the table.

He didn't want the book talk or any other controversial
subject to impinge on the tranquility he was enjoying. But he
asked anyway, "And what might that be?"

Steve, munching on the shrimp, said, "What happens to us after we die?"

He felt a sinking feeling in his stomach. *This guy keeps pushing me to tackle things I'm not prepared to.* "We leave the experiment."

"Okay. Then what happens?"

He shrugged and said emphatically, "I haven't the foggiest idea; it's immaterial. Furthermore, it doesn't interest me in the least."

Steve asked, "Why aren't you interested?"

He gestured in frustration. "Because, at the very best, trying to delve into it'll be an exercise in futility."

Steve countered, "You mean fantasy, conjecture, don't you?"

"I guess so." The resignation in his voice reflected the realization that Steve wasn't going to let up on the questions about that subject.

Steve cajoled, "Oh, come on. Let's see what your reasoning and imagination can do. Go ahead, fantasize away."

He thought, *I'll play along with him. We're relaxing and not going anywhere; the poor guy's finally on the mend and just wants some harmless banter for entertainment.* "Well, since you're like a nagging toothache that must be dealt with, we'll take a shot at following a human to the other side and develop a scenario based on the thinking I've already done; then we'll see where it leads us."

Steve grinned with obvious satisfaction. "Good. Who do we pick?"

Without hesitation, he pointed a finger at him. "You. Let's follow you to the other side."

Steve was taken aback. "Me?"

He said in a matter-of-fact tone, "Sure, why not?"

Steve raised his eyebrows and smiled.

Don put his drink down on the table and shifted to a prone position on the lounger. "Okay, let's assume you just died. You'll be one of the countless humans with independent minds who've crossed over. Since we're trying to evolve to the desired state through experimentation—through trial and error—it stands to reason that all you dead people will share and pool your experiences somehow to facilitate learning and progress. Of course, being out of the experiment, you'll know everything."

Steve was listening intently. He rubbed his chin. "All that may happen. But the first thing I'll do is see how Erika and Kitten are doing in heaven."

"There's no heaven or hell. There can't be."

"Yes. You're right. Sorry, I forgot we're playing by your rules."

He nodded and said, "Of course we are. My guess is you'll know they're absolutely fine the instant you leave the experiment. By now, they're probably on other assignments on different planets in the universe."

Steve's frown betrayed his skepticism; but he said nothing.

Don felt things were getting serious. "By the way, even if there were heaven and hell, what makes you think you'll end up in heaven and not hell?"

Steve appeared to relax; he smiled. "Get back to your less-than-inspiring scenario."

He took the cue and tried to emphasize the point he'd been trying to make. "Once you're out of the experiment, you know everything about it—earth, other planets, universe, humans, other life, you name it."

Just then the jogging couple appeared on their return journey and again waved to them; both waved back.

Steve said, "Who collects and pools the information from the dead?"

He wasn't interested in expending energy on that question. "Beats me. Perhaps no one: The experiment may be self-adjusting and self-correcting. Look, let's see if we can paint a picture in terms we understand: Our experiment is housed in a room in a laboratory building. You entered it through an adjoining separation chamber which blocked your awareness that you're a god. Once your time in the experiment as a human is up, you're going to leave it through an adjoining return chamber where you'll regain the awareness that you're a god."

Steve gave the thumbs-up sign. "Visualizing a lab helps a lot."

He acknowledged with a smile. "Super. At some point, I suppose everyone leaving the experiment somehow exchanges information, especially those who may have unusual or extraordinary events to report."

Steve seemed to be enjoying himself. "And who do they report to? I'd say some sort of committees, wouldn't you agree?"

He said, "That works for me. Let's call them ... ah ... planet councils. In that case you'll appear before the earth council."

Steve looked surprised. "Why would I do that?"

He stroked his beard. "Quite simple: the Zeller Foundation. It may end up having an unimaginable impact on mankind's thinking and behavior."

Steve was visibly pleased with Don's high expectations of their foundation. "With you at the helm, it most certainly could."

He continued, "Maybe the council members will be impressed enough with you to listen to your bitching about violence and rethink earth's design."

Steve's face turned grim. He said through clenched teeth, "Maybe I'll convince them to vaporize the punks who shot Erika and Kitten."

He sensed Steve's emotions stirring; he didn't want that. So he smiled and tried a humorous dig at his own ex-wife's attorney. "While you're at it, ask them to vaporize a certain divorce lawyer too."

Steve laughed and said, "It's tough to let go; but it's tougher to forget. That shyster made quite an impression on you." He got up and picked up a fresh wine bottle and went to work on it with a cork screw.

Don grinned as a small piece of bruschetta disappeared into his mouth. He realized their conversation was off on a tangent—and liked it. "Just think what we humans are capable of. Mankind can and may annihilate itself and the world. But it may also be the one to find the ultimate answer."

Steve's voice dripped with good-natured sarcasm. "Nothing like straddling a fence."

He shook his head and felt he had to elaborate. "I'm not straddling anything. I'm only speculating that other worlds may not offer one or more of the emotions and traits we have here that almost always demand action—love, fear, cowardice, hate, compassion, greed, curiosity, ambition, judgment, to name a few. Consequently, while these planets may have happy and content species that are not self-destructive like humans, they also may never seek or chart a new path that'll reach the objective precisely because they're happy and content."

Steve smirked. "So they stagnate—blissfully. That surely calls for your semi-separated gods to do their thing."

He laughed and said, "Quite possible, only as a last resort. An intervention might help on a planet, but it also has the potential of introducing unwanted bias that could compromise the results there."

Steve squinted and looked at Don. "Suppose the intervention failed the dumb, fat and happy species, what would you do with a planet like that?"

His nonchalant response was accompanied by gestures. "Easy. Depopulate it or terminate it, possibly by hurtling it toward a black hole."

Steve smiled and picked up a shrimp. "Extreme, but I see your point. Let's hope mankind won't stagnate. Okay, now back to after we're dead. What next?"

He closed his eyes and used his fingers to rub his temples. He was feeling tired, and a bit drunk. "Um, I don't know . . . perhaps we all return to the experiment . . . could be back on this earth; could be some other planet in the universe."

Steve chimed in, "I get the picture. We share our experiences, maybe get some rest and then return to the lab for new assignments."

He said with tongue-in-cheek, "Precisely. And in your case, because you've decided to sink a fortune into studying what humanity's up to, you'll choose to return to the earth."

Steve retorted, "Damn right I will. I'll have another reason to come back here: To keep an eye on you to make sure you don't screw up the Zeller Foundation."

Both laughed.

Neither was aware that Nanny had appeared behind them and both jumped when she leaned forward and said in a loud voice, "Hey, you two. Time to stop talking out here. If you don't come in now and eat dinner, I clean up and go to bed; and then you will have to find your own food." Without waiting for an answer, she started transferring everything from the table onto the tray she'd brought with her.

Steve shrugged and said, "I guess it's time to eat."

8
Return

STEVE FELT REJUVENATED and relaxed as he sat at the head of the oval table occupying a corner of his spacious office at Zeller Enterprises on Fifth Avenue. He didn't show any lingering scars from his intense grieving of the loss of Erika and Kathy as he looked at the other four sitting at the table. "All right, it's late and this marathon meeting's just about over. We've thrown around a lot of numbers and zigzagged through a bunch of issues. But all that was worth it because we've arrived at a consensus. Victor has signed the bid papers prepared with remarkable speed by Barney. Now, they're in front of me for my signature. But before I sign, I'll quickly recap our joint position on this very exciting investment:

We believe the bankrupt Centomat Company's true value is two hundred and twenty million dollars, liquidation value is eighty million and debt is one hundred and thirty million. We've agreed to enter a bid of eighty-three million dollars. Am I right so far?"

"Some think the value of the company is much higher— but that's fine, continue," said Victor Wolfe who was leaning back in his chair at the other end of the table. He appeared tired and relieved at the anticipated end of deliberations.

Jack Wolfe and Barney Williams merely nodded. Alan Wolfe, too, nodded, but glanced at his wrist watch; impatience was written all over his face. Joan Winters, the ever-efficient secretary, remained expressionless; but her eyes made a momentary stop on each person and then looked down to write on a notepad resting on the table.

Steve continued, "It's also agreed that this will be our one and final bid to be submitted by the deadline of 4:00 p.m. today, which is about an hour from now. Any final questions or comments before I sign?"

There was silence. He reached for the pen and signed the bid document.

Barney jumped out of his chair and grabbed the document. "I'm on my way." He rushed out of the room.

Steve was amused at his dramatic departure. He smiled and said, "For all our sakes, I hope he doesn't get stopped for speeding. Gentlemen, all we can do now is wait. Let's break and meet here at 4:30, so we hear the news from Barney together."

Joan stood up and addressed everyone. "Gentlemen. After you've freshened up, please go to the VIP lounge where I've arranged for you to relax with cocktails and snacks and then enjoy a steak dinner."

● ● ●

Victor and Jack were already sitting on a sofa with drinks in their hands and engaged in a conversation; their plates with appetizers sat on the coffee table. Steve was at the bar watching the bartender mixing his dry vodka martini.

The lounge door opened and Alan walked in.

Steve turned his head and looked at him. "Boy, you sure left the meeting in a hurry. I thought you were scrambling to get to the restroom; but I didn't see you there."

Alan reached the bar. "Scotch, please," he said to the bartender and then, facing Steve, made a nonchalant gesture. "Oh, I
had to make a couple phone calls. Joan set me up with an office."

Steve accepted the martini from the bartender. "Was one
of the calls to Carl Wyler?"

Alan turned red and gave him a sharp look. "Huh? Of
course not. Now why the hell would you say that?"

He was seething. He thought, *You lying slime bucket!* But
outwardly he simply smiled and said as he walked toward the
appetizer table, "Forget it. Just joshing, that's all. I know Carl
would stoop to anything to know our final bid before he and
his backers submit theirs. It's an open secret he wants the
Centomat he's bankrupted. As its CEO, he knows the real
value better than anyone else. And you being his yachting
buddy and all that . . . as I said, just kidding."

Alan said nothing but his stern eyes followed Steve even
as the bartender tucked a drink into his hand.

• • •

Alan entered Steve's office. Joan got up from her desk, closed
the office door behind him and left the reception area. Steve
looked up from a document he was writing on and waved him
to a chair.

Alan said, "I understand you have something to discuss
with me."

Steve removed the document from the desk. "Yes I do.
Make yourself comfortable. Did you have enough to eat?"

Alan sat across from Steve; the elegant mahogany desk-
top between them was bare. Steve placed on it a large, brown
envelope he pulled out from its side drawer.

Alan eyed the envelope. There was detectable suspicion
in his voice. "Yes. Food was plenty and delicious. What's this

about? Joan would only say that you want to talk to me about something—alone."

Steve nodded. "You'll understand shortly the sensitive nature of this meeting. Would you like a drink?"

"No, I'm fine. What do you have?" Alan made no attempt to mask his impatience.

He wasn't in any hurry: He was savoring the moment. With a broad gesture, he asked, "So . . . what do you think Carl's bid would be?"

Alan's eyes widened and he exploded, "How the hell should I know? Are you again insinuating I gave Carl our bid number? Goddamn it, Steve, you're totally out of line. Sure, he and I hang out. So what? That doesn't mean I'll screw Wolfe Financial Services or my family and, above all, my father?"

Steve's nostrils flared. He gave Alan a menacing stare, but kept his voice calm. "No, but you'll screw me."

Alan's eyes narrowed and he leaned forward. "I *did not* give Carl our number," he said through clenched teeth.

Steve kept his eyes fixed on him. "Alan, spare me the bullshit. Okay? We both know you like to screw me over every chance you get. Am I right?"

Alan glared at him. "You've stolen my place in the family and the business."

He shook his head. "I stole nothing. You and your stupidity forced Helmut to give it to me."

Alan retorted in a contemptuous tone, "Ha. You were nothing, and before long you will be nothing. But, the scum that you are, you used Erika. You seduced her and then married her only for money and control of my father."

Steve could no longer conceal the hate for his nemesis sitting across the desk and struggled to control his urge to pounce on him and choke the life out of him. "That's it, you no-good, lying traitor. No more games."

As Alan watched, he undid the string on the envelope, pulled out a miniature recorder and slowly placed it on the table. He felt euphoric as he said, "For your information, Joan's a very resourceful and tech-savvy secretary. She set you up in an office she had bugged. You used the company-provided cell phone. She not only traced your calls, she taped them. This tape has the goddamn call you made to Carl. Listen." He pressed the play button and leaned back in the chair.

By the time the twenty-seven-second tape ended, Alan's handsome face had turned gray; his forehead glistened and a drop of perspiration formed on his temple and edged down his cheek; his shoulders drooped; and he'd sunk into the chair. He looked small. Steve watched his metamorphosis intently and waited for him to acknowledge defeat.

Suddenly, Alan jumped out of his chair and, pointing a finger at Steve, he sneered, "You bastard. You're trying to destroy me."

He was taken aback by Alan's display of the cornered rat syndrome. But his face hardened instantly. "Sit down," he ordered, "and put your finger away, if you know what's good for you." His voice was decidedly menacing.

Alan's face turned white; he lowered himself slowly back into the chair. They'd had plenty of unpleasant and unkind exchanges before, but that was the first time Steve had threatened him.

Steve regained control of himself. He relaxed his grip on the arms of his chair, but kept his eyes fixed on Alan; his voice was normal once again. "Let's keep this conversation civil, shall we? The outcome of our chat is entirely up to you: The consequences for you could be severe or mild; the choice is yours. And, don't for even a second think Helmut can bail you out of this one. So tell me, what did Carl offer you?"

Alan raised hands in resignation. "Nothing. I just wanted you to lose. I guess the only winner today turned out to be Carl."

He relished the pain in Alan's voice and couldn't help smiling. "Not by a long shot. You see, my gut told me you and that low life would conspire against me. I decided to listen to it and set out to turn the tables on both of you."

Alan was shaking; beads of perspiration were rolling down his temples. He asked in a low voice, "But how? Our bid was eighty-three million; his was eighty-six."

His voice was smug. "Ah, but our bid wasn't eighty-three. You see, I had Barney prepare two bid documents: a mock bid document from Wolfe Financial Services for eighty-three million, which we all discussed and Victor and I signed; and the real bid document for ninety-three million dollars from the Zeller Enterprises, which none of you saw and which required only my signature. The higher bid was justified because, I, like Victor, think the company's worth a lot more. Barney submitted the Zeller Enterprises' bid, of course." He looked at his watch and added, "The deadline's past. Your buddy Carl's about to get the bad news."

Alan sat with his head down; he looked every bit a beaten man. He asked, "What do you want me to do?"

He became somber. At that moment, he felt nothing for Alan—no hatred, no anger, no mercy. "Absolutely nothing that you don't want to. Just understand one thing: I want you're resignation from Wolfe Financial Services immediately. Use whatever excuse you want. If you don't, I'll expose you and destroy you. But if you resign without a fuss and forever stop inciting Jack and messing with me, you'll walk away with a generous financial package; still enjoy Helmut's good graces and share in the family fortune; and this whole affair will remain our little secret."

"What about Joan or Barney?" Alan asked. His hands were trembling.

Steve pointed to himself and replied, "You have my word. They won't talk."

Alan nodded and looked at him. "I think we can work together."

He stood up and said, "I know we can. Remember, we're family. I'm glad we had this chat." He held out his hand.

Alan pulled himself out of the chair and leaned forward. He shook hands with him and, with a pained look, turned around and left without another word.

He sat back and rested his head on the chair; he closed his eyes. He'd finally neutralized Alan; it had taken him years to do it—but, it was over. He felt indescribable relief. His mind drifted back to his childhood, to the day he vanquished the oversized school bully and rival, Jody. He smiled.

• • •

When the word about the creation of Zeller Foundation got out, the financial community took note with mixed feelings. Everyone was impressed with the magnitude of the endowment; some expressed skepticism about the value of the foundation's mission; and others were stunned by the realization that the Steve Zeller they'd known for so long as a tough, merciless, shrewd businessman had a softer side to him. A few clients of Wolfe Financial Services, concerned about their investments, worried that the tragedy of losing his wife and daughter may have blunted his competitive edge and dampened his single-minded desire to win. However, on balance, most clients were unfazed and came forward with their own contributions to the foundation.

Marty Coleman was a long-time client of Wolfe Financial Services. He was a fifty-five-year-old bachelor. In his early thirties, he'd managed to scrape together meager savings, which he put into penny stocks. His high-risk move paid off, and he turned to Wolfe Financial Services to manage and invest his fortune.

A month after the foundation was announced, Marty called Joan to tell her he was on his way to meet with Steve. As usual, he didn't specify the purpose of the meeting, and half an hour later he showed up. He walked into Steve's office with a big smile, sat down on the comfortable, maroon leather sofa across from his desk and said, "Hi, genius."

"Hi, Marty. It's nice to see you. What brings you here?" Steve got up and walked around the desk over to his muscular, deep-tanned client with peppery gray hair and mustache. They shook hands and he sat down in a tub chair next to the sofa.

Marty fixed his solemn eyes on him and said, "I'm here to return the favor."

He was perplexed. "That's nice of you. And what favor is that?"

Marty shed his mock somberness. "Helmut and you've made me a pile of money over the years—probably enough to buy Cuba from Castro. So I've decided to offer a token of my appreciation."

He waved his hand and said, "It's our job, Marty. You don't have to—"

Marty interrupted him, "I know, I know. But hear me out, will you? I want to help you perpetuate the memory of your beautiful wife and your delightful daughter. I think you've channeled your grief in a creative and constructive manner. I want to donate to the foundation . . . er . . . a headquarters built on eighty-five acres."

He couldn't believe what he was hearing. He was silent for a while, absorbing the shock. Then he said in soft voice, "Wow, Marty, that's fantastic. Where?"

Marty was beaming. "You know I have a three-hundred-plus-acre estate in New Rochelle. I live there, but most of the acreage just sits there doing nothing. I've been thinking about, maybe, donating some of it. So I took a look at it, and guess what? I found I could easily carve out and donate an eighty-five-acre piece on a hill away from my house. There's a wooded barrier isolating it from the rest of the property. The headquarters would have a panoramic view of the Long Island Sound. Ideal location for some serious contemplation, don't you think? You've got to see it."

Still stunned, he struggled to find words to express himself. "I . . . wow . . . Marty, I don't know what to say . . . Marty, thank you. Thank you so very much."

Marty laughed. "Nah, it's my pleasure. Look, I must run. We'll talk some more soon, and I'll take you out there," he said, standing up. As he shook Steve's hand, he added, "I'm not doing this just for you, understand? I don't have a family of my own; so, all this makes me feel really good. Honestly, I should thank you for letting me help. I'll see myself out. Bye."

Steve didn't move and was speechless. *Am I dreaming? This guy just donated to the foundation a headquarters and prime piece of property in a wealthy suburb of New York.* It took him a minute to digest the full impact of what had happened. He regained his composure and hurried to his desk. He couldn't wait to break the momentous news to Don and Helmut: Their foundation had a prestigious, permanent home.

• • •

Marty Coleman was a determined and impatient man. He threw himself into creating the headquarters for the Zeller Foundation with the same zeal he reserved for his prized endeavors. Before Steve and Don had a chance to even meet and drink a toast to his generosity, Marty had commissioned a leading architectural, design and construction firm to work with Don to define the short- and long-term needs, and left no doubt that he wanted to break ground without delay. In a month the architect was able to present renderings of three building options in park-like settings. Everyone liked the three-story, three-wing building with a striking exterior of glass and stone.

The chosen building had the shape of half a hexagon. It was positioned on the hill so each of the three wings had an unobstructed view of the Long Island Sound. The center wing was the main section and entrance; it had a spectacular atrium with reception area, a conference center, meeting rooms, and executive offices. A spiral staircase and two glass elevators led to the upper floors. Prominent in the center of the atrium would be a life-size bronze sculpture of Erika and Kathy standing on a pedestal. The mother and daughter would look exactly the way they did on the fateful day the bullets struck them—walking hand-in-hand and smiling at each other. Steve had commissioned the sculpture and decided on his inscription on the plaque: *In celebration of the lives and the memories of Erika Wolfe Zeller, my beloved wife and mother to my children, and Kathleen Margaret Zeller, our sweet first-born and sister of Todd Helmut Zeller and Jeffery Stanley Zeller.* The inscription ended with his name: Steven Raymond Zeller. He'd asked Helmut to write an inscription on behalf of the Wolfe family.

The main wing was named "The Wolfe Wing." The other two wings, housing libraries, laboratories, meeting rooms, and study rooms for a variety of disciplines, became "The McCoy Wing" and "The Coleman Wing."

The construction firm maneuvered through the bureau-cratic maze with masterful expediency and managed to obtain the excavation and grading approval by early spring. The per-mit arrived on a Thursday; Marty decided to break ground the very next day, Friday, at six o'clock in the evening. Everyone agreed with Marty's suggestion for a simple groundbreaking ceremony attended by a few contributors and friends, fol-lowed by a small celebration at his house. He noted that the foundation would get all the publicity it would want by mak-ing the dedication ceremony of its headquarters an elaborate media event.

• • •

Steve steered his four-month-old black Porsche off Interstate Route Ninety-Five clogged with evening rush-hour traffic and onto Route One. It was five thirty. He said to Don sitting next to him, "Boy, I'm glad we're out of that damn traffic."

"Yeah. It's less nerve-wrecking from here to Marty's estate."

Soon they were traveling on the small hilly roads of New Rochelle. A few patches of melting snow still dotted the land-scape and edges of the country roads. They came to a hand-painted sign at the beginning of a dirt and gravel road. It read "Zeller Drive."

Don said, "We're here."

The sign amused Steve. The idea of Zeller Drive appealed to him. He turned the car onto the road freshly cut through a heavy, overgrown brush and pointing uphill. He pulled into a makeshift, muddy parking lot full of luxury cars. He got out of the car and looked around. He saw a large mass of people milling around at top of the hill and scowled. "So this is Marty's idea of a small ceremony. I should've known: Nothing he does is small."

Don, too, appeared surprised. "Hell, he and I've been working very closely on this whole thing, and I had no idea he was thinking this big." Then, shaking his head, he put his hands up and added, "This guy's something else."

Steve was annoyed and stared at the crowd. "We should've invited our families."

Don nodded. "Yeah. We should have."

They walked toward the crowd gathered around a bulldozer, and saw Marty beckoning them with a hard hat and a shovel in his hands. "You're on time. Grab hard hats and shovels. It's show time."

The groundbreaking was simple and quick. Photographers were everywhere snapping pictures. Marty and Don said a few words, and both pointed to Steve as the prime driving force behind the creation of the foundation. He smiled and bowed in acknowledgement to a resounding ovation from the gathering, and was thankful not to be making a speech.

Marty closed the ceremony by thanking the attendees and left. The crowd began dispersing into the cars to head for Marty's house where a party was underway. Don started to chat with the representatives of the construction firm.

Steve took the opportunity to walk to the highest point on the hill, and surveyed the scenery with a sense of total satisfaction: *Soon we'll be back here to dedicate the building and make the foundation a reality.* He stood there with his thoughts, enjoying the beauty around him: The sky was painted red, purple and blue by the sun's imperceptible descent behind the trees; fog was rolling into Long Island Sound; and lights on Long Island glimmered through the enveloping haze. *A perfect spot for a memorial to Erika and Kathy,* he thought. He could see their laughing, bubbly faces, and became lost in his memories.

Don's voice broke his trance. "Hey, Steve. Are you ready to leave?"

He replied, "Yes. Let's party."

• • •

Marty's house looked like a towering, dark stone castle flanked with turrets. It was tucked away on the side of a hill, among dense evergreens and lush gardens. Steve handed the car keys to one of the valets and he and Don walked on cobblestones to the massive, arched mahogany entrance.

A man in black tie, tails and hat opened the door for them and said, "Gentlemen. Welcome to the Coleman residence."

Once inside, they found themselves in a huge rotunda; on each side of the house's impressive entrance was a curved stairway hugging the circular wall as it rose to meet the common landing on the second floor. From the landing's center a straight stairway led up to the next two floors. Cream-colored plush carpeting was everywhere; it looked striking against the dark mahogany entrance, banisters, doors and windows. A mixture of colorful modern and impressionistic paintings covered the walls between oversized stained-glass windows throughout, creating the look of an elaborate art gallery. Modern and traditional furniture was spread around the room; and five ornate crystal chandeliers, augmented by wall light-fixtures, illuminated the space. Straight ahead, at the other side of the room stood a large fireplace with a dark mahogany mantle, and on its left side sat a grand piano, which was being played by a gray-haired man in a tuxedo. Under the right stairs was a long bar with three busy bartenders wearing red bow ties, and under the left stairs two chefs were serving an expansive array of foods. The servers moved around with grace, attending to the guests—some sitting, most milling around—in the mammoth room, on the stairs, and on the second-floor landing. The dress code seemed to be what each guest wanted it to be, so long as the clothes were of an upscale or designer variety.

Marty saw them from the other side of the room. He worked his way to them through the crowd; he was animated. "Hi, guys," he said and, beaming at Don, continued, "Everything's going like clockwork. I bet you'll be in your headquarters by the year-end."

Don said, "Super. I'm looking forward to it."

Marty motioned to a waiter carrying a tray of champagne. When the three had glasses in their hands, Marty raised his and said, "A toast to a great beginning."

Steve and Don, too, raised their glasses, and all three took a sip.

Steve said with a feeling of satisfaction, "From what I see, with the right investments, Don's going to have an annual operating budget of about five million bucks. That and your gift of headquarters most definitely make for a great beginning."

Marty put his hand on Don's shoulder. "Looks like you're in good shape. By the way, I understand you've come up with a way to select the Think Tank—I assume that's the name."

Don said, "I've not come up with the name for the think tank. Anyway, I've decided on a two-phased approach."

Steve looked at Marty and interjected, "What little I know about it sounds good."

Marty took another sip of champagne and said in an apologetic tone, "Look, Don. So far, every time we've met, we've barely had enough time to talk about what my focus is: the foundation headquarters and issues surrounding it. How about giving me a peek at your efforts to assemble a think tank?"

Don put his glass on the bar and gestured. "Here's my thinking. First, I want to assemble a selection committee of prominent, freethinking theologians, scientists, astronomers, and philosophers. They'll help me fine-tune the mission and initial objectives of the think tank; firm up the disciplines we should start with; draw up candidate qualifications; identify candidates; and, of course, select the think tank—things like that."

Marty raised his eyebrows and asked, "Isn't that asking a lot from them?"

Don replied, "No because they'll be compensated very well for their efforts."

"That's good. Will they be disbanded at that point?"

"Not quite. I'll use them to help the new think tank members work through the next phase."

"And what's that?"

"The phase two puts everything in place for the think tank to start working on its tasks and objectives. That means setting up labs, libraries, computers and systems—everything."

"What's the timetable for all this?"

"Phase one's pretty far along. It should be wrapped up in two months. Phase two should take about six months. With the headquarters being ready by the year-end, I expect our work to be well underway by the spring of next year." Don had a hint of determination in his voice.

Marty's tone was complimentary. "Huh, just about a year after breaking ground. Not bad—not bad at all." Turning to Steve, he said, "I know things have been pretty rough for you. But you owe it to yourself to have some fun, ol' boy. It's time." Then, gesticulating, he said to both in an earnest voice, "Now, it's time to eat, drink and celebrate. Please, I insist."

Both patted Marty on the back and nodded.

Marty gulped down the remaining champagne in his glass and said, "I always say: Enjoying life is serious business." Then he walked away to socialize with his other guests.

Steve scanned the room; he was impressed. "Boy, this guy sure knows how to throw a party. Lucky bastard has remained a bachelor; what a life he's living."

Don seemed to agree with his assessment. "And what wealth, what popularity, what broads. Everything's super."

Both laughed and headed toward the buffet spread as Don added, "I'm told his parties are never boring or elegant; but they're always colorful, free-spirited. He has a reputation for owning a superb wine collection, which he shares freely with his guests."

"We'll soon find out firsthand," Steve said as they plunged into the sea of lively guests. "You're right about the crowd he's invited."

For the next two hours they drank, had *hors d'oeuvres* and mingled. Steve started to feel good and relaxed; he moved away from Don, who'd become engaged in a cozy conversation with a sharp-looking blonde, apparently an old acquaintance. He walked around, enjoying more—a lot more—fine wine. The feelings that had remained dormant in him for over five months started to awaken: He started to notice beautiful women as he used to, and exchanged flirtatious smiles with more than a few.

When he got in the vicinity of the fireplace, a strange feeling came over him. He felt a pair of eyes following him. He couldn't resist turning his head. His eyes made contact with those of a stunning redhead in a black evening dress enhanced by a pearl necklace and earrings. The mature look on her oval face with full lips and soft features was made more alluring by the healthy tan that covered her petite body. He walked to within a few feet of her. She was holding a glass of white wine and sitting next to a long-haired young man wearing a black bow tie and jacket. Steve took him to be her date, gave him a quick once-over, and caught snippets of his conversation. He surmised the guy was a talking idiot—a bottomless well of trivia found at any large party—who'd corralled two polite elderly gentlemen.

Steve turned his attention back to the redhead, and returned her undisguised gaze; she smiled at him. It was an invitation he couldn't resist; he smiled back. The woman stood up and walked over to him.

He said, "Hi, I'm Steve Zeller."

"I know. I was at the groundbreaking. I'm Denise Mann." She held out her hand.

So, she already knows who I am. Steve shook her hand. "Nice to meet you, Denise. What did you think of the groundbreaking?"

Still maintaining eye contact, she replied, "Nice ceremony, exquisite location for the foundation and memorial for your wife and daughter. You're quite a determined man."

"I wanted to do something . . . nice, something lasting. I had a lot of help," he said and added, "You know, I can't take my eyes off you. I hope I'm not making you uncomfortable."

Denise put her hand on the top of his jacket lapel and moved it down in a slow, gentle motion. "I've been staring at you. Are you uncomfortable?"

"No," he replied as he smiled and thought, *Where's this going? Should I push small talk? Nah, my mind can't take it, and I don't want it . . . she's what I want; I can already feel her body joined to me.* He decided to be bold. "Let's go somewhere quiet where we can get to know each other."

She looked at him for a moment with a faint smile. "I know just the place. One moment." She walked back to her escort who was still holding court, picked up her purse and whispered to him. He nodded without interrupting his inane discourse. Then she walked past Steve, motioning him with her eyes to follow her.

They ended up in a study in a secluded part of the mansion she seemed to be very familiar with. She locked the door. Steve put his arms around her from behind and kissed her neck. She turned around and looked deep in his eyes. "You don't waste any time, do you? I'm glad."

He pulled her to him. "You're so beautiful, so irresistible."

She led him to a black leather sofa. They embraced and their lips locked into a lingering, passionate kiss. Their lovemaking was explosive and rushed.

Afterward, as they straightened their clothes, Denise said, "It was wonderful. We should do this again without worrying about someone barging in."

He nodded. "You're right."

Denise said without hesitation, "Let's go to my place."

"Now?"

"Yes, now."

He asked, "But what about your date?"

She said in a dismissive tone, "He's just an acquaintance. Don't worry about him. I'll make an excuse and leave."

His carnal desire was strong. But something didn't feel right to him. He'd just experienced sexual fulfillment, but not emotional intimacy; and, emptiness gnawed at his heart. *Why am I feeling this way? I've never needed emotional connection during sex before? What's different now? Is it too soon after Erika?* He needed time to think. "I drove here with a friend. We're going on a business trip early tomorrow morning."

She raised her eyebrows. "On a Saturday? Hell, you have a girlfriend. I should've known."

He shook his head. "No, I'm not involved with anyone. We should get together again."

She looked into his eyes for a long moment and said, "Yes, we should." Then she kissed him and, opening the study door, walked out.

• • •

When he returned to the party, he saw Denise sitting next to her escort, whose new hostage was an awfully bored-looking young man. She looked tranquil.

How can she be that way? Damn, I'm anything but calm, marveled Steve as he stood near the piano and studied her. She gave him a warm, momentary glance—the only sign of acknowledgement that they'd just shared an intimate experience. He knew he could still change his mind and spend the night in her inviting arms. But he couldn't bring himself to do it.

He had to find a way to slow down his pulse and shake the conflicting thoughts nagging him. He decided he needed a drink and walked away. At the bar, an empty stool and a prompt bartender greeted him. He munched bar-nuts and downed two glasses of the finest wine from Marty's private collection. Then he moved on to cognac, his favorite drink. He was on his third cognac when he felt a hand on his shoulder and turned around.

Marty had come up behind him; he appeared to have been enjoying his own party. He said with a broad grin, "Glad to see you having fun."

Steve nodded. "I sure am. By the way, this is a great party."

Marty said, "Thank you, ol' boy." Then he lowered his head close to his ear and added in low voice, "Look, I'm having a small group over for dinner next weekend. You're invited, and Denise will be there."

Steve shook his head and smiled. *Damn. This guy doesn't miss much.* The thought of meeting Denise again and getting to know her better appealed to him. He said, "Thanks. I accept the invitation. Tell me about Denise."

Maintaining a discreet tone, Marty said, "Denise is a fun person. She's sharp and a good friend." He paused and looked at Steve.

"And?"

"And beyond that, you can find out for yourself next week when you're sitting next to her during dinner." He grabbed and shook Steve's hand. "Got to circulate, ol' boy. See you next Friday, six o'clock. It's casual dress." Then, without waiting for his response, he disappeared into the throng of his guests.

Steve stood up; he had to take a moment to steady himself by holding on to the back of his stool. He realized he'd had one drink too many; it was time to leave. He looked around for Don.

• • •

Only the roar of the powerful Porsche engine broke the stillness on the dark, winding and hilly road; and the car's two shafts of light weaved in and out on their downward path. Steve felt contented as he manipulated the steering wheel. After speeding through a tight curve, he said, "Boy. This beauty sure hugs the road. I'll keep it around for a while."

Don's eyes were closed, and his head was lying back on the headrest. He asked, "What did you think of the party?"

Steve was exuberant. "It was fantastic. Damn, I had more than enough booze to float away, and so did sixty or seventy others dispersed in that mansion. But, guess what? I connected with a delicious and elegant redhead, Denise—Denise Mann. We enjoyed a few private, intimate moments. I'll get a chance to meet her again next week; compliments of Marty."

"That's super. Like Marty said to you early in the evening: It's time."

"And how about you? Who was that hot-looking chick you latched onto?" he asked, again savoring the memory of his sensual encounter with Denise.

Without moving or opening his eyes, Don replied with a smile, "The blonde was Ann Harper. Obviously, I didn't have as good a time as you did. But would you believe we went to the same high school? She was very popular—dated only jocks. Anyway, she just got out of a long, bad marriage. One of Marty's friends brought her to the party to get her back into circulation."

"Thanks to you Ann didn't circulate much, did she?" he joked.

Don grinned. "No. We hit it off and she agreed to go out with me tomorrow."

"I bet she couldn't resist you, especially after you informed her that you suspected she was a goddess."

Both laughed.

After a brief pause, Don said, "This is weird. All of a sudden my mind's gone back in time to our chance meeting in front of the bulletin board in the NYU student center. I can't explain why. Anyway, that meeting appeared to be a pretty minor event at the time, right? But look what it's led to: you've become a powerful and filthy rich man with a beautiful family; a thirty-five-million-dollar foundation—maybe sixty with Marty's contribution—to study the purpose of human life; and me, a floundering, wanna-be intellectual, becoming the head of that foundation. Pretty impressive, huh? I mean, who would've thought all this would happen? Man, it's super. This demonstrates what we've discussed before—that nothing is insignificant." Then, after a momentary pause, he asked, "By the way, do you know the most important thing you've given me?" His voice cracked.

"No. What?" Steve was surprised to hear him getting emotional.

Don replied, "Pride, by making me the guardian of Todd and Jeff. Now I feel I have a family."

He was relaxed; he was listening to Don as he negotiated a curve without easing up on the accelerator. In a calm voice, he said, "It was a no-brainer for me. I know that if I'm history, my sons will have a wonderful, caring guardian in you. It'll be great for the kids, of course, but I'm not so sure it'll be great for you."

Don opened his eyes and looked at him. "And why won't it be great for me?"

He replied, "Kids require a lot of attention—you know, discipline and things like that. Moreover, being tied to two kids could cramp your style."

Don closed his eyes again and put his head back on the headrest. "No, it won't. But, just so you don't have to worry your dead little head, I'll say this: I'll quit the singles scene and marry a woman with strong maternal instincts to help me fulfill the guardianship role. Now what do you have to say?"

He smiled and said, "Let's hope you won't have to make that sacrifice for a long, long time. In the meantime you're free to visit my kids anytime you want. Oops, this is one hell of a curve."

Steve was fighting to keep his eyelids open. He'd missed the road sign that warned about the sharp curve to the right and the speed limit of twenty-five miles per hour. He was doing sixty, and the Porsche was already in the left lane, the lane for oncoming traffic, before his drunken brain could react. He put his foot on the brake pedal and pressed down. At the same time he steered hard to the right. "Better get back in my own lane. Who knows what nuts are out driving tonight?"

"You mean nuts like you," Don said.

He made no comment. He returned his foot to the accelerator.

There were a few seconds of silence. Then, the car's passenger-side tires started bouncing on the uneven shoulder. Don opened his eyes. He lifted his head and saw a tree rushing toward them. He shouted, "Watch out!"

Don's scream pierced the seductive sleep about to envelope Steve. The very next thing Steve heard through the fog in his head was a crunching boom and felt himself lurch forward violently against the seatbelt. Everything went blank.

9
Somewhere

DON'S SCREAM BROUGHT Steve back from his trance-like state. He opened his eyes. He saw he had company: Four of the five empty chairs were occupied. Those who were sitting in them, at times, squirmed to get comfortable or made momentary eye contacts with one another. An awkward silence prevailed.

Not a very social bunch, he thought. "Hi. I'm Steve Zeller."

The four looked at him for a moment; then lowered their eyes without saying anything.

He didn't feel slighted. *The dead are from all over the world. Maybe, English language is a problem for these guys; and maybe they're uneasy, confused—perhaps a bit more than I am.*

He surveyed the people in the circle, trying to zero in on someone with whom he could start a conversation. As he focused his eyes on them—one by one—they returned his stare, and immediately he picked up basic information about them: The teenager with sad eyes was Oku, a refugee from Africa; Antov—a six-foot-tall, muscular blond man—was a Russian hero in his mid-twenties; Rani was a twenty-year-old, olive-skinned Asian prostitute blessed with alluring innocence; and, from Arkansas, was Willie, a wiry young gangster with long hair, deep penetrating eyes and a prominent, jagged scar extending from his right cheekbone to the corner of his mouth.

Despite one failed attempt, Steve decided to try again to coax the group—even one person—into chatting. "Look, guys. Just think of what's going on. Here we are, total strangers thrown together for the first time. And yet I feel like I know every one of you, and can access your past if I want to. Do you feel you know me? Say something—anyone." He raised his hands and added in an animated voice, "Why the hell am I asking you? Christ, I already know what's on your minds: You're so anxious about what's behind the exit doors, and how we'll be judged, that nothing else seems to register in your brains. You know, like you, I'm worried too; and it seems you're not quite sure about the mind-reading ability we've picked up—in fact you're unnerved by it. I know you are. Damn it, will someone speak up?" He shrugged his shoulders and waited.

But no one said a word.

"Just my luck. I'm stuck with these dumb bastards," Steve muttered to himself with resignation as he folded his arms and sat back.

His last words elicited an immediate reaction from Willie: clenched teeth and a menacing glare. He also got a steely stare from Antov, who'd leaned forward. It was quite obvious they were offended by his unflattering utterance. He made a mental note of their hostile reactions, and responded by leaning forward and looking directly and sharply at them. The standoff of unblinking stares dragged on for a few long seconds before the three lowered their eyes and again settled back in their chairs. Steve knew he'd made two enemies.

Oku and Rani were reluctant witnesses to the tense scene; but Steve could tell they didn't sympathize with him.

He became worried: He couldn't afford to ignore the obvious ill-feelings his unfortunate confrontation had generated.

Damn, that was a dumb thing to do . . . what was so important about talking to these schmucks? The last thing I need at my judgment trial is a bunch of weirdos who don't like me. Who knows, now just out of spite one of them might decide to compete or pick a fight with me; or, another screwball might just shoot his mouth off against me. No, I can't . . . I won't let them jeopardize my chance at getting into heaven. I must get enough dirt on them to neutralize or discredit any shithead who dares to speak against me. I hope there's enough time to take a peek at their miserable lives before one of the blue uniforms joins us to start the trial. His eyes scanned the room. The activities he'd noted before he became preoccupied with his life review were continuing unabated: the myriads of five-person meetings moderated by the staff; people displaying varied emotions with infinite levels of intensity; the constant influx of dead people in white gowns and sandals into the dome; and, the dead in an unending line leaving the dome through one of the two exit doors.

Once again, Steve closed his eyes. Then he switched on his mind to review the life capsules of the silent four with whom he was about to share his final moments and, perhaps, compete or quarrel—Oku, Antov, Rani and Willie.

10
Oku

THE LIFE IN Oku's village was serene. Of course, the oven-like temperatures and stifling humidity were facts of life, and so was the stark scene of villagers toiling on farms to feed their families as the merciless sun baked their bodies. Everyone was poor; but no one starved because everyone cared—and shared. People lived; people worked; people died; and the restless youth left to seek fortunes elsewhere. There was laughter, and there were tears. But serenity, above all, was the characteristic that predominated there; and, life flowed like a calm river.

The thirteen-year-old Oku had an easy disposition and was quick with a smile or laughter. Whether he was out playing with his friends or clinging to his mother for comfort or helping his father with chores, he always felt safe.

"Oku. Come out, you sleepy head," shouted Oku's impatient friends as they milled around outside his hut.

"Coming," he shouted back, and continued gulping down rice and fresh milk from a bowl as fast as he could.

Soon, he was outside with his friends and, like them, was shirtless, shoeless and wore tattered short pants. They hurried to their favorite spot—a shaded, swampy area near the only well the village had for its water supply. Besides being an obvious focal point for the people, that shady area was also the coolest. The children spent countless hours playing there, and the surrounding air would be filled with their laughter and mischievous shrieking.

Two hours later, Oku's father, Sari, a slight, balding man with a gaunt face, walked by the swamp and saw the youngsters engrossed in a tag game. He called out, "Oku. I need your help with chores on the farm. Will you come with me?"

"Yes, Father," Oku replied. With a proud smile on his dark brown face exposing pearly white teeth, he turned to his playmates and said, "I have to go. I must help my father."

He felt special when his father would ask him to work on their meager farm at the outskirts of the village. His chores were the less strenuous things he and his father could do together, like collecting cow chips for fuel, feeding their two cows and securing them for the night. He loved it when his father interrupted the chores to play with him, give him bear hugs and talk to him. Sari always seemed to have time for those bonding sessions with him.

That day, they worked on clearing out weeds, ate lunch, wrestled playfully, and did more weeding until mid-afternoon. Then Sari said, "It's time to get out of the sun. Let's head home."

Oku held Sari's hand as they started to walk. He looked up at him and said, "Father, a dream came to me last night."

"Oh? What did you dream about?" Sari's eyes widened.

Excitement rose within Oku. "Remember you told me about shining machines that can fly like birds? My dream had one big flying machine, way up in the sky and . . . and you know what? I was sitting in it."

Sari looked intrigued. "Is that so? What was inside the machine? Do you remember?"

He replied with pride, "I remember everything. It was very large inside; very pretty colors—red, green and orange. There were lots of people in nice robes sitting inside. I was wearing a new robe and . . . and we were eating chicken."

Sari's face lit up. "Praise the Lord! Chicken. That's so expensive. You must have a lot of money."

"I don't have money. It was a dream, Father," he said and laughed.

Sari smiled. "Yes. But if you work hard and go to school, your dream will come true; you'll earn plenty of money and then really go up in the sky in the flying machine."

"I want to go to school. It will be fun." His young mind was already conjuring up fantastic adventures.

Sari said, "Tomorrow I'll tell you about a very big village. It's called a city, and that's where the school is."

Oku would concentrate with a sense of self-importance when his father explained new things to him; his friends' fathers didn't do that. As he mulled over the new topics his father promised to discuss with him, his eyes wandered onto an unusual sight. "Father, look."

Sari turned his head to where his son was pointing. In the distance, at the edge of the farm, he saw four young men in fatigues, looking in their direction; they were carrying machine guns and machetes. One of the strangers waved to them, and then the four turned around and melted away into the thick brush.

Oku was curious. "Who're they?"

"Just some people from another village." Sari's tone had changed and his face had hardened.

"What were they carrying?"

"Ah . . . probably something to hunt with," Sari said and knelt down. He put his hands on Oku's shoulders, looked deep into his eyes and said, "Oku, listen to me. You won't squander your life in this village like I did. I wanted to leave and be successful; but I kept procrastinating until it was too late. You'll work hard and study hard. I'll tell you about the big world outside our village; I'll get teachers who can explain wonderful things to you and broaden your mind. You'll have a bright future in a faraway land. I promise."

Sari's intensity scared Oku; he became tense. "Huh? What?"

Sari seemed to realize the effect he was having on Oku. He recovered control of his emotions and laughed. "Don't worry your smart, little head. Forget what I said now. You'll understand everything when you grow up." He stood up and patted Oku on the back. "Now let's go; your mother must be wondering about us. It's getting late."

Sari's reassuring tone relaxed Oku

The rest of the way back to the hut, Sari was quiet; his face was somber.

• • •

".... So, brothers and sisters, of course, you think your life is good. It's because you don't know what a good life is or can be. See what I mean? The corrupt leaders and parasites in our government have been stealing the wealth of our country. They are destroying our—yours and mine—dignity and chance for a better life. We must not let that continue. No, we must not. We must demand a more equitable sharing of the wealth: We must be handsomely compensated for long hours of hard work, sweat and sacrifices. Yes, we must do that. No longer will we tolerate those who steal our prosperity, justice and future; the days of their tyranny, and our ignorance, are over. Stand up and fight for your rights: Remaining an apathetic, sleepy village is no longer an option. You are entitled to freedom and democracy—now and forever. The time for revolution is now. Don't worry, my brothers and sisters, your village and hundreds of other villages like yours will be a part of the revolution very soon; so, join us and prosper. Power to the people!"

The young, bright-eyed outsider in fatigues had appeared on a motor scooter from nowhere. He made the impassioned speech to the whole village gathered at the well and drove away.

The villagers were confused: Why were they being asked to care about things that didn't matter to them? They already had a full and peaceful life. One elder made an ominous prediction: Greed and lust for power, coupled with ideological fervor and ravings, weren't going to be denied; things were going to change.

And change they did. Within months of the young man's speech, the better life they "deserved" was forced on them.

The serenity was shattered.

• • •

The whole village was burning; the massacred bodies lay everywhere. It was the price the entire community was paying for its neutral stance in the civil war.

"Son, come here," Oku's sobbing mother, Mona, called out. "Your father is asking for you." She was cradling Sari's bloodied head in her lap as his mangled body lay on the ground, and life was ebbing from him.

Rebels had dragged Sari out of the hut in the dark of the night and hacked him to the point of death with makeshift hatchets, as the shrieking Oku and Mona huddled together and watched in terror. When rebels torched their hut, they had to get out. Oku saw and grabbed the spear his father kept next to the door to fend off an occasional threatening wild animal. They sought shelter under a nearby tree. When Sari was left to die, Mona rushed to him.

Two of the perpetrators stood a few yards away from Oku and his parents and watched them with glee. When Oku made an attempt to leave the sanctuary of the tree to walk toward his parents, one of the rebels stared at him and shook his head. Then, with a broad grin, he brought the hatchet to his own neck and made a slicing gesture with it and started walking toward him.

Oku, then barely fourteen, froze with fear. He felt an uncontrollable urge to urinate—and he did.

"Oku, come quickly," Mona shouted once again.

But the petrified Oku couldn't speak or move; he just stared at the approaching man.

When the man got close, he said, "I see you have a spear. Are you brave enough to use it?" Then he laughed and placed a hand on the shaft of the spear and pulled the spear's point to his chest. He stopped laughing and his face turned stern. "Go ahead, plunge the spear into me. I split your father's skull; he's going to die. Spear me; show some guts, boy." He laughed again and released the spear. Then, he walked away.

Oku remained motionless and speechless.

The two revolutionaries chatted and lingered a while, then left. Mona continued wailing and wiping blood off Sari's face with her shawl.

Long minutes passed; Mona had stopped crying. "Oku, please come help me lift your father," she said.

The teary-eyed Oku's paralyzing fear had subsided enough for him to inch his way to his parents. He was shaking and couldn't bring himself to look at his lifeless father, sprawled face up on the ground, and covered with the drying blood that had spurted out of the deep gashes on his chest, face and head.

Rebels had ordered the surviving women and children to leave the area by daybreak—or else. The terror-stricken families were mourning and scurrying to bury their dead before fleeing.

The huts were gone; the livestock was gone; and the village was gone. The survivors' cries of anguish filled the air.

Mona again said aloud, "Come, Oku. We must quickly bury him and leave."

Terror had numbed Oku; etched in his mind was the horrifying final sight of Sari flailing against the merciless attackers. He couldn't comprehend Mona's repeated urgent pleas for help.

The grieving Mona had to struggle alone to drag Sari's body into the shallow grave she'd dug to bury it.

• • •

The scorching sun was relentless. Oku's mouth was parched. He tried to chew on the dry grass, which did manage to activate his salivary glands; but when he tried to swallow, a sharp pain in his throat interceded, and he was forced to spit the grass out. He gave up and lay there, looking in the direction of his mother.

Mona was rolled up into a ball. Her face was hidden; only slight movements of her ribcage revealed she was alive.

Miles of grueling march from their village and lack of food and water had exhausted them. The blinding sun and his distended belly forced Oku to lie on his sides, which had started to ache. His feeble body couldn't hold itself up; he couldn't even chase away the flies feasting on his open sores and cuts. So, he lay there, waiting for someone to come and help him and his mother. Waiting was the only thing he could do.

His mind had started to roam. It kept drifting back into a not-too-distant past where laughter was everywhere; where surroundings were cool, green and secure; and where love was plentiful, and food always enough. He could see himself as a happy thirteen-year-old, full of life and dreams. He remembered the faraway, fascinating places his father told him about, and the visions he had about going there in a flying machine. And, of course, he looked forward to attending school in a big city.

Mona was motionless; she'd been that way for some time. She was dead.

Mona wasn't the only one lying near Oku. A whole mass of humans was scattered around him, most dead and the remaining few too spent to plod to the refugee camps miles away.

Hours passed. Then, a sudden distant roar disrupted the deathly stillness; the noise grew louder, and Oku saw bellowing dust following a jeep that was speeding toward him. It squealed to a stop about a hundred feet from him, and two uniformed men got out. He could hear their conversation.

One man said, "My God. Look at these poor bastards. They have finally succumbed. After all these days of starving and marching in this dust bowl, they are still many miles away from food and shelter."

The other man grimaced. "Hundreds of corpses—women and children. Ugh. Better call this in and request a mop-up operation."

"Sure, but why not first take a quick look around? Some wretches are still alive; quick treatment might save a life or two. It'll be hours before medics can get here."

The other man nodded. "Damn. Look at the open sores and blisters on their feet."

The two moved around, scanning the grisly scene. Among the still bodies on the ground, they heard a faint, sporadic wheezing sound; they followed it. It led them to an emaciated four-year-old child who was laboring to breathe.

"This girl is barely alive. You start giving her medical aid. I might as well go ahead and notify headquarters," said the first man as he rushed to the jeep.

The second man worked at a hurried yet methodical pace to stabilize the girl. Her wheezing stopped and she fell into a deep sleep. The man called out to his partner, who was searching for more survivors. "We saved one. This child will live."

Oku watched the man revive the girl, and he heard the two men's excited talk as she slept. They were about forty feet away from him. He wanted them to know he was alive and needed help; he, too, wanted a chance to live. He opened his mouth in an attempt to speak, but couldn't. Instead, he coughed and felt a piercing pain in his throat. He tried to lift his hand to grab his neck, but it stopped in mid-air and slumped lifeless to the ground.

For Oku, everything was serene once again.

11
Antov

FOR THE TWENTY-FIVE-YEAR old Antov Suryevo, the seven-year journey from a farmhand to a highly success-ful operative in the FSB, the Federal Security Service of the Russian Federation, had been a thrilling adventure. The life he was experiencing was nothing he could've imagined when he was growing up in a nondescript village of a hundred or so farmers and laborers in the southern region of Russia. His austere upbringing and the back-breaking work to live off the land had prepared him well for the physically and mentally arduous activities of the secret services. But the attribute that stood out and defined him was his unquestioning, single-minded loyalty to his motherland. And, while investigating him as a potential recruit, the FSB had taken note of the zealot in him and concluded he'd be ideal for counter-intelligence.

During his probationary period after intense training, he realized he had no compunction committing all sorts of atrocities and murders to eliminate threats to his country. He focused on the precise mechanics when he pried finger nails off his subjects or twisted their necks—his preferred method of killing—and watched them die.

But now he sensed trouble. Though he was shrewd enough to realize the price of becoming a hero was to pay homage to certain superiors and give them full credit for his accomplishments, he couldn't bring himself to comply. His handlers were unambiguous in passing on warnings of grave consequences from unnamed superiors. Furthermore, the innocuous tests to gauge his loyalty had uncovered a troublesome pattern of individualism and independence, and he'd failed to demonstrate a propensity for corruption. The bottom line was he lacked the weaknesses required of an FSB hero. The FSB had made an error it couldn't admit. Antov was certain a campaign to liquidate him would start soon, if it hadn't already.

He didn't know what they'd do to eliminate him or how they'd do it. He trusted his instinct; it kept him on guard, and told him the attempt wouldn't be overt. The FSB's disciplined training was also coming in handy: It had taught him to screen and assess everyone's character as a matter of habit. He'd concluded that he might be able to trust a handful of individuals, and only three of them implicitly—his parents and his fiancée Larissa. He didn't even trust the only other member of his close family, his older brother, who was a farmer without ideological convictions and scruples. The two had nothing in common and, when they lived under the same roof with their parents, they barely tolerated each other.

He'd decided against sharing the burden of his suspicions about the impending trouble with anyone. For the time being, it was enough for him to know that his parents would be there if he needed them; and he also had Larissa for moral support, emotional security, and love.

He'd met Larissa when he first arrived in Moscow, and attended an orientation seminar and banquet arranged by the FSB for its new recruits. She was one of the many female administrative assistants in the FSB bureaucracy ordered to attend and mingle with recruits to make them feel at home. They met again when he was accepted as a full-fledged operative. It didn't take long for the two to fall in love. While she knew he'd work on field assignments, she wasn't authorized to know what those assignments or duties would be; and neither broached the subject. As their love blossomed, she became a constant source of strength and support for him. She was his exquisite, soft flower; and he couldn't imagine a life without her.

They spent evenings together at her apartment. She was an excellent cook; he marveled at the breadth of her culinary knowledge and skills.

Her apartment, like every low-level bureaucrat's subsidized residence, was small, austere and painted white. It contained dark brown furniture devoid of any style, and had a bedroom, a bathroom, and a living room that included a kitchen and eating area; the only window in the apartment was in the bedroom. Larissa had used her creativity and flair for decorating to make the apartment comfortable and cozy. It had become a love nest for them; they cherished their long evenings there—unwinding after work, dining, talking, laughing, holding hands, dreaming, making passionate love, and formulating plans for their life together.

The quiet war with his superiors was starting to gnaw at Antov's nerves. He felt like a boat docked in a slip being rocked and shoved against the pilings with increasing frequency from the approaching storm. His temper was getting short; his quick, handsome smile had become scarce; and he'd become moody. The stress had become much too onerous for him to handle alone.

One evening, he was stretched out on the couch and following Larissa's movements in the kitchen area as she prepared dinner. He couldn't hold back any longer; he said in a somber voice, "Larissa, I must talk to you now, please . . . I have to tell you . . . things."

She studied his face for a moment. Then she wiped her hands on her apron, turned the burners off, and said, "Finally you're ready to talk to me about what is upsetting you. Good. You certainly haven't been yourself lately; I have been worrying, and waiting for you to say something."

Antov felt uncomfortable. He closed his eyes and didn't speak.

As she walked toward him, she asked, "Antov dear, what is it? Oh God, is it about us . . . about me?"

"No, no, it's not us, or you—nothing like that." He took a deep breath. "I . . . I am in serious trouble with some of my superiors."

By then Larissa was sitting next to him and holding his hand. "What do you mean? That cannot be. You're one of their top operatives." Her eyes were wide with astonishment, and her voice had deep concern.

He pushed strands of long, soft red hair back from her face with gentle hands and sighed. "I have become a threat to their authority, and they have no choice but to strike back."

Larissa looked at him with compassionate eyes and said, "I just cannot believe what you're saying . . . not possible. Darling, they adore you. You have said so yourself."

"Most do. But some want me dead."

"How do you know? Has something been said?"

Antov shook his head. "No. No one has uttered a single word. In fact, everyone is very polite—too polite. But I just know . . . have a strong feeling—instinct, you know."

Larissa held his hand and asked, "What kind of assignments have they been giving you?"

He pulled back. The question surprised him. "How can you ask me such a thing? You know we can't discuss that. Only the top FSB hierarchy and select party members are privy to that."

"I am simply trying to understand what's making you their target. If—"

He interrupted in an adamant tone, "I will not put you in any jeopardy. Anyway, I am certain that the whole problem is not my assignments; part of it—most probably a large part—is me."

"This is so unfair. Can you approach someone . . . someone powerful, who likes you, to protect you or help you?"

He shook his head. "I think that would be a grave mistake."

Larissa began to cry; her stark fear was evident in her eyes. "Antov, I do not know what I will do if something happened to you."

He put his arm around her, gave her a gentle hug, and gazed into her eyes. "Nothing will happen to me," he said through clenched teeth. "I can take care of myself."

Larissa clung to him, with tears streaming down her cheeks. "Quit the FSB. Just quit—or at least the field assignments. Request a bureaucratic job, here in Moscow."

"Why should I do that?" He was surprised at her suggestion.

"Part of your problem is connected to your assignments, yes? So, if you stop doing them, you will be out of the limelight. That will signal to your enemies that you're not hungry for power and, therefore, not a threat to them; and they will soon forget you."

He forced a weak smile. "Good logic, darling. But, what you ask is not possible; I cannot do it."

"Yes you can, Antov, yes you can. You will be alive and we will have a wonderful life together."

But he wasn't in a mood to give in. "Do not worry, dear. I will identify and handle my enemies—whoever they are. Just wait and see."

She said in an agitated voice, "Why are you so . . . so hard-headed? You know they are going to kill you. Do you wish to die? You must defuse the situation somehow; you must do it. I mean, you have to show them that field assignments are not important to you."

Antov didn't say anything; just shook his head. *Wrong, Larissa, wrong! Assignments are very, very important to me ... I will not give them up.*

Resignation replaced agitation on Larissa's face. "Okay, okay, do as you please," she said, "but, you must do one thing for me: You must agree to move out of your apartment and stay with me."

"Why?"

"You will be safer with both of us in the same apartment. Your enemies will realize we're lovers and wonder what secrets you've shared with me. In that case, don't you see, they will have to liquidate both of us."

"You really believe that?" He was skeptical, but paying attention.

She replied, "Yes I do; you know how the party detests messy situations. And the last thing the FSB wants to do is to irritate the party. Now, would it not be strange if two FSB employees—a hero and a bureaucrat—died or disappeared at the same time from the same address? No one in the FSB would be comfortable explaining that. Do you agree?"

Grasping the wisdom of her argument, Antov weakened. "But we're not married. People will gossip, and ... of course, our parents would object."

"But you would be safe," she said with teary eyes, as she kissed him.

Antov kissed her back and relented. "All right, I agree to stay in your apartment, if that will make you feel better."

They held each other in silence. Antov felt the oppressive tightness in his chest waning: He was no longer alone in the fight of his life. He closed his eyes; his peace of mind that had eluded him for months was returning to him.

• • •

The spacious and dimly lit ballroom in the elite part of Moscow was filled to capacity with the Kremlin's most powerful dignitaries. The bright white light flooded the podium and special guests on the stage. This was the most important annual event hosted by the FSB to showcase its very best recruits, and to congratulate itself for making the world safe for Russia.

The master of ceremony introduced the next speaker. "And now, with great pleasure and pride, I present to you a very remarkable operative. You judge for yourself the merits of this exciting young man. Please welcome Antov Suryevo."

The crowd responded with an obligatory and restrained applause.

The six feet, three inches tall, blond-haired Antov rose from his chair on the stage and bowed in the direction of his superiors sitting in the front row of the large assembly. Then he turned and confidently walked erect to the podium. As he adjusted the microphone higher, he looked around the elegant room. The faces of his audience were difficult to see— they were masked by the glare of lights focused on him. He had a boyish grin on his ivory white, handsomely rugged face that glowed with excitement. He spoke in a slow, deliberate tone.

"Distinguished Guests, it is an honor to speak to you. It is my humble duty to announce that our beloved Russia is much safer today; it is so partly because my field assignments of the past year and a half have been successful far beyond my most optimistic expectations. To date, I have had the good fortune to neutralize fifteen German spies, and to infiltrate and expose a subversive Chechen organization. And, crowning those achievements was a bonus catch: I identified and caught a dangerous and slippery CIA spy entrenched right here in Moscow. He had lived under our very noses under the guise of a family man and entrepreneur. He is now in our jail, where he cannot be a threat to us. Credit for all I have accomplished goes to my esteemed superiors; I am indebted to them for having faith in me, and giving me the opportunity and honor to serve our great country. I hope to remain worthy of their and your trust and confidence. I salute them and you."

The audience broke out into a thunderous applause.

Flushed with pride, Antov acknowledged the prolonged ovation with a slight nod. Then he walked back to his chair and sat down. He looked down at his superiors. All of them had joined in the applause for him; most were smiling and nodding; and the rest were staring at him with cold eyes and painted smiles.

He felt he'd earned a hero's ovation; he was proud to have met his challenges in a flawless and efficient manner. His intensive training as a FSB operative and total loyalty to his country were paying off. But, he also knew that the applause from his superiors with the frozen smiles was for proper appearances; after all, he was their man and, with the recognition of his exploits, he was enhancing their stature in the eyes of the party's top echelon.

• • •

After the ceremonies, as the guests and the FSB chatted and enjoyed caviar and drinks, some of Antov's superiors retired to a small conference room for a private meeting. Their conversation had an air of urgency.

"Did you hear that arrogant bastard taking all the credit? 'Successful far beyond my most optimistic expectations,' he said. I mean, he has already anointed himself a hero. Remember, I had predicted he will be trouble."

"We must approach this situation calmly—"

"Calmly? Of course, you want calm now. You are the one who insisted it would be easy to control this immature twenty-five-year-old. Just a loyal farmhand with nerves of steel and a killer instinct, you said."

"A hero must be one who can be controlled . . . er, someone who demonstrates blind obedience. Antov has the capacity to go it alone, and he has proven that. So I think, at some point soon, his individualism will clash with our authority, and then things would get messy, very messy."

"We must not forget what he has accomplished for us."

"What he has accomplished for himself, you mean?"

"I say he is uncontrollable . . . just trouble."

"Huh. Someone should have dealt with this fanatic by now."

"Please. No one is to blame. We were all taken in. He is very smart, and gets results."

"That he does. But, unfortunately he has an independent streak."

"Once people put him on a pedestal as a hero, confronting him will be political suicide."

"He must be stopped—now. I always say: An ounce of prevention—"

"Yes. Prevention is the answer."

"I will put it bluntly: Antov must die."

Everyone nodded and said, "Agreed."

They all emerged from the conference room laughing, smiling, making small talk, and melted into the noisy crowd.

• • •

Antov and Larissa had retired to the bedroom after a long evening of celebration.

"Larissa, I wish you had been there when I was presented that," said Antov with pride and pointed to the plaque sitting on the oversized chest of drawers at the foot of the bed. The plaque proclaimed him the outstanding citizen of the year. Antov continued, "You want to know the truth? I would happily do what I did for the Motherland without all that honor; I really mean it . . . I would even sacrifice myself. But it sure felt nice to be appreciated."

Larissa was lying on her side, cuddled next to him. Her head was resting on his shoulder. As she watched her hand roam on his chest, she said, "I am so happy for you. Whatever you did, it must have been very important—and heroic—for them to honor you so greatly." Then she added with a mischievous smile, "That explains only a part of the time you spent away from me. What did you do with the rest of it, chase women?"

He laughed and played along. "Yes, but I found none as good as you."

"You rascal, I will take that as a compliment," she said in an exaggerated husky voice.

He grinned and pulled her closer.

"I love you, Antov. I love you so much," Larissa said, while she kissed his cheek and continued rubbing his chest.

He was feeling sanguine. Pointing to the two empty glasses on the small square nightstand, he said, "Let us have more vodka."

She raised her head. "No. You've had enough."

"Umm . . . just one more toast to this unforgettable moment of success, love, happiness," he pleaded.

Larissa stood up and brought her lips close to his ear and said, "Very well, we'll have one more."

Antov remained motionless, and allowed his mind to once again savor the accolades bestowed on him by the party bosses that day.

Larissa returned and handed him a glass. "Here is your vodka, darling." Then, she nestled close to him with another glass in her hand, and said, "A toast to you."

He raised his head and the glass. "To us."

They took long gulps and put the glasses down. Antov pulled Larissa close to him and both lay back on oversized, fluffy pillows. He closed his eyes and savored the warm sensation of vodka permeate his body.

Twenty-six seconds later, Antov suffered a massive heart attack. When his convulsions stopped, he shuddered and was dead. Within an hour and a half, the poison he drank with the vodka would break down, and there would be no trace of it left in his body.

Larissa arranged him in a restful, sleeping position. She disposed of the remaining vodka, washed the glasses, turned off the lights, and went to sleep on the sofa.

The next morning, she phoned her doctor and said in a sobbing voice, "Something is terribly wrong. I cannot wake Antov. Please come quickly."

Then she dialed a private number at the FSB headquarters. When her contact answered, she said, "It is over," and added with a sigh, "and so are the two most boring years of my life. I hope my next assignment will be more exciting."

She hung up and sat down on the sofa to wait for the doctor to arrive.

12
Rani

"LOOK, MOTHER, A doll!" Rani shouted, breathless from running.

"Calm down, child. Where did you get it?" Veena asked without looking up from the threshold she was sweeping the dirt over and into the street.

Rani pointed and replied, "There, at the end of the street, in the garbage pile." Then, clutching the doll to her chest, she asked in an excited voice, "Can I keep it, can I?"

"Let me take a look." Veena grimaced and picked up the doll with two fingers. She inspected it and held it close to her nose for a moment. Then she said in a disgusted voice, "Child, this is filthy . . . ugh, smells so bad."

"I will wash it. Can I keep it after I clean it? Let me keep it. Please, Mother, please." The animated Rani danced around Veena.

"All right, you can keep it, but only if you can wash the filth off," Veena said. She noticed the excitement in her ten-year-old daughter's eyes, and was unwilling to deprive her precious child the pleasure of playful moments with her newfound treasure.

With shrieks of joy, Rani rushed into her dark, cave-like apartment in the dilapidated two-story building. She returned with a remnant of a bar of soap, snatched the doll from Veena's fingers, and ran to the community water tap. She was in luck: There was water. She scrubbed and washed the old frazzled doll covered with a thick coat of dirt and grime. She spent over two hours cleaning and combing it and transformed it into a soft, fresh-smelling, cuddly companion.

• • •

Veena couldn't stop the tears from flowing; her own memories had resurfaced as she watched her daughter's reaction to a doll discarded by another child. She remembered throwing away her old dolls and toys as a child growing up in luxury. Her wealthy family lived in a lush resort-like area of Goa, a town on the west coast of India, which was favored by foreigners because of relaxing white beaches and plentiful drugs. At fifteen, she was given in an arranged marriage to a rich man twice her age. Two years later she was raped during a home invasion. Even though the culprit was caught and confessed to assaulting her sexually, her husband considered her soiled and sent her packing to her family. Her parents promptly unloaded her in marriage to a young man of meager means and few skills by giving him a handsome bribe called a dowry. She was ordered not to have any contact with the family. She accepted the cruelty of fate and society without a word of protest and started serving her sentence of a grim life of poverty in the slums. Furthermore, she was pregnant with a child—a gift of rape. When her daughter arrived, she named her Rani, a Hindi term meaning 'queen.'

• • •

Rani had to fend for herself because her parents worked long, hard hours for the family's mere survival. Like other slum children, she spent most of her time on crowded streets. The streets adopted her and watched over her. Everyone noticed her love for soft and cuddly things: She was always patting and hugging stray pups and kittens.

People noticed Rani because of one other thing: She was a captivating beauty. Though she grew up in rags, dirt and poverty, she stood out and appeared to be miscast in the role of an urchin. Everyone sensed that she was destined to rise above the slums; but to what heights was a topic of scores of debates.

The poor in Rani's neighborhood, like the poor everywhere, had time for such debates. Somehow, such occasions provided expression for their own fantasies that they couldn't, and wouldn't, realize. The very thought that someone in their midst might have a chance excited strong emotions tinged with envy; and they had to talk it out because, while their minds dwelled on hope—even though it was someone else's—they escaped the hopeless reality around them.

Rani didn't have long to wait for her chance: A benefactor appeared when she was twelve. Kishore Senna was a wealthy, middle-aged family man who owned a jewelry store and a large, fortress-like estate. Everyone referred to him as 'Kishore Sahib'—'sahib' or 'master' being a term of respect. He'd observed Rani playing in the streets whenever he was chauffeured through the city in his black Mercedes to go on business trips. With much anguish and guilt, her parents accepted his offer to give her a position and shelter in his house. He promised them that he'd treat their daughter as one of the family. Her parents, not wanting to stand in the way of her good fortune, dismissed her tearful pleas to remain with them and forced her to go with him to become a companion and babysitter to the two toddlers in his home.

Rani helped to take care of the children until she was fourteen. Then, Kishore seduced her and made her one of his mistresses. This change in her status exposed her to high society; more and more, well-heeled men started to desire her and, with Kishore's acquiescence in exchange for favors, ended up acquiring her. She aroused and satisfied lust as only she could. Her beauty and prostitution took her higher and further away from her heritage of poverty and hunger.

It wasn't long before she ceased to look forward to her parents' routine visits which had become awkward, emotionless—and yes, stressful— encounters. She decreased the meetings in frequency and, finally, stopped them completely. She was enthralled with the world of lust and luxury, and her parents, or any other reminder of her painful past, had no place in it.

By the time she was twenty, she had eased into the role of a Madam with a stable of young women eager to sell themselves to escape poverty. She entertained only the most powerful and their clients; and a lot of those clients were foreigners seeking to act out their erotic fantasies in an exotic surrounding.

● ● ●

"I have a very important business associate visiting me from Europe. He calls himself 'The Shark'. He will be here tomorrow to close a major drug deal and I want every one of his needs taken care of. I choose you to make sure that that happens and he leaves here a happy man, no matter the cost." Kishore's hands rested on Rani's shoulders and his eyes bored into hers as she sat in a chair in his office with him standing over her.

Accustomed to such demands from him, she put her hands on his and said, "Of course, Kishore Sahib. Just tell me how I can help."

"The Shark prides himself for having bedded virgins all over the world. The youngest virgin he claims was thirteen. Plus, his taste runs toward unorthodox sex; says he likes to experiment. He has intimated that this time he'd like to try a ten-year-old."

Rani didn't like what she was hearing. The memory of being seduced at age fourteen by him came rushing back. "Sahib, that is too young. I'm not sure a child at that age can cope physically or mentally with her body—"

"Listen to me, Rani. This deal is going to be the most lucrative my partners and I will be concluding. If this deviant wants a ten-year-old girl, then we must get him a ten-year-old girl. It is a small price to pay. Tell the parents of the girl you will make it worth their while. Remember I said 'whatever the cost.' The Shark must leave here happy. You understand?" Kishore's hands had tightened on her shoulders and his tone had become firm—almost threatening.

Rani knew enough not to press her objection further and relented. "I understand, Kishore Sahib. I will arrange everything."

"Good." Kishore released his grip on her shoulders and walked away to his chair.

• • •

Rani's sense of urgency increased as her speeding car neared its secluded destination.

At seven o'clock in the evening, she had dropped off the Shark and Shanti at Kishore's cabin, tucked away forty minutes' car ride into the mountains. She'd made sure the cabin was well-stocked with food and drinks, and told them she'd return in the morning to fix them breakfast and give them a ride back.

Around midnight she was startled out of deep sleep by the ringing of the phone. On the line was Kishore. "Get to the cabin immediately. I will meet you there," he said and hung up. Ever since that call, her pulse hadn't stopped racing. When she reached Kishore's property, she saw his station wagon parked next to the cabin porch. She raced to the door; it was ajar. Inside she saw the Shark in a robe sitting on the sofa. The robe was unable to fully cover the rotund belly of the deeply-tanned, balding, middle-aged, short pedophile. He was speaking in a low voice to Kishore, who was standing next to him and quietly listening.

"What's going on? Where is Shanti?" Rani said aloud and, without waiting for an answer, she rushed into the bedroom.

The diminutive Shanti lay naked on her back over the rumpled white sheet covering the king bed. Her head rested on a large soft pillow; her eyes were wide open and staring at the ceiling. Her legs were apart, exposing blood stains on the white sheet.

The sickening sight stunned Rani. All she could do was whimper and utter in barely audible voice, "Shanti, Shanti, little angel. What have I done? Oh God, what have I done?"

She felt a hand on her shoulder: Kishore had followed her into the bedroom. With watery eyes, she said, "Look at what that monster has done to the sweet, innocent Shanti: He's murdered her. I promised her parents that I would keep her safe . . . that I would bring her back to them safely. God! Why did he have to kill her?" She broke into violent sobbing.

Kishore patted her shoulder and said in a soothing voice, "It was an accident. He says he drank a lot and gave Shanti some to relax her. After he finished with her he passed out on top of her for some time. When he rolled off of her, he noticed she was not breathing."

As she listened to Kishore, her grief gave way to anger. "I will make that bastard pay for this."

Kishore's tone changed: It became firm and unemotional. "You will do no such thing. You will stay here and clean her up and make her body presentable for her parents. Then you will tidy up the place. Dr. Mathew is on his way here to attest to the death of Shanti being the result of unexplained embolism or such; that should appease the family. Also, I am doubling the stipend you will give to the family; I will have the cash in your hands when you take the child to the family. As for the Shark, he will be out of the country in a few hours."

Rani was enraged even more by Kishore's detached attitude and insensitive tone. She shot back in a defiant, loud voice, "No more orders from you. I said I will make that scum pay, and I will. I am going straight to Sharma Sahib to report the murder." With that she rushed out of the room.

• • •

A young beggar, with his body covered by tattered shorts and undershirt, walked to a dozen or so street dwellers bunched together in the shadow of a building, trying to escape the punishing sun, and said, "Have you heard? Rani's been arrested."

"What? Our Rani arrested? Not possible; you are mistaken," an old man said in disbelief.

"It is so. It is all over the bazaar."

"But why?" someone asked.

"Police Chief Sharma had her arrested for whoring and selling drugs," the boy replied in an animated voice as if doing an exposé.

"Selling drugs? Everybody is doing it. And whoring? What of it? She has been whoring since she was a child. Sharma lost his virginity to her," someone said with irritation in his voice.

There were disgusted looks and head shaking.

Puffing on a frayed and mangled *hookah,* one man with weathered face and white beard said, "That cocaine-addicted pig Sharma sold the body of his own kid sister to gain favor and power from politicians. His own sister! What possible reason that . . . that bastard has to arrest Rani for prostitution and drugs?"

There were more sighs and comments as others in the group started to absorb the gravity of the news.

"This will destroy her life."

"That spineless bastard has gone mad."

"Poor Rani—so young and fresh, never a sharp word, always smiling, always sensual. Praise God."

"Oh Almighty *Bhagwan.* Please protect our Rani."

"Amen."

• • •

Rani was starting to wake up. She felt numb and disoriented. She opened her eyes slowly: The light hurt her eyes. She saw she was lying on the floor of a dungeon-like room. She noticed she was naked, and her clothes—ripped and bloody—were strewn around her; she heard herself making uncontrollable, incoherent sounds.

Her mind was becoming clearer. She closed her eyes to concentrate, and she started to remember:

When she had reached the police station, she was met by three men at the entrance who identified themselves as detectives in the Criminal Investigation Division. They informed her she was under arrest and they were taking her in for questioning. They became rude and contemptuous when she insisted on seeing the Police Chief Sharma. Out of desperation, she warned them she had powerful contacts and they could face severe consequences for their bad behavior. They only laughed and whisked her away to a heavily guarded fortress-like bungalow outside the city and brought her into the inhospitable room she was in. Once there, they told her their orders were to allow no one to get near her. They also announced that their reward for arresting and guarding her was to enjoy her as they pleased. She was horrified. They ripped off her clothing and proceeded to repeatedly take turns with her to satisfy their gluttonous sexual appetites. But she remembered that, after numerous assaults, mere sexual gratification hadn't been enough for the last detective, a short, muscular young man with a cold stare. He was sadistic, and had satisfied his lust to inflict pain: He used his hands, teeth and a small, sharp, curved dagger to bloody her whole body. At first, her incessant shrieks filled the air. Then, finally, her merciful brain blocked out all signals of pain from her flesh, which was being torn to shreds at a leisurely pace. She blacked out.

Rani's mind snapped back to the present; she felt herself being dragged. Her senses were starting to come back; the all-pervasive pain was returning; she felt cold. She opened her eyes and saw two detectives dragging her by her arms into a well-lit room. They deposited her nude body on a chair. Facing her, beyond a huge, dark, mahogany desk, sat the lean and bearded Sharma, staring at her with emotionless eyes.

Rani was elated to see him: Sharma was a client—and a friend; she felt certain he'd save her from her tormentors. She looked at him with pleading eyes and asked, "Why? Why did they do this to me?"

Sharma replied in a calm voice, "You broke the unspoken rule."

She began to sob and said, "What rule? I did not break . . . any rule. Sharma, I was coming to you . . . for help . . . to report the murder of Shanti, a ten-year-old child, by a foreigner who is here to buy drugs. I . . . I wanted you to arrest him for killing one of our innocent children."

Sharma stroked his beard with slow, even motion. "He was buying drugs from me and my partners. Rani, I know this is confusing for you, and that is precisely why, my dear, you should have stuck to what you are good at: selling pleasure. Instead, you branched out into making moral judgments and demanding justice. No one asked you to do that; Kishore Sahib even ordered you to desist from acting on your threats. And now, you must die for it."

As Sharma spoke, Rani's optimism started to ebb and, by the time he finished, she was overcome with stark fear. Her body trembled; her voice became frantic. "Sharma, no . . . please let me explain. Horrific sight of Shanti lying dead shocked me. My . . . my emotions got the better of me. I procured the ten-year-old for the foreigner; I was devastated and felt responsible for her being dead. And . . . and I was enraged at the pedophile for smothering her to death. As *Bhagwan* is my witness, I wasn't thinking clearly when I defied Kishore Sahib. You must believe me, Sharma . . . you know me . . . I never demand anything . . . or confront or judge anyone. Am I right? Please, I beg you not to kill me . . . please."

Sharma spoke in a slow deliberate voice, "I cannot let you leave here after what has happened, now can I? It is out of my hands. You do understand that?"

Rani's pleading grew shrill. "Please, Sharma, have mercy. Please, Sharma, please. I am afraid to die. Do not kill me. I am not a threat to you or anyone else. I will do anything you say."

Sharma raised his eyebrows and gestured. "Well, if you swear you will never utter a word of this—"

"Yes, yes, I swear, I swear in the name of the Almighty. I will never speak of it to anyone. Please, I pray to you." Rani's naked body was shaking from uncontrollable sobbing.

Sharma sighed. "All right, Rani, you will live," he said in soothing voice. He raised his eyes to the detective standing behind Rani's chair and added with a nod, "Let her go."

Rani felt hope surge through her entire body. Her every nerve was tingling when she felt a sharp new pain in her back and chest. She looked down and saw the point of a sword emerging between her breasts. The next moment, she was dead.

Sharma didn't move a muscle; he simply stared at Rani. After about three seconds, he raised his hand and made a dismissive gesture. Two detectives lifted her lifeless body out of the chair. As they dragged her away, a trail of blood oozing out of her chest followed them.

13
Willie

RED CREEK WAS one of the small, nondescript towns in Arkansas. It was home to seventeen thousand people who depended on the rice and cotton farms and the poultry factories for their livelihood. Interstate Route Forty grazed the north end of the town. On either side of the interstate sat strip malls studded with liquor stores, fast-food places, and bars. Not far from the highway were small streets lined with trailer parks and dilapidated houses.

Willie lived in one of those houses with his parents.

One clammy, ninety-plus-degree summer afternoon, the seven-year-old Willie was helping his father, Joe, put away tools in the garage.

Joe was a middle-aged, flabby and graying production-line worker in a nearby poultry factory. On that day, he'd grunted and cussed his way through the replacing of a leaky radiator hose on his fifty-five Chevy parked in the dirt driveway overrun with weeds. He slammed down the hood of the car and said, "The bitch's finally done." He wiped the sweat off his face with his filthy shirtsleeves, picked up his beer bottle and two wrenches and walked into the garage. There, he handed the bottle, with a swallow of warm beer left in it, to Willie. "Finish it off," he said.

Willie took the bottle and sniffed it; the beer smell didn't appeal to him. "I don't want to."

It was quite clear Joe was surprised by his son's refusal. "Don't recall giving you a choice, son. Aren't you thirsty?"

"I'll go inside and drink water," replied Willie, feeling uncomfortable.

Joe, looking irritated, raised his eyebrows and said in an adamant tone, "You'll drink beer; you hear, boy. It's a man's drink. Now, drink up."

Willie grimaced, but inched the bottle up to his lips. He took a small sip and promptly spat it out.

Joe was enraged at what Willie did. He grabbed him by the neck and snatched the bottle out of his hand. "When I say drink, I mean drink. Don't you dare stop till the bottle's empty." Then, he forced the bottle into his mouth.

Willie was scared; he somehow swallowed the warm, disgusting beer. But, even before Joe could remove the bottle from his mouth, he started to heave. Within seconds, he was vomiting, bent over with hands on his knees. He didn't hear Joe shout, "Why, you son-of-a-bitch," but he felt six or so stinging lashes from Joe's belt. His loud cries from the sharp pain and fear brought Edith, his scrawny mother, running out of the house.

Edith's protective arms engulfed Willie, who was howling in pain. With bewilderment in her eyes, she shrieked at Joe, who was trying to avoid eye contact with her, "What happened? Why has he thrown up? Are you trying to kill him with that belt, you good-for-nothing drunk?"

Joe growled and said, "Get out of my way, woman. Your son's too goddamn sissy to give himself a chance to like the good, ol' American drink." Then he stomped into the house without paying attention to Edith's further rebuke.

Willie was eight before Joe pressured him again to drink beer. One Saturday afternoon, they were watching a Razorback football game on television. Joe opened two cans of beer and handed him one. Willie started to feel nauseated. The smell of beer brought back a vivid memory of the vomiting episode. Staring at the beer can, he pleaded, "Dad, it's yucky; I hate it. It makes me throw up. Could I have a soda?"

Joe gave him a menacing look. "Son, if you're smart, you'll finish the can without any more lip," he said, as he held his own beer resting on his potbelly. The can and his belly moved to the rhythm of his strained breathing.

Edith was hunched over her ironing. She scolded Joe in a shrill voice, "Leave the boy alone, you hear? I don't want him to grow up and be a drunken maniac like you."

"Oh, hush, woman. This boy has to learn to be a man—you know, take care of himself. A couple belts of beer never hurt no one."

"It helped you none. All you do is get loud-mouthed, mean and ornery," the feisty Edith said, without looking up from her ironing.

"Enough of this yakking from you," he said glaring at her. Then he turned to Willie and smiled. "You know what, boy? Me and you are going to be drinking buddies. C'mon, son, let's raise hell together."

Willie was scared; he took a sip and managed to keep it down. He looked at his towering father, who was nodding at him with a smirk of approval. He felt a surge of pride, and relief.

• • •

Willie was drinking hard liquor by age ten, and doing drugs by eleven. Girls came later—much later. He was busy impressing his father with the tough-guy image required of him. He hung around the unsavory element in the streets and soon gained acceptance in the neighborhood's gang of juvenile thieves, drug-pushers and junkies. He couldn't stand going to school. He knew his father, too, couldn't care less about his schooling, as long as he didn't let anyone push him around, and did manly things. So, whenever he was caught cutting classes, the standard excuse he gave his father was that he'd gone hunting with the boys. Joe would then order the reluctant Edith to write a note to the school with a drummed-up reason for his absence.

One late afternoon, Willie, then thirteen, was sitting on the front steps of his house and waiting for his friends when Edith returned from her errands.

As the frail Edith eased herself up the steps, she said, "Hi, dear, now don't be out too late."

"Hi, Mom."

"I'll save you some supper."

"Okay, mom," said Willie, without looking at her. He heard the front door close behind her. He sat motionless with his head leaning toward the house; he strained to eavesdrop.

"So, woman, you went and saw the school principal this morning. Willie told me all about it."

"I couldn't write lies in the note today. I just couldn't do it. Joe, our boy needs to be in school—studying—and not on the streets."

"You told the principal I've been allowing Willie to cut classes—"

"No, I didn't. The boy's telling stories."

"And you told him I made you write lies in the notes. Goddamn bitch, how could you do that to me?"

There was a loud bang; something was knocked over.

"I wouldn't do that, Joe. You got to believe me"

Willie heard sounds of slaps, blows, piercing cries—all intermingled and in quick succession. Then, only the sobs and painful wailing of Edith remained. He heard Joe shout, "Woman, if you ever talk to anyone in school again—anyone, I'll kill you. You hear? I'll kill you. Now fix me supper." Willie heard his sobbing mother scurrying in the kitchen. He had a smile on his face: He hoped his father's violence and threat would deter her from smothering him.

Minutes later, a noisy old convertible, belching smoke, pulled up with four rough-looking youths in it. All were chewing gum and moving their heads to the beat of loud rock music emanating from the car radio. Willie jumped into the back seat and the convertible sped off, squealing tires and leaving behind a cloud of dust.

• • •

Edith made valiant efforts to keep Willie in school; but she failed, largely because of Joe's contempt for schooling. She'd also tried to control and guide him away from her husband's gutter behavior and influence. But Joe wore her down; he ignored her, and beat her. She lost the battle to save Willie. She died of cancer when he was sixteen; but she'd given up on life a long time before her death. Willie paid little attention to her when she was alive, and quickly forgot her after she died.

• • •

Willie parked his souped-up Ford Fairlane across from the school ballpark. He and his three gang members in matching brown leather jackets got out and approached a muscular young Latino in a black T-shirt who was conversing with two white men standing under a basketball hoop. Willie pretended to be surprised. *"Amigo,* what's going down? I thought last week I told you to stay out of my territory."

The Spanish gangster swaggered around to face him and pointed a bobbing finger at him. "I can't do that, man. You know, there's enough business here for both of us, man. Everything's cool."

Willie remained calm. "You don't hear so good, *Amigo.* I said nothing about enough business for both of us, did I? No. I said this is my territory and . . . *you* don't deal in my territory."

"And I say me and my friends'll do business here. That's it."

"Okay. Let me put it another way." Next instant, his fist smashed into the face of the Spanish guy, knocking him unconscious.

Willie's friends, with hands on the guns in their jacket pockets, had taken positions in front of the other two intruders who could do nothing except clench their teeth and fists and watch.

Willie turned to the shaken friends of the man lying senseless on the ground with blood trickling out of his nose and mouth. "Get that piece of shit out of here. If I catch your candy-asses here again you'll leave in body bags." He surveyed the audience that had gathered around him. A large number of school kids—his customers —witnessed the whole incident. *This is a great message for the pretty boys. It'll keep 'em in line; they'll buy drugs only from us,* he thought.

It didn't take him long to become a symbol of fear in Red Creek, and run the most vicious gang, which was also the sole distributor of narcotics. By age eighteen, he'd been arrested numerous times on charges of drug trafficking and violence. But none of the charges could be substantiated, and he was

never convicted. He was living and doing things simply to satisfy his ego and his appetite for excitement. His father didn't
matter to him anymore.

• • •

The three friends were relaxing in the best hotel suite Red
Creek had to offer. The two-room suite had a musty smell of
cigarettes, gasoline and humidity; it had run-down furniture,
and stained linen and carpets. The hotel was a part of the
truck-stop complex on Route Forty. Willie was sprawled on
one bed, and Chino and Bud were stretched out on the other.
They were high from cocaine and beer. The prostitutes had
just left because it was eight o'clock on a cool, late-fall Friday
evening—a prime time to get paying customers.

Willie was restless. "I need action. Let's go." He jumped
out of the bed.

Bud asked in a tired voice, "Go where, man?"

"Let's go teach the ol' bitch at the liquor store a lesson.
Nobody messes with me."

Bud said, "She didn't mess with you, man. She just didn't
let you take beer without paying cash. She doesn't care who
anybody is. Man, sometimes she even forgets where she is.
That flake's over seventy years old. Forget her, man."

Willie was adamant. "No. She'll pay for disrespecting me
in front of people."

Chino said in a cajoling voice, "There was no one else—
only us, man. Aw c'mon, Willie, give it a rest."

He glared at his friends. "No. I say let's go—now," he
said as he sifted through the leather jackets on the couch and
picked up his own.

The three piled into Willie's Ford and rode in silence, listening to the rock-and-roll music. He parked the car across

the street from the Discount Liquor Store. They waited for the customers to leave. When only one customer was left in the store, Willie said to Bud and Chino, "You wait in the car. I'll be right back with the booze and cash the bitch owes me."

He entered the store. He saw the thin, hunch-backed woman with a heavily creased face standing behind the counter. She was eyeing him as she chomped on her toothless gums. Willie walked over to the wine racks and pretended to look at some bottles: He had to wait for the customer to leave. He moved down the aisle to the whiskey bottles. He noticed the customer was at the counter paying for his purchases. He picked up a whiskey bottle and walked toward the counter as the customer walked out the door. With a slight smirk on his face, he asked the woman, "Remember me, bitch?"

The woman stared at him and replied in a shrill voice, "I recognize you, you punk. Got smart with me this afternoon—tried to get free beer."

By then Willie had taken out his gun and reached the counter. With cold eyes fixed on the woman, he said without emotion, "I'll teach you a lesson for messing with me."

The old woman waved a trembling finger at him, and her voice got shriller. "Don't you point that thing at me; you scare me none. I've sent the alarm in already, and cops'll be here any second. You good-for-nothing—"

Willie snapped from rage and drugs. He said, "You old bitch." Then he cracked the woman's head hard with the gun. She let out a piercing cry and fell to the floor. He looked over the counter, and saw her moaning and writhing there, with blood trickling from the side of her head. He put the whiskey bottle on the counter, pocketed the money from the cash register, and fired a shot into her. As he picked up the whiskey bottle, he heard sirens; he ran out of the store. He reached the car and was about to open the door when he saw two state troopers a few yards away, rushing toward him with guns drawn. His mind went blank.

The next thing he heard was Bud, in the front passenger's seat, screaming at him: "Get in, man. Let's get out of here!"

He saw the two troopers lying on the ground; one was twitching, and one was still. The gun in his hand was empty, but his index finger kept pulling the trigger.

Once again Bud shouted, "C'mon, man. Let's go."

He jumped into the car and floored the accelerator. He felt as if his brain was in a fog, and shook his head to clear it.

Chino in the back seat was shaking with fear. "You killed two cops. You dumb bastard, you killed two cop!"

With perspiration drops trickling down his temples, Willie shouted, "Just shut the hell up. We got to stay cool, man. We got to get out of the town, fast."

"Where can we go?" asked Bud.

"I don't know. Shit, let's head for the Ozark Mountains . . . best we stay on back-roads till . . . till we hit some big city up north. Then, we ditch the car and hole up somewhere."

As the Ford Fairlane was disappearing into the dark countryside, the police and detectives were converging on the grim, bloody scene the three friends had left behind.

• • •

"It's cold back here. Put the heat on."

"Chino, the heat *is* on."

"Just jack the damn thing up, man."

"Schmuck," said Willie as he complied. He knew his friends were very nervous and afraid. His own hands were shaking. Actually, he was shaking all over—from excitement, not fear. He was experiencing a rush from playing over and over in his mind the scene of killing the old woman; he felt no remorse.

Bud asked in a shaking voice, "What's the matter with you? Why did you have to kill the old woman? What were you trying to prove, man?"

Willie answered with emphasis, "I told you already. She pissed me off."

Chino leaned forward and said in a loud voice, "Then you waste two cops. You don't jump in the car and run, you kill two cops."

Irritated, Willie said, "They were state troopers and, for Christ sake, don't scream in my damn ear. Sit back."

Chino mumbled something and sat back.

Bud banged on the dashboard with both hands. "We're going to die. Cops'll kill us for sure."

Willie said with confidence, "They can't catch us." Then he threw the gun in Bud's lap and added, "Here, load it up."

Bud looked surprised. "What you want with the gun, man? You ain't picking a fight with no more cops."

Willie clenched his teeth. "Don't argue with me. Load the damn gun."

Bud shook his head, opened the glove compartment, and reached for the ammunition.

Chino continued to express displeasure at Willie. "Your macho shit's done it this time. Goddamn it, they'll get us for what you've done."

Willie was exasperated. "Damn it, Chino. Just clam up." He speeded up the car on the straight road through a dense forest.

A blanket of clouds blocked the light from the moon and stars. Inside the dark car, silence prevailed for two to three minutes; then it was shattered by Chino's frantic voice from the back seat. "Cops! They're behind us."

Willie looked in the rearview mirror and saw two head-lights and a flashing red light closing in fast.

Bud became frantic. "Get out of here,"

Willie pressed his foot on the gas pedal. The Fairlane roared and pulled away from the pursuing county police unit.

Bud and Chino chanted: "Go! Go! Go! . . ."

Willie turned on the high beams to push the darkness farther away down the straight road. With his eyes squinting and the car flying forward, he was able to detect a hint of flashing lights. Tense with excitement, he said, "Roadblock!"

"Now what, man?" Bud asked.

Willie laughed. "They can't stop us, man; we'll go right through. Hang on."

Chino implored, "No, no, don't. Stop! Stop!"

Willie ignored him; his mind was made up. He rolled down the window; picked up the gun with his left hand, cocked it and held it outside the window. With his right hand clutching the steering wheel, and accelerator at full throttle, he aimed the car at the roadblock. The next instant he had a sinking feeling in the pit of his stomach: His Ford was losing power. He looked at the gas gauge; its pointer was on empty.

Chino shouted, "The cops are closing behind us."

Bud grabbed Willie's shoulder. "Hit the gas!"

Willie said through pursed lips, "Can't; we're out of gas."

He brought the Ford to a screeching halt about fifty feet from the roadblock. Blinding headlights from the front and behind lit up his car.

A state trooper, manning the blockade, spoke through a bullhorn: "Come out with your hands up."

"We can take them," Willie said with conviction.

Chino was trembling. "You're crazy, man. I'm outta here."

Bud's forehead was covered with sweat. "Me, too. I don't want to die."

Willie smiled with a determined look. "All right, guys. You win. Let's go."

The three doors opened. Chino and Bud emerged with hands up in the air.

Willie started to emerge with one hand in the air and shouted, "Don't shoot." The next instant he dropped to the ground and fired shots at the headlights pointed at them. He thought he could make a run for it in the darkness. He managed to hit three of the six lights.

But by then the barrage of return gunfire had cut down the unarmed Chino and Bud, and made a mess of the Ford. Willie lay in a pool of blood. Bullets had struck him on the right shoulder and thigh, but he was alive.

A county policeman grabbed him by the collar and dragged him away from the Ford to the roadside. "You goddamn low-life, got your two buddies killed for nothing, huh? I've got a good mind to put a bullet in you and end it all."

Another policeman said, "Simmer down. Just handcuff the bastard."

"Oh, I know. I'm just spouting off. Shit. All this . . . such a waste."

"This dope-pushing murderer's finally going to get what's been coming to him for a long time. No judge or jury'll be able to let him go free this time."

"Damn right. Now he's responsible for five deaths. Well, well, well. We finally won't have to worry about our bad boy Willie anymore."

• • •

The time for Willie to receive the lethal dose had arrived. He'd put on a brave act until then—cussing, laughing and joking— even with the priest, who tried to give him the last rites. As he lay strapped on the gurney in an aseptic, all-white room, he saw solemn faces watching him through the glass windows. He couldn't recognize anyone.

Then—imperceptibly—the transformation set in. He was overcome with a sudden fear and felt tightness in his chest: He was afraid to die. He felt alone; he closed his eyes. He was no longer a tough man of twenty: He'd regressed, and his mind was that of a child craving a protective and comforting hug. He started shaking, and tears streamed out of his closed eyes.

Willie felt a prick in his arm that was being held steady by a firm grip. He opened his eyes and saw a plastic tube connecting his arm to the I. V. bags hanging from a metal stand. He saw liquid dripping into the tubing. He turned his eyes toward the man holding his arm. The man was looking at him with sympathy in his eyes. Willie felt a connection with him.

Long moments passed.

Then Willie said in a shaking voice, "Dad. I'm afraid. Please don't let them hurt me. Please, Dad—" He couldn't keep his eyes open. His agitation started to subside, and soon he went to sleep. He was no longer afraid.

14
Somewhere

STEVE HAD KEPT his eyes closed while his mind sped through the life capsules of his group members. At the end, he felt confident and relieved: Now he had sufficient ammunition to fire back if one or more of them would be foolish enough to start taking shots at him.

He finally opened his eyes. He noticed Antov was sitting upright with folded hands, glum face, and eyes focused on the floor; Oku was frowning and looking straight ahead, while his left leg shook, betraying nervousness and anxiety; Rani was staring at the people leaving from the exit doors; and, Willie sat with hands behind his head and his intense eyes surveyed others in the circle.

What's with these guys? Why don't they speak? Since his attempt to start a conversation had been rebuffed by them and had ended up being a tactical blunder on his part, Steve decided not to repeat the fiasco and tried to occupy himself with watching the staff welcome an unending flow of people into the center. But his impatience was mounting and making him nervous. *What's the holdup with the damn review? Why won't they get on with it?*

Suddenly, Willie broke the silence. "Man, this is great!" He was grinning and wasn't speaking to anyone in particular;

his eyes continued to dart from person to person. "This just came to me: I've got a fifty-fifty chance of walking through the right door into the arms of an angel. Can you believe that? Man, I've never had such high odds before and had to fight for everything I got. Ma always said: 'Be good and you'll go to heaven.' Ha, good thing I didn't listen to that square woman; and, actually, I told her to shove it. Man, getting this kind of odds after death makes me feel glad I did all the fun and exciting scenes, you know—"

Steve looked at Willie in disgust and interrupted him in a sharp voice, "Oh, shut the hell up, will you? Who said the odds for you are an even fifty-fifty? What do you think they do, just toss a coin to determine your fate? For all you know, they may have already judged you, and decided to burn your sorry ass in hell. You know, a punk like you doesn't deserve a choice or a chance. You should burn in hell for the lousy things you've done in your blasted short life—murders, rapes, drugs."

Willie ignored the blistering tirade and said in a smug tone, "Odds are fifty-fifty, man, because I get to pick the door."

"You moron, if you pay attention to what's going on around here you'll see that you have nothing to do with picking a door. You see that door-lady there? She'll push you out a door based on the judgment already passed on you here. Willie Boy, they'll pick the door for you—the door to hell. Now what do you have to say?" Steve couldn't bear the thought of a low-life like Willie having the same chance as he did to get into heaven. To him, luck had nothing to do with going to heaven or hell.

Willie said nothing. He had stopped grinning; it was obvious that his spirits were sagging, and he was grappling with Steve's dire assessment of his fate.

Oku's face had turned thoughtful as he listened to the exchange between Willie and Steve. "There is no way they will send me to hell: I have done nothing wrong. You just wait and see. When I go through the door, my mother and father will be waiting on the other side to take me to heaven."

Antov looked up from the floor and said to Oku, "Excuse me, but there is no heaven for you. You did not honor the wish of your father to talk to him because you were too scared of the rebels and could not walk a few yards to where he lay wounded. You urinated in your pants out of fear and left the village to run away from the revolution of the people. All that means you are a coward. Also, you were not very smart to not join the rebels, because all that did was get you and your mother killed. Is that not so? The important question for you to answer today is: What did you accomplish in life on earth to deserve a place in heaven?"

Oku became defensive. "I wanted to learn and do big things, but I didn't have a chance to do anything: I didn't have time."

Antov didn't seem sympathetic. "How long you were on earth means nothing. But it seems to me you had plenty of time to learn to be afraid."

Steve, with a refreshed memory of his own life, cut in, "I accomplished a lot." He was pouncing on a ray of hope and trying to convince himself. "With all the good I did for society and my family by making myself successful, there's no way I'd be condemned to hell."

Willie sneered. "Bullshit, big shot; hell is for exactly the people like you. You had everything; you didn't need to sin, but you did anyway. You knifed people in the back in business; lied and cheated to get your way and make big bucks; kicked your relatives' asses when they were down; and screwed around with broads right under your wife's nose. At least I had the guts to face the people I whacked and admit what I was. And I didn't have to sneak around and cheat on my wife because—very simple—I decided to remain single, and just screw. Also—"

Antov didn't let him finish. He pointed an accusing finger at him and Steve, and said with disdain, "You both did contemptuous and cruel things for personal gains. For that you must be judged harshly." Then he added with pride, "Yes, I too did cruel things; I killed more than once. But it was never for personal gain. I did it for my country, for the revolution, and for my party. Whatever I did I did to rid my country of its enemies; that was a noble cause. There is no question I'm a hero, and that will guarantee heaven for me."

Steve and Willie stared at Antov, unconvinced. They shook their heads, but neither said a word.

But Rani, who'd been silent until then, said in an accusatory tone, "How the three of you can even dare to think about being allowed to enter heaven? You have cheated, you have killed, you have caused suffering to your loved ones and others; and it matters not why you did those heartless things. The ones who will go to heaven are those who suffered at your hands and at the hands of people like you. I was raped, tortured and killed; I suffered a lot. Now, my suffering will end forever, and I will be with *Bhagwan*. And you? You'll be reincarnated back to earth to pay for your sins."

Steve was irritated. *So, this olive-skinned broad thinks she's on a higher moral ground than I am. Well, screw her.* He said in a sharp voice, "Now you listen, cutie. First of all, you believe in reincarnation; we believe in hell. But, that aside, one thing is certain: neither is heaven. Second, it's odd that you, a member of one of the vilest and most depraved professions in the world, are passing judgment on us. You were nothing but a well-paid whore and pimp running a prostitution and drug ring. When you foolishly messed with the wrong people, you had to pay with your life. Was it unfortunate? Yes, absolutely. But does it qualify you to enter heaven, nirvana, whatever? I wouldn't be too sure if I were you."

Rani grew vehement. "But I led the only life I was trained for right from childhood. My parents gave me away because we were very poor, and *Bhagwan* knows I was forced into prostitution."

Willie covered his mouth to muffle his laugh. "Sure He does, baby. He also knows that you renounced poverty and your parents when you got a taste of riches. And, by the way, what do you think I was trained for? Priesthood? Huh? Maybe a . . . a rock star, or a scientist? So, why would I go to hell for the crummy things I did? My father forced me to learn those things when I was only a kid. He beat the crap out of me if I didn't drink, do drugs, watch him abuse women, and mess with guns and knives. There was no room for a Boy Scout in our house, you know?"

Silence fell over the group.

Steve realized he'd just participated in sniping and character assassination—the very behavior his instinct had forewarned him to expect from his group members. *Okay, so everyone tried to smear others to bolster personal odds of ending up in heaven. But, did this competition to look better really help, or did it make us look like petty schmucks? What would happen if we're supportive of one another?* As he struggled with his creeping ambivalence, he looked at the group members. He detected no one in the group was afraid anymore, but the defensive and confrontational tone of the conversation had lowered everyone's spirits, and the mood had become morose.

He said to Oku, Antov and Rani. "It's surprising how well you three speak English."

All three raised their eyebrows and looked at him.

Rani said, "I know some English; but I am speaking Hindi—we are all speaking Hindi."

Antov was emphatic. "I only know Slavic, and I understand everybody here."

"What is English?" asked Oku.

Willie broke in with a bewildered look, "Wow! Looks like we can understand and speak all languages."

Once again, everyone became quiet. They looked at one another, obviously confused and needing time to digest the revelation made by Willie, who sat back with eyes closed.

Steve withdrew to his own muddled thoughts. *Things are happening too damn fast. It's uncanny how others and I've learned to understand different languages so quickly. Wow, being dead does have advantages—all these new powers. Too damn bad you have to be dead to get these abilities. Umm . . . there seems to be a common thread in all this. Communication? Yes, that's it. These new abilities are promoting communication by removing barriers. And, of course, one other thing's happening: Our lives are completely exposed. Everyone knows everything about everybody, even our thoughts.*

He took a deep breath as his mind changed its focus. Once again it dwelled on the people leaving through the two exit doors—the only way out of the dome. *I've got to find a way to leave through the right door,* he thought with his anxiety returning.

His mind flashed back to when Don McCoy was discussing material for a potential book with him. He remembered Don speculating or arguing that every human was a god. *What a laugh. I'd love to see his face when he gets here. It'll be a rude awakening for him. Poor Don. Just look at us: We're definitely not gods. If we were, we wouldn't be waiting around here to be grilled and judged by others and face those blasted two doors, and whatever may be behind them. Sorry Don, old friend, you*

*and I aren't gods and this isn't our experiment. It's a good thing
we set up the Zeller Foundation. I hope the work you do there'll
help you figure out the whole mess.*

The waiting was getting tiresome for Steve; he wished
they'd hurry up and get the group meeting going. He again
tried to keep his mind occupied by looking around at other
groups and eavesdropping on a few conversations. But he
soon tired of that activity and reverted to thinking about the
long discourses he'd had with Don about religions, birth-life-
death and violence. He chuckled when he remembered the
questions Don couldn't handle, such as: If we're gods, then
what are other creatures, such as animals, insects and birds?
Are they gods, too? He also appreciated Don's simple answer,
"I just don't know."

• • •

After what seemed like an eternity to Steve, a person in the
light-blue uniform walked over to the group and sat down in
the sixth chair. He was pleasant, and addressed the group
with a smile. "Hello. I'll be your host during your brief stop
at this center. We realize you've been through a lot—life and
death; and now you're subjected to strange happenings and
new powers without preparation. I apologize for the resulting confusion and apprehension on your part; but it can't be
helped. I'll try to make our time together as comfortable
as possible. By the way, since you're still more proficient in
speaking rather than engaging one another with your minds,
we'll continue our discourse verbally."

Steve asked, "Why do you call yourself a 'host'? Why not
what you really are: a judge?" His boldness was returning.

The other four trained their eyes at the host. Antov wore
a frown, and Willie, a smirk.

The host made eye contact with everyone and said in a reassuring tone, "Please remain calm and listen. We've already compiled a complete chronology of everything that happened to you and everything you did on the earth. So we're not here to discuss that. Right now you're being given a chance, like everyone who has passed through here—"

Steve couldn't help interrupting. "Speaking of passing through here, does everyone who dies pass through here?"

"Yes, every human being—no exceptions."

"In that case, my wife and daughter were here about six months ago. I want to know if they're okay."

The host said, "Erika and Kathy went through here less than a minute ago; they are just fine."

Steve said with exasperation, "A minute? You didn't hear me correctly. I said they died six months ago."

The host's tone remained unchanged and accommodating. "I heard you correctly. But, the dimension of time we are in here is different. The time on earth goes by considerably more rapidly than here: A year on the earth translates to about a minute here. I am sorry; I should've anticipated the confusion." The host paused and looked around at the group.

All remained silent; their brains were clearly straining to digest the host's new revelation.

Steve realized his thirty-five years on the earth equated to just over a measly half an hour in the new time-dimension he was in. Intrigued, he gestured toward the group and asked, "What about the five of us?"

"What about the five of you?" the host asked back.

"Are we here together because we left the earth about the same time?"

The host replied, "Not necessarily. Though one of you may have arrived here within minutes or seconds of another, some

of you died years apart. Again, that's because of the difference in the time concept here and on the earth."

Antov said, "Something I must ask: Are the five of us here
because we all died from unnatural causes—you know, execu-
tion, accident, starvation?"

The host shook his head. "Your coming together as a
group wasn't planned; it was a random occurrence."

Antov was unconvinced. "I cannot believe our sitting
together is only a coincidence?"

"Yes, it is." The host looked around and waited for more
questions.

Steve wanted to pursue the subject further, but changed
his mind and asked, "Which door did Erika and Kathy leave by?"

The host answered, "Erika left by the red door, and Kathy
by the white door."

Steve was shocked. *Why didn't they leave together? Why
were they separated? How could they have been judged differently?* He became quiet and shook his head, unable to come
to terms with what he'd heard. He began to brood over the
fate of Erika and Kathy: *Which one was sent to hell? Why? It
couldn't have been Kitten: She was such a gentle, loving child.
And . . . and how could it be Erika? She was so uncomplicated,
kind-hearted, committed; so dedicated to helping the homeless
children and charities. This is bullshit—judging two pure, loving,
giving individuals so differently. Damn it, it makes no sense.* The
more he dwelled on the fate of his loved ones the angrier he
got. He blurted out, "How can they leave by different doors?
What kind of asinine judges you have here?"

The host looked at him with sympathy. "Steve, every life is
unique, and is treated as such."

Steve retorted, "As it should be. But you do agree that
both, Erika and Kathy, deserved heaven, don't you?"

He realized the futility of his diatribe and the fact that he had insulted the hosts. The consequences for him could be disastrous. He softened his tone. "Enough said."

The host nodded at him and then said to the group, "Now, let us go back and pick up where we left off. Ah yes, I was saying that every one of you has an opportunity to share any thoughts, impressions, perceptions, or feelings that are meaningful to you, or were meaningful to you in your life on earth. To accomplish that effectively, we must keep a few simple ground rules in mind: anything you say is strictly voluntary; my job is to listen, document, and facilitate the group's interactions. I may, from time to time, ask questions to help you explore further, expand, or clarify your thoughts. I won't judge or critique you or your remarks. I can't engage in any discourse or answer questions about your lives' journey up to this point, or the final leg waiting for you beyond this point; and finally, you must not challenge or criticize one another."

Steve remained dubious. "Excuse me for not buying the explanation you just gave for this gathering. It seems like this is a court, and you want to hear my side before deciding on the door to send me through. From where I sit, that's passing judgment to send me to either heaven or hell."

The host smiled. "You're entitled to your opinion about what's happening here. As a matter of fact, a majority of people passing through here feel the way you do about these proceedings. And that's fine, so long as we follow the process in an orderly fashion while you're here."

"Thanks for actually following the ground rules you just laid out. You didn't take issue with my opinion. I'm impressed," Steve said, softening his tone further. Then, without waiting for the host's reaction, he asked, "Can you tell me if I'll see my Erika and kitten again?"

Oku's face lit up and he said in an emphatic voice, "And I want to see my parents."

"Before I head for heaven, it'd be kinda fun to stop by hell for a moment and run into my old man," Willie said with a snicker.

The host signaled them to stop talking. His voice was compassionate, yet firm. "Your questions and requests are perfectly legitimate. But, for me to say anything about them would be a violation of the ground rules. I ask you to be patient; you'll have all the answers shortly."

Oku and Willie became quiet and settled back in their chairs.

Feeling sheepish, Steve said, "I'm sorry."

The host acknowledged his apology with a wave of his hand and asked the group, "Should we start our discussion now?"

The five nodded.

"Well then, who wants to go first?"

Steve answered, "I will. Frankly, I've got to get something off my chest. It's been driving me crazy for the last few months."

The host gestured to him and said, "Please go ahead."

"I'm angry at God's warped sense of justice on the earth: I'm angry with Him for the senseless deaths of my wife and daughter. Why does He stand idly by while innocent and helpless lives are destroyed, turned upside down, or cut short by the scum He's created, who often escape punishment and live to a ripe old age in comfort and luxury? Why? It just doesn't make any sense to me."

The host said, "I understand your anger. But, hard as it is for everyone, there is a sound reason for not interfering."

Steve's voice was emphatic. "That's a lot of bull. All God has to do is demonstrate His sense of justice by handing out harsh and public punishment to some of the lowlifes. That'll send a clear message to every murdering punk and coward and the world will be a much better place for all of us."

The host countered, "The religious leaders and—"

Steve knew what was coming and it irritated him enough to interrupt the host. "Why not communicate directly to people? Why religions and the self-appointed 'chosen' mortals have to act as His intermediaries and the deliverers of His message? That only makes His message susceptible to errors, ambiguity or misinterpretation. And worst of all, the violence goes on."

"Your opinion has merit."

Steve raised his hands in exasperation. "Does He really need *me* to point that out to Him? Unbelievable." He added a forced smile to his face and continued in his sarcastic tone, "*And*, by the way, all this indirect communication ends up getting Him a free pass from the confused people who don't know whether to revere Him, fear Him or love Him. When one child's born healthy or rich and the other's born deformed or poor, people shield Him with platitudes like, 'Life isn't fair,' or, 'God has His reasons,' or, 'God has a plan.' Humans also feel compelled to put a positive twist on His inconsistencies. Let's take an example of an earthquake: Life crushed out of hundreds, thousands of people by crumbling buildings is accepted as 'God's Will'; and the rescue of a few mortals who are buried alive under the same falling debris is hailed as 'A Miracle' attributed to 'A Merciful God.' People either don't want to or don't dare to see the irony or absurdity of those characterizations. This type of behavior by someone other than God would be considered callous, shallow and capricious."

The host said, "So you want God to demonstrate justice and consistency on the earth. Am I stating your view correctly?"

"Yes, you are," Steve replied.

Rani, looking more relaxed, said, "I do not feel angry with the Almighty as Steve does. After all, He created us. But I do feel that He must enunciate directly to us all a set of rules that humanity must live by. Selfish people, and even some good ones with mistaken beliefs, do a lot of horrendous things in His name."

"Don't you already have rules and codes of conduct?" the host asked.

Rani answered, "Yes, but they are man-made or, as Steve said, The Word of God is filtered to us through a chosen few; their interpretations pass as His rules."

The host asked, "What would His rules do for you?"

Rani was ready with her response. "They would eliminate confusion, mistakes, conflicts and violence arising out of warped or erroneous interpretations. Had such rules existed, people would not have dared to murder me."

Willie nodded and said, "Right on, baby. If God had rules for everyone to follow, I would've had a different and productive life, and my old man would've been history long before he corrupted me; maybe he'd have become a good-hearted, loving father. Man, who knows what I could've accomplished if my father and society hadn't failed me? The damn society wrote me off when I was just a peewee kid; and then, when I turned bad, it used all its energy to catch and punish me. But really, in a way I'm glad I was killed off early. If not, I would've brought pain, misery and death to a lot more people—all because of the way I was brought up. And guess what? I'm counting on God to take that into account before I'm judged."

The host smiled at him and posed a question to the group: "Is it possible for humans to come up with a unified, ethical code of conduct?"

Rani replied, "Not so long as there are self-centered or well-meaning-but-misguided people who are slaves to their egos and agendas."

"Does anyone disagree with Rani?"

The four shook their heads and Willie said, "Man, even if that was possible, it'll take a long, long time to come up with one."

Steve noticed that the group members were calm; they were actually listening to one another's views. He saw that even Willie was no longer defensive or abrasive, and had become thoughtful in his interactions with the others. He felt the host's reassuring demeanor had a lot to do with it. He also observed the host was sitting back and allowing the conversation to take place at a relaxed pace.

Oku, who'd been listening to the exchange between the group and the host, spoke up. "I am very resentful that I was not given a chance to live a full life. But still more important is this: I cannot understand the mass destruction of life. I do not care if it is nature causing famines, fires, epidemics, floods—things like that—or humans causing wars."

"Does the destroyed life get replaced?" the host asked.

Steve replied, "Probably. But here's the question for you: Why put in an effort to create millions of humans and animals, then turn right around and, kaput, destroy them in one fell swoop, or squeeze the life out of them slowly through starvation, as was the case with our friend here." He pointed to Oku, and added, "All this destruction, to what end? I think, from God's point of view, such actions would be so pointless, so senseless."

Antov picked up the thread of the conversation: "I support the feelings expressed by the others. I don't understand why God chooses to keep humanity in the dark about practically everything."

The host remained quiet and smiled at him.

Antov continued, "I grew up believing firmly in my sacred duty to the Motherland, and did everything to fully discharge it. I even executed our enemies."

"You were extremely proficient at your job," the host said with a hint of praise in his voice.

"Thank you. You would think God would be pleased with what I did. But He did not do anything to stop the selfish, insecure, power-hungry bureaucrats from murdering me; He even allowed them to corrupt the woman I loved into carrying out the cowardly and heinous deed."

The host nodded. "Your death was unfortunate and untimely."

"Right now, where am I headed—heaven or hell? I am not sure, and that is unfair. If I had known the purpose of God in creating us, I would most definitely not be in this predicament. I would have known how I would be judged, and lived my life in such a way that a place in heaven would have been assured for me. I think God owed me that much," Antov said.

The host's eyes narrowed. "Besides God telling you, is there another way to learn the purpose of creating humans?"

Antov paused for a moment before answering. "Other than the continuing self-serving, muddled and haphazard attempts by all types of humans, the only thing I can think of is what Steve has left behind: the Zeller Foundation."

Willie's tone was wistful. "It's too late for us. But Steve's foundation may eventually wind up helping people answer a lot of these questions."

Steve's first impression of Willie had been negative and, until then, he'd distrusted him. But he acknowledged his comments with a nod, and felt a surge of pride.

The host smiled at Steve. "Antov and Willie are right: You've left the earth quite a legacy. I've noted it down as a special event."

Steve accepted the compliment by smiling back. "What's a special event?"

"Simply put, it's an activity that's the first of its kind, and has the potential to dramatically change the direction of thinking and endeavor of humanity. Your foundation definitely falls into that category."

Steve felt modesty creeping in; he changed the subject. "If it's okay, I'd like to give you my take on the previous points raised by the group."

The host said, "Go ahead."

"I'd like God to maximize the value of humans. Everyone should be put on the earth with a clear understanding of God's expectations of him or her and be allowed to live a full life to accomplish as much as possible."

Antov nodded. "Just look at us. The lives of all five of us were cut short."

Steve continued, "My wife and daughter, too, died before experiencing full lives; I wanted to raise my sons and see them take over my financial enterprises; and I wanted to help my foundation achieve prominence. No one will ever know how much more every one of us would have accomplished with a full life."

The host said, "For example, Willie could have charted a more productive life—different from the one of killing or destroying others."

Steve glanced at Willie. "Yes, of course, if he'd been properly advised of his mission on the earth."

"True. I believe you've made your point." The host smiled and looked at the others to see if they had further comments. Taking the cue from their silence, he said, "Perhaps it's time to talk about something else. How about sharing your thoughts on your accomplishments, relationships and emotions—whatever you want. Who wants to start?"

Oku clasped his hands. "I accomplished nothing, but I did one bad thing: I was very afraid when they dragged my father out of our home and beat him. I did not—could not—go to him as he lay dying because I could not move from fear; and after that I could not even bear to look at his bloodied face or help Mother bury him. I still have the anger and shame I felt after that. But the worst thing for me was the feeling of helplessness, and I wish God had done something to help me." He stopped talking; a teardrop rolled down his left cheek.

Steve was moved by Oku's emotions. "Don't be too hard on yourself. You were only fourteen. Even adults couldn't stand up to those murdering rebels."

Antov said with a pensive look, "I, too, have much pain at the breach of trust by my fiancée. I trusted her with my life, and she poisoned me. And God did nothing—no warning, not even a hint. For that I am angry at Him."

Willie tried to console Antov. "Hey, look, man. Your life was full of great exploits—some against my country, unfortunately. But, man, no one can take them away from you, right? As for God, He was no help to any of us."

The conversation had upset Rani. "I think God is too heartless to do anything, and He has abandoned the earth and everything else He has created."

Steve said, "Rani, I couldn't agree with you more. I've already expressed my feelings about life, and God. I hope He's listening; His creation and His act need a lot of work."

The other four nodded. They'd reached a point where they treated one another with respect and understanding. The cutting remarks and personal attacks were gone, and they were raising one another's spirits with supportive comments.

The host appeared to be pleased. He said, "I must congratulate the five of you. In the short time you've been together, your transformation has been remarkable, to say the least." Then with a smile he asked, "Does anyone have anything else to say?" He saw the five shaking their heads. So he continued, "Very well. Now you're ready to resume your journey. I enjoyed our time together, and thank you for sharing things that are important to you. That means a lot to us. Now, it's time for you to leave. Please go and stand in the line, and the doorperson will escort you to your exit door. Goodbye."

That ended the session. They got up and hugged one another and the host as they walked past him to take their place in the line. They knew everyone's overriding concern: "Now what will happen to me?"

· · ·

Steve was next. The doorperson was walking toward him after having escorted a frail, old woman to the white door. "Well, this is it; here we go," Steve said under his breath. He was shaking with anxiety and anticipation.

The doorperson reached Steve and whispered in his ear, "Red door. Please come with me."

Steve followed her. He was numb, and his mind a complete blank. She opened the door. He had to squint as he gazed into the bright light engulfing him. He moved forward, and the doorperson walked away to escort another individual from the line. The light started disappearing with the door closing behind him. As he stepped outside the doorway, he understood everything: Both doors led to the same place. He smiled and said, "Don was right."

Epilogue

HUMANITY ALREADY HAS the tool it needs to identify and achieve its true purpose: the brain.

56389288R00163

Made in the USA
Middletown, DE
14 December 2017